Praise for
The Grindle Witch

'Bravery and loyalty take on ancient evil in this shocking, breath-taking thriller.' *Bookbuzz*

'A spooky chiller told with real verve.' *Financial Times*

'If you enjoy a good, edge-of-the-seat horror story, *The Grindle Witch* is for you. I loved it.' *The Bookbag*

'This is a thrilling and imaginative supernatural story which keeps the reader turning the pages from start to finish. Alongside the excitement of the action and drama, there are some beautifully evocative descriptions of the countryside and a sense of connection with nature – even if parts of that nature are dangerous.'
School Librarian

'*The Grindle Witch* is one of the best books I've ever read.' *KidAround*, young reviewer

Also by Benjamin J. Myers

The Bad Tuesdays Sequence

Twisted Symmetry

Strange Energy

Blood Alchemy

The Nonsuch King

A Crystal Horseman

The Spiral Horizon

You can find Benjamin J. Myers on
Facebook and Twitter @BenjaminJMyers

The Grindle Witch

BENJAMIN J. MYERS

Orion
Children's Books

Orion Children's Books

First published in Great Britain in 2015 by Orion Children's Books
This paperback edition published in 2016 by Hodder and Stoughton

1 3 5 7 9 10 8 6 4 2

All characters and events in this publication, other than those clearly
in the public domain, are fictitious and any resemblance to
real persons, living or dead, is purely coincidental.

A CIP catalogue record for this book
is available from the British Library.

ISBN 978 1 4440 1172 2

Printed and bound in Great Britain by Clays Ltd, St Ives plc

The paper and board used in this book are from well-managed forests
and other responsible sources.

Orion Children's Books
An imprint of
Hachette Children's Group
Part of Hodder & Stoughton
Carmelite House
50 Victoria Embankment
London EC4Y 0DZ

An Hachette UK Company
www.hachette.co.uk

www.hachettechildrens.co.uk

To Ted and Granny

Prologue

The way from the village of Grindle to the hamlet of High Wicton is over hills and across fields, along a track treacherous with hoof ruts. Then it winds down through the woods that cluster the sides of the Deepfold Valley. On a bright summer's day the woods are cool and damp and dappled with dark shadow. At night they are black, so black your thoughts seep out of your head and your body might as well not be there at all.

Where the path crosses the Deepfold river there is a narrow hump of a footbridge. Cross the bridge and climb the thick woods on the other side of the valley and the way levels out in wet fields below the half-dozen stone cottages that are High Wicton.

Old Tom Moore stops on the hump bridge and listens to the sound of the river, the only clear sensation in all this night. It is a distant rush and rumble and it comes from far beneath him, from tunnels worn through the limestone twenty metres below the boulder-strewn riverbed. This is the way of the Deepfold river. At Wicton

Mill, a tumbledown ruin half a mile upstream, the river vanishes, sinking suddenly below its rocky bed which fills only when torrential rains gorge the Deepfold Valley with roaring water.

Only three nights ago, a storm like no other Tom has known poured itself into the Deepfold, ripping down trees, smashing chunks of earth and rock from the wooded cliffs and filling the valley bottom with a white fury. But already the waters have sunk back beneath the earth, leaving only their murmur winding through the trees.

A ghost of a river, thinks Tom.

He leans against the parapet of the bridge, tiny at the bottom of the valley, and tilts his head as he catches a scrape of earth. That's what it sounds like: stone skittering over stone, among the trees on the other side of the river.

'Stone don't go falling on its own,' mutters Tom and he screws up his eyes at the secretive darkness. He feels the darkness stare back, giving up nothing, and he grunts, imagining a mole, or a badger snouting through the roots which drape the rocks like long fingers.

The stale tang of beer clings to his jacket after an evening's drinking at The January Gallows but behind the beer he smells smoke: coal smoke caught on a tongue of mist, drifting up the valley.

The blacksmith is at work.

Tom has been to the forge, from time to time. It's half a mile downriver from the bridge. The path becomes a track, then barely a fox trail and then you come to a solitary outcrop of stone filled with a red heat: the final place before the trees close ranks, shouldering over rock and blotting out everything but the murmur of the stone-bound river. Hidden by the Deepfold Woods, beyond the reach of any road, yet always the forge is glowing: smoke curling from the tall chimney, furnace roaring, hammer striking in the rock fist of the smith.

Who goes that way? wonders Tom. *Who takes trade to this edge of nowhere?*

Sometimes a farmer with an old nag, half lame, or a smallholder looking to fix a battered gate. But Tom has seen things in the forge that have nothing to do with farmers, or smallholders, or horseshoes or gates. He has seen the cold glint of steel blades, the yellow of gold, bronze amulets, spear heads like iron leaves and, beneath heaps of sacking, armour. And always the smith is busy, and always he is silent. In all Tom's wanderings to the forge, never has the smith spoken of his customers, or from which side of the woods they come.

Tom shivers, although the summer's night isn't yet cold.

It's the cave. The cave always gives him the shivers. Tor Cave, a yawning mouth of stone gaping above the woods, an elbow of rock jutting into the sky, high and solitary.

Tom glances upwards. All he can see is night, but he scowls as if the cave alone is responsible for all this darkness, as if this night has poured out of its great black throat.

Time to go home, says the voice in his head and, with a scrape of boots, Old Tom Moore shambles off the bridge and into the hazel thickets at the foot of the climb. Through the hazel he goes, into the woods and up the pitted track.

The climb is steep. Tom likes to take his time, but not tonight. Tonight something tells him he must climb quickly. He mustn't linger in the woods.

Rocks catch his boots, roots turn his ankles and spindle-tipped branches scrape the back of his neck. Tom curses and stumbles, and stumbles and curses, and then, louder than his grumbling, he hears branches creak and the leaves rush with a wind that isn't there. To his right, a stream of stones tumble, chasing one another down the slope.

Something's moving: moving as quickly as he is.

Tom goes faster, loping upwards, half running although the way is steep. He chews curses and his throat is dry.

Faster.

His toe stubs on a root and he stumbles, breaking his fall with outstretched hands that are left flaky with leaf mould.

Stupid old fool, he tells himself. *That's what they call me, and they're right. Stupid old fool to be afraid of the dark.*

Tom has spent his life around these woods. He knows them. He knows there's nothing to be frightened of.

'Think of something nice,' his ma used to say when he

was small enough to sit on her knee. 'Nice thoughts chase away bad ones.'

Tom thinks of tea brewing on the hob. That's what he'll do as soon as he's home. He'll fill the pot, bang it on the stove top and make some tea. Strong and sweet.

'Hurry home, hurry home,' he chants as he climbs.

Nearly at the top now. His eyes are full of night, too thick even to see the trees and their ivy-lashed boles. But he knows the way. He knows there isn't far to go. He knows that in another twenty metres the rough path will break out of the trees and he'll be into the fields. He'll wade through the wet grass and in no time he'll be in High Wicton.

And then he realizes, the woods are still. The silence presses into his ears like thumbs. He stops, hands on knees, breath like a hacksaw in his throat, the only sound in all this night. His eyes are wide open but useless.

Something's watching me.

Tom knows this as surely as he knows these woods.

He coughs and spits and thinks of the tea he'll make when he gets back to his cottage. Only twenty metres to go.

Tom is about to set off when he hears the clatter of stones and a thudding over the earth, like a miniature avalanche rolling towards him. For a moment he thinks of turning and bounding back down the hill, helter-skelter, and then he smells sheep. The pale shapes rush past him, haphazard, grunting under their breath.

Silly old fool. You've got yourself into a right state. Think of the nice things.

But a bad thought creeps up Old Tom's spine and gnaws the base of his skull.

What made the sheep run?

Tom knows that sheep don't run through trees in the dead of night: not unless something's spooked them. Something that's driven them towards him. Something that must be coming his way.

Get out of the woods.

With a certainty deep as blood, Tom knows that he has to get out: get out of the woods and up to the fields. He'll be safe in the fields.

Get out of the woods. Get off the path.

He scrambles off the path and begins to claw his way upwards. Brambles snare his ankles and score his wrists but hot fear gives him strength. A branch spears into his jacket pocket and for a couple of seconds he thrashes like a hooked trout, arms flailing. Then *CRACK* and it snaps and he is staggering upwards again.

The air is full of snapping branches now.

He is sure he can see where the trees end; where they stand like sentries at the bottom edge of the fields. But now a shape moves between the far trees and Tom's legs fail. The shape is quick and loose as rags and black as a crow's wing, as if the pitch mouth of Tor Cave has thrown down a coil of darkness all its own.

Tom is on his knees. Weak. Slack-mouthed.

The darkness rears before him, blotting out the wood and then the night itself.

Across the fields, the people of High Wicton are sleeping. But in the Deepfold Woods there is the smell of earth, the taste of blood and bone, and a screaming that no one hears.

Jack Jolly blinked awake. The daylight here was so much brighter than the city. It filled the window casement furnace-white until he had rubbed the sleep from his eyes.

Birdsong, and the smell of baking.

He looked at the clock by his bed: 6.45 a.m. Every morning since they had moved here it had been birdsong and the smell of baking. The birdsong he understood; along with cows, crows, the sound of distant tractors and nights that were as dark as locked cupboards, birdsong was one of the things you got when you lived in the countryside. But he hadn't expected the baking.

Jack soaked up the light that poured in through the window. He was glad it was morning. Before they'd moved here, to the countryside, night and day were mostly a matter of whether you turned the lights on or off. But out here, night wasn't just a different time, it was a different place: an alien place. Even the house was different at night, so different that Jack had decided that there were actually two houses: a day house and a night house. Always he was relieved when it turned back into the day house.

He swung out of bed, roughing his fingers through his straw hair as he swayed over to the window, ducking to avoid the low beams of the attic bedroom. The wooden floor was warm under his bare feet. The window opened stiffly, the peeling frame catching on hairy creepers that strung the mullioned ledge. Jack leant out and, satisfied that no one had been muck spreading, he heaved in a lungful of air.

Morning mists were drifting clear of the treetops in the Deepfold Valley. Jack hadn't been into the valley. There was a footpath that led from Grindle down to the Deepfold but although he had acquainted himself with the village, its churchyard and meadows, he hadn't taken the way down to the woods. Not yet. He'd only been living in the house in Grindle for a couple of weeks. There just hadn't been time to explore the woods with their gnarled trees and gloomy hollows and quiet watchfulness. All fourteen years of his life, Jack had been a city person, existing in a world of perpetual neon. There was no rush to submerge himself in the perpetual night of the woods; he'd tackle them when the time was right.

His eyes lingered on the cave that gaped above the far slope of the valley, black as the inside of a monk's hood. Its near side was a sheer escarpment that soared high above the woods, a towering cliff of cracked stone sprouting haggard shrubs. At its summit there was a precipitous ledge from which gulls dived into the valley below. The drop made Jack's stomach turn. The morning was heating up already but the cave defied the sun with a solitary coldness, hoarding its shadows, storing night within the vault of its belly as day unfurled.

Distant, out of sight, a tractor coughed and droned. Closer by, a farm dog barked. Jack tugged the window shut and hunted for socks.

Downstairs, in the long kitchen with its cool, broad flagstones, his mother was baking. Again. She'd baked every morning since they'd moved here. It was as if she believed that baking was expected of her now that they were living in the country. Broken egg shells, two mixing bowls and an exploded bag of flour cluttered one end of the wooden table.

Jack dumped his school bag by a table leg, and the floor replied with a mushroom cloud of white powder.

'Baking,' explained Mrs Jolly, breathlessly.

'I can see,' coughed Jack. He assembled a plate of toast and carrot cake.

Cake for breakfast: at least some things are looking up, he decided.

His mother was at the sink now, cutting flowers. 'Picked them from the garden, this morning.' She brushed her palms across her apron, then thrust the flowers into a vase and sniffed them extravagantly. Jack raised his eyebrows. His mother never used to arrange flowers at breakfast. Then again, she never used to bake cakes.

It's like she's at a theme park, he thought to himself. 'I bet you'll want a cow next,' he observed, through a mouthful of carrot cake.

Mrs Jolly ran a hand through her ash-blonde hair, flouring it a little, and smiled at her son brightly. 'And risk you selling it for beans? No chance.' Then she sighed and stared absently out of the window. 'But it is beautiful here. Everything makes sense. I feel like I've lived here all my life; like I'm meant to be here.'

I liked where we were before: my friends, the street lights, being in a place where mobile phones work, the general sense of civilization. But Jack knew how much being here mattered to his mother so all he grunted through the stodgy wedge of crumbs was, 'Great cake.'

The house didn't help. The Old School House. They were renting it until they found somewhere to buy, and it came complete with contents: dark oak chests, panelled wardrobes that smelt of beeswax, a study crammed with leather-bound volumes, sombre oil paintings in gilt frames and, at the top of the mahogany staircase, a stuffed hawk on a fluted pedestal with piercing eyes of amber.

But it wasn't the antique contents of the antique house that put Jack on edge (although the hawk with its unblinking eyes could be unnerving late at night); it was the noises. The house was full of noises where there shouldn't have been noises at all. When you ran the taps, the pipes clanked, when you opened the heavy doors, they groaned and when you did nothing, absolutely nothing, when you just lay there in the dead of night, the floorboards creaked with the memory of ancient footsteps.

'The last day of term,' announced Mrs Jolly, brightly.

'Hmm.' *How can I sound so glum about the end of term?* 'Perfect,' said Jack, in a renewed attempt to strike the expected level of delight.

'I thought the end of school was a good thing?' His mother sat down opposite him with a big mug of tea. She'd removed the apron but flour still tumbled from her blouse and into her tea, onto her dark jeans.

The end of term would normally be a good thing but, on this occasion, Jack had mixed emotions. They'd only moved here two weeks ago. Two weeks hadn't been much time to make friends, and everyone at school knew each other so well they were slow to let him in. They acted like he was different just because he'd come from somewhere else. It was going to be a long and lonely summer.

Jack crunched on toast. 'Where's Dad?'

'At the village hall.'

Jack made a noise that meant, 'Why?'

'They needed a doctor.'

'Who needed a doctor?'

'The police.'

Jack chewed his mouth empty and swallowed a lump of toast that was so dry it made his throat hurt. 'Why?'

'You shouldn't take the music player. You'll lose it.'

Was this a deliberate attempt to change the subject?

Jack sighed and tucked the headphone cable back inside his blazer. 'Everyone's got them, Mum, and no one loses them.' He folded a piece of toast into quarters and put it whole into his mouth.

'You and that cave have a lot in common,' remarked Mrs Jolly. Jack didn't need to ask which cave she meant; there was only one cave. Strange how much space it took up in his mind.

'I don't know how you're such a rake when you eat so much.' His mother got up and ruffled his hair. 'Don't you ever comb it?'

'Why the police, Mum? Why did they want *Dad*?' Jack wanted to know. His dad was a pathologist; he specialized in dead bodies, not living ones. There was only one reason why the police would want the assistance of a pathologist. Jack stood with a loud screech of his chair, swilled down the toast with orange juice and wondered what was in the village hall.

'Do you want me to drive you over to the bus stop?'

'No. Thanks, Mum, but I'll cycle.'

Every day he'd cycled over to the bus stop on the main road to Leek, leaving his bike round the back of the one shop which served the local villages: villages which were cast about the deep hills like lost pebbles. There were two other students who caught the bus. They were both his age and in his class and the last thing Jack wanted was to turn up at the stop, chauffeur-driven, after they had cycled there. And anyway, today he might take a detour: a detour via the village hall.

Curiosity killed the cat, said a voice in Jack's head. Jack ignored the voice.

'Text me when you get there,' said his mother. 'To the bus stop.'

She was worried, Jack could tell that.

Why was she worried? What was in the village hall?

'There's no mobile coverage,' Jack reminded her.

Mrs Jolly looked a little crestfallen at this reality of remote living, but only for a moment. 'Well, be careful. Watch out for cars.' She opened a cupboard that was packed with home-made cakes. 'Do you want to take some?' she asked, hopefully.

'It's OK, Mum,' said Jack. 'I'll make it through the day.' Cake for lunch *every* day hadn't made it any easier for Jack to establish that he was no different from everyone else at school. He kissed his mother goodbye.

Watch out for cars? Watch out for cow-muck would have been better advice. Jack wheeled his bike from the shed, noticing how yesterday's dung had dried to a harmless brown crust on the underside of the frame. He kicked it loose, then pedalled slowly. The lazy click of the gears was loud in the summer morning. He stopped short when he came to the village hall.

Two police cars, a dog van, a liveried transit van and two jeeps choked the narrow road. A couple of uniformed officers stood outside the main entrance and sitting on a bench that had its back to a wall spread with climbing roses was another officer, this one with a rifle across his thighs. He watched Jack cycle by and Jack could see himself reflected in the lenses of the officer's sunglasses.

'Hello,' said Jack and the officer nodded.

A pathologist *and* armed police: Jack didn't have to ask to know he wasn't going to be allowed entry.

He freewheeled past the hall, breezily looking into the green middle distance, exuding a lack of interest in the clustered vehicles, the police officers, the rifle. But, once out of sight, he turned sharp down a back lane whose cobbled surface and troughed gutters dog-legged in the direction he had just come: too narrow for cars, too deep amidst weeds and stone walls to be watched from the road, Jack jolted his way to the back of the village hall.

The end of the building was flush with the dry-stone wall that marked one side of the lane. Jack used his feet to brake the bike beneath a half-open window, high in the wall. He could hear voices from inside. They were muffled but it was so quiet in the lane that he caught snatches of what was being said.

'Savage.' A male voice Jack didn't recognize. Deep.

Hoarse. Tired, maybe. 'Twenty-three years in the force and I've never seen anything like it. *Savage*.'

'It was discovered in the woods below High Wicton, early this morning,' continued a second. 'Found by a farmer.'

'Poor bugger,' muttered the hoarse voice.

Jack guessed that these were police officers speaking.

'We believe his name is Tom Moore.' The second voice: sharp, precise. 'Tom Moore didn't return home last night, and his cap was found near the body.'

'Near the *remains*,' said the first, quietly.

Then Jack heard his father's careful, measured tones. 'Dirt in the wounds. Stone in the bone.'

The clink of metal, an object on a tray perhaps, and immediately Jack thought of operating theatres and the rattle of sharp instruments.

What were they doing inside the village hall?

'An animal, Doctor? Could it be an animal that's done it?'

Jack wanted to see what was happening. He wanted to see what had been found, what they were looking at. But the window was too high to look through. However, if he propped his bike against the wall and stood on the top of the frame, then maybe . . .

He pushed it hard against the masonry and tested how secure it was with his foot.

'We think it could be some kind of beast.' The sharp voice. 'A big cat perhaps, driven out of the caves after all the flooding.'

Jack glanced up, then down the lane. He was alone.

'There's meant to be over thirty big cats on the loose across the country at any time,' continued the voice. 'Panthers, pumas, stuff like that.'

'Animals bite limbs,' Jack's father said. 'They tear throats, rip open bellies. Animals don't do *that*.'

Footsteps and then the sound of running water. Jack knew that his father was washing his hands. Two flies buzzed around the open window, dancing madly in the warm sun.

Holding his breath, Jack pushed up as gently as he could until he was standing on the top of the bike frame. The bike seemed secure: only his knees were shaky. He rested his cheek against the rough brick, steadying himself.

'We've called in marksmen, anyway,' the first officer was saying. 'Two in the woods and two at the mill, patrolling the country round about. For a couple of days at least. And we've commenced a full investigation; we're ruling out nothing. We're grateful for your assistance, Dr Jolly. The village hall isn't your ordinary morgue, but these aren't your ordinary circumstances.' The man hesitated and then asked, 'But if it isn't an animal, can you tell us what *did* do that? What weapon, maybe?'

Jack stretched up, palms flat against the wall. He inched his eyes level with the sill until he could look down, into the room below.

'A lawnmower?' His father was wearing a lab coat and was drying his hands by a metal sink. From the toys heaped against the far wall, Jack realized that normally this room would have been a crèche. 'No. I can't help with a weapon.' Dr Jolly tossed the crumpled towel onto the draining board. 'What leaves splinters of stone in bones?' He turned to face the two plain-clothes officers who were standing by a table. 'He's not been stabbed or shot or strangled or poisoned or killed in any of the various ways that your everyday psychopath enjoys. This is worse. Far worse. If you want my opinion, and it isn't a technical one, I'd say he's been shredded.'

Fingertips clinging to the ledge, Jack looked at what was on the table.

It was a steel-topped surgical table, wheeled in to turn the crèche into a morgue. On it there lay a body wrapped in a zip-fastened sheath of heavy-duty polythene. A body? Well, from where Jack was clinging to the windowsill, it looked more like a long roll of shrink-wrapped flesh and bone.

One arm lay free of the polythene along the steel table-top and the gory head was facing Jack. An eyeball dangled. It regarded Jack solemnly.

I've got my eye on you, Jack Jolly, it seemed to say.

Toast, cake and orange juice filled Jack's throat. He slapped his hand across his mouth to stop himself from throwing up. With his weight released, the bike slipped down the wall, saddle scraping, chain rattling. Swallowing back vomit, Jack's palms scraped down the wall too as he tried to break his fall. He landed on the bike, grazing his ankles on the pedals before thudding onto his backside.

Had his father spotted him up there, the moment before he fell? Jack didn't waste time worrying about this.

With a burning throat and a mouth that tasted of cheese and nail varnish, he yanked up the bike and peddled out of the lane with a reckless clatter. He cycled hard until he was out of the village and coasting off the top of the hill, towards the bus stop on the high road. He closed his eyes and the fresh air of the moor blew cool across his face. But inside his head there remained a body, shredded and wrapped in polythene.

Leila was at the stop. She stood with her bag between her feet and her hands in the pockets of her school blazer.

Jack raised a hand briefly.

Leila didn't wave or shout anything back. She just watched his approach, dark eyes unblinking. A gust of wind whipped Jack's straw hair across his face, unkempt, but Leila's black, cropped hair barely ruffled.

The coolness of the moor, and seeing Leila at the stop, felt good. The appearance of Rakhman from where they left their bikes behind the shop didn't.

Paddy Rakhman.

Rakhman walked to stand an arm's length from Leila and watched Jack's approach with the same silent regard. But the effect was different. His eyes, equally dark, made Jack want to look away. His scoffing silence always made Jack talk too much: talk too much and feel stupid. He was as tall as Jack but bigger, broader. His hair was as black as Leila's but longer, and whereas Leila's skin was bone-pale, Rakhman's was olive-dark.

Paddy Rakhman, son of Fergus Ben-Nazim Rakhman, landlord of The January Gallows, Grindle's public house, whose red hair, red beard and red temper kept his drinking den clear of all but the most hardened regulars.

Patrick Ben Fergus Rakhman.

Nemesis.

Rakhman dropped his bag to the floor with a thump, claiming the space where he planted his feet. But Jack noticed that Leila continued to watch *him*. She ignored Rakhman.

'Hi,' said Jack, with a wave of his hand.

Why did I do that? he thought, as his front wheel caught a pothole, almost flipping the bike off balance. He grabbed the handlebars with both hands, controlled the wobble and skidded past the stop with his face fixed in a ludicrous grin. Leila and Rakhman stared back.

The arrival of the idiot, thought Jack, still grinning.

He freewheeled past the stop, secured his bike round the back of the shop, then shouldered his bag and came to stand with the others.

'Hi,' he said, breathlessly. He hesitated for a moment before standing beside Leila, between her and Rakhman. Immediately, he felt awkwardly close to both of them.

'Hi,' said Leila, quietly.

Rakhman looked at him but said nothing.

Rakhman's black hair was shoulder-long. It was against school rules, but Jack knew that school rules didn't matter to Paddy Rakhman. Everybody was scared of him and he was scared of nobody. People told stories about him in whispers; they'd warned Jack about him, about how nothing frightened him.

There was this scrap yard on the edge of town, right, and the owner was a nutter. He nicked a bike off of some kid who'd upset him and put it on top of the scrap pile and nobody dared get it 'cos he had dogs, big dogs: Dobermans. But Rakhman went down there and he climbs the fence and legs it to the scrap and up the pile. He gets the bike and when he's legging it back the dogs come for him. They chase him to the fence and Paddy lets 'em get his hand, just so he can beat 'em off with the bike. That way he was free to climb back out, which he did, right, with the bike still over his shoulder.

Jack tried not to look at the thick white scars that webbed Rakhman's left hand, but he didn't move away, however uncomfortable it was to be near him. His own right ankle was throbbing where he'd grazed it against the bike chain, so he tugged up his trouser leg to reveal a claret scab that had already hardened.

'Fell off my bike,' he half-laughed, immediately regretting this admission of stupidity. *Rakhman gets savaged escaping with a bike; I get savaged* by *a bike.*

'Fell off your bike?' queried Rakhman, wearily and with a slight shake of his head. He turned his dark eyes to the moor over which Jack had just ridden and sighed.

Why me? asked Jack, inside his head, glancing sidelong at the broad, dark shape of Paddy Rakhman. *I haven't fallen out with you. I haven't done anything to you. If it wasn't for this bus stop, I wouldn't come anywhere near you. So why've you got it in for me?*

Leila's feet were close to his. Not for the first time, Jack noticed how scuffed her shoes were and how the hems of her trousers were worn and a little too high.

'How come you fell?' she asked, and inwardly, Jack thanked her for that; thanked her for breaking Rakhman's merciless silence.

It wasn't the first time that Leila Jones had helped him out. Since his first bus ride, she'd been all right with him. Paddy Rakhman didn't frighten her, which made her different from most other people at school: that, and how quiet she was.

Quiet? *Strange* was how other students treated Leila, and they were as careful with her as they were with Rakhman. But Jack didn't think she was strange. She didn't have all the stuff that most other students had: the phones, the music, the clothes. But what she didn't have didn't seem to bother her, and that went for friends: she didn't try very hard to make them. But she seemed OK with him. She made him feel less awkward, less of an outsider, than most of the other students did. Jack wasn't sure whether she actually liked him, she wasn't *that* friendly, but when he weighed it all up, he realized that he liked her.

'Skidded on some gravel,' said Jack, in answer to Leila's question. *I was standing on the bike and fell off* would have sounded ridiculous.

Silence. Leila and Rakhman were both masters of silence. Jack wasn't. And he needed to talk about what was inside his head. He could see it still: that dangling eyeball staring back at him.

'You wouldn't believe what I just saw in the village hall,' he declared.

'A dead body?' suggested Rakhman, not taking his eyes from where low clouds scudded over the moor.

Jack choked back the question, 'How'd you know that?' Of course Paddy Rakhman knew. The January Gallows sat on a rise on the edge of Grindle, before the road climbed up to the moor. It looked down, into the village. The Rakhmans could see everything. They wouldn't have missed the cavalcade that had assembled outside the village hall that morning.

'Old Tom Moore,' whispered Leila. Jack couldn't tell if she actually was whispering or whether the wind had snatched the name from her lips as soon as it had been uttered.

'You know what happened?' he asked.

Leila's eyes turned to his and they were so dark and so bright. '*No one* knows what happened.'

Jack thought of the handful of cottages that were High Wicton and how they huddled on the back of a hill among the moors and the woods. That was where Leila lived and it seemed a long way from anywhere.

The heavy roll of tyres on tarmac. Theirs was the first pick-up so they could sit on the bus wherever they liked. Jack sat by Leila, a couple of rows behind the driver. Rakhman sat in the row behind them. He switched on his music as soon as he had thrown himself across the double seat, leaning against the window. The grazing drive of thrash metal competed with the droning engine of the bus. Jack knew that Rakhman couldn't hear him talking with Leila so, while Rakhman closed his eyes and filled his head with noise, while the bus shuddered up and down the hills to Leek town and filled with students, while the morning grew warmer still, Jack told Leila about what he had seen and what he had heard in the village hall, and all the time, Leila listened in silence, rocking as the bus rocked, sometimes rocking against the window and sometimes against Jack.

It was the last day of term, a half day, and coming back in the bus was like sitting inside a hot tin can. The heat was killing. Only Paddy Rakhman looked at ease, stretched out across a double seat, eyes closed as he listened to his music, sleek, dark hair swept back and olive skin glistening with a thin sheen.

Like a big cat, thought Jack. *Like a panther.*

Rakhman's lashes parted and he eyed Jack darkly. Jack sank back into his seat.

Like a mouse.

As soon as they came to the final stop, their stop, Leila surprised Jack. Her hand found his wrist. It was hotter than he had expected such pale skin to be and she whispered in his ear, 'Do you want to go for a ride? Over to mine?' She glanced at the drowsy figure reclining across the seats behind theirs. '*Quick!*'

Apart from one journey in the car with his father, Jack hadn't been across the Deepfold yet. And the thought of what might be out there, what had torn Old Tom Moore to tatters, was stalking inside his head; that eyeball in particular wouldn't stop ogling him. But it was the middle of a summer's day. And he was being asked to go for a ride with the girl who'd spent the last forty-five minutes swaying gently to and fro against him and who Jack liked more than anyone else he could think of. So it didn't take half a blink for him to say, in a whisper, 'Yes.'

Jack and Leila were through the doors as soon as they parted, blazers stuffed into their bags, and the bags across their backs. In a frenzy of rattling they had their bikes unlocked and were half-pedalling, half-kicking them away as Rakhman sauntered round the corner.

He watched them depart with a poker face, not in any hurry himself, but Jack could feel Rakhman's eyes hot on his back until he and Leila had crested the hill above Grindle village.

They freewheeled down the hill, Jack following Leila as they sped past a tumbledown shell of a farmhouse, broken stone walls scattered along the roadside and sprouting grass. Where the road came off the moor and into the village, it split. Jack's way home was dead ahead but Leila leant into the bend, taking the road right and round the front of The January Gallows, her wheels spraying loose pieces of tarmac. Jack's brakes squealed as he followed.

It was four miles by road from Grindle to High Wicton. First the road took them over sloping meadows of thistle and yellow-headed ragwort and then it hurtled them down and into the woods in a steep zigzag. The sky vanished behind a cathedral canopy of gnarled treetops, branches thick and crooked as old hammer beams. Flashes of light pierced the tangled roof in narrow lances, dazzling Jack.

In the depths of the Deepfold, an arched stone bridge carried the road high over the dry riverbed. And then began the upwards climb.

She does this every day, thought Jack in thigh-burning purgatory. *Twice.*

Leila was waiting for him when he emerged from the

trees in a crawling swelter. They cycled along a lane with dry-stone walls. The lane looped round the back of the low slopes which eventually led up to Tor Cave. Above the cave a chain of rooks smudged the blue sky, their grackle cries echoing across the valley.

Seven cottages, Jack counted as they crossed the final fields before High Wicton. Not much bigger than barns, dark-stoned and strung in a skewed line. Each stood in its own small plot of land and even on a day as hot as this, two had faint trails of smoke rising from their twisted chimneys.

'Here.' Leila stopped beside a retaining wall of rough-hewn rocks at the foot of the front garden of the second cottage along. Her cheeks were flushed but her cropped black hair was stubbornly unmoved. Jack was panting and his unkempt thatch of yellow hair was plastered to his face with sweat.

'Good,' he gulped, trying to sound less breathless than he was.

A little girl in a grimy dress was skipping in the lane. She stopped and stared at Jack darkly.

'Hi, Liza,' said Leila. The little girl looked at Leila, smiled and began to skip again.

They left the bikes propped against the front wall and walked up the shallow steps to the path. Jack noticed that the shutters were closed on the front windows of the next cottage along.

By his side, Leila looked at the shuttered windows in thoughtful silence. 'Tom's,' was all she said, before leading Jack round the side of her own house and into the back garden.

'Hello, love.' It must have been Leila's mother, or maybe her grandmother. Jack wasn't sure because, although Leila was his age, this woman looked quite a lot older than his own mother. Her hair, mostly grey with a few strands of blonde, was tied in a ponytail and she wore a washed-out blouse and old jeans with soil-caked knees. On her hands were gardening gloves and she was holding a pair of secateurs.

Kind eyes, thought Jack. They were blue.

The woman put an arm round Leila's shoulders and pulled her close, whispering, 'I'm glad you're back safely.' The kind eyes glanced in the direction of the house next door: the house where Old Tom Moore had lived.

It seemed that everybody knew what had been done to Tom Moore. But no one knew *what* had done it. Maybe the answer to that gory puzzle was here, in High Wicton.

The sun hammered the hills. Jack's mouth was dry. *Maybe I'm standing close to a piece of the puzzle right now,* he thought.

'You must be Jack. Leila's told me about you. I'm Leila's mum.' The woman held out a gloved hand and Jack felt himself blush as he shook it.

'Hello, Mrs Jones.'

It was a small garden with a bean patch to one side. Washing hung on a line at its far end, which wasn't very far away. A lean-to greenhouse was propped against the back wall of the cottage. Someone was moving amongst the plants within.

'Dad.' Leila could see where Jack was looking.

A head emerged from the sliding door, grey hair in a ponytail but dark-eyed like Leila. 'Hullo,' said Mr Jones, flatly.

'Hello,' replied Jack.

Mr Jones shifted uncomfortably where he stood. 'Er . . . tomatoes.' He jerked an elbow at the interior of the lean-to. 'And sweet peas . . . got to look after them . . . Sorry.' He became a shadow within the greenery again.

'Go and get something to drink,' suggested Mrs Jones with her fresh smile, before returning to the bean patch where she'd been working. Jack followed Leila into the house.

The walls must have been very thick because the rooms were even smaller than Jack had expected. The tiny windows had deep ledges that were crowded with books, dried flowers, candlesticks, mugs and whatever else needed somewhere to be left. The inside of the house was dark and cold. Cold radiated from the flagstone floors with their threadbare rugs, and out of the exposed stone walls.

'Here.' Leila handed Jack a glass of water after the tap

had stopped clunking. She opened a cupboard. From where Jack stood, it didn't appear to contain much more than a couple of boxes of cereal. He thought of the warm kitchen in The Old School House and how it was crammed with cake. Then he looked again at Leila's frayed trousers.

Leila found half a packet of biscuits and offered it.

'Thanks.' Jack was hungry but he only took one.

Silence: apart from a loud crunching that filled his head.

I sound like a horse that hasn't eaten for a week.

It took forever to finish crunching the biscuit and then there was more silence. When he looked at Leila, her eyes made him feel as if he were about to fall although he was standing on solid flagstones. He glanced out of the kitchen window and saw the figure of Mr Jones within the lean-to, moving amongst tendrils of greenery.

'Does he spend a lot of time with vegetables?' asked Jack.

A whole minute of crunching and that is the best you can come up with? Inwardly, Jack shook his head at himself. *You are a hopeless case, Jack Jolly.*

Leila sighed.

And now she's wondering why she brought you here. One more question like the last and she'll be begging you to leave.

But Leila wasn't sighing at Jack's apparent interest in vegetables.

'Dad's got to go to work.' She bit her lip.

Jack nodded sympathetically, although he had no idea what the problem was. 'What does your dad do?'

'Not a lot. He struggles with stuff.' Leila stared out of the window as she spoke. 'So he doesn't have a proper job. But he does two nights a week in the forestry.'

Jack nodded, realizing at once what Leila was thinking. Fear crept across the kitchen flagstones from her to him like a sheet of frost.

'The forestry's about two miles that way.' She nodded at the hills beyond the fields at the end of the small garden. 'Twice a week, Dad's there from ten 'til six in the morning. He sits in a Portakabin all night to make sure no one steals machinery for the logging. He's security, supposedly, although he doesn't do much except drink tea and listen to the radio. But it's night, see? It's forty minutes to walk there, over the hills, and then he's on his own, out there in the forestry, until morning.'

Jack swallowed biscuit crumbs that went down like dry grit. 'It's the opposite direction from the Deepfold,' he offered, encouragingly. 'And maybe,' he added, 'your dad could skip work for a couple of weeks?'

Leila's dark eyes stopped him from saying anything else.

'We *need* the money.' She looked down, in the direction of her scuffed shoes.

Please don't be embarrassed, Jack whispered to her in his thoughts. But he knew to say nothing.

'And it don't matter where the Deepfold is. He has to go out; out *there*,' and she looked up, glaring at the window. 'He has to go out at night. Anything could happen to him. *Anything*.'

Old Tom Moore, shredded and wrapped in thick polythene on a steel table said that she was right.

Leila breathed in, slowly. 'But it's nearly another week before he goes again. Maybe they'll have got whatever did Tom by then.' She looked at Jack.

'Yeah,' Jack agreed, as keenly as he could. 'They probably will have.'

'Come on,' said Leila and they went through to the front room, leaving thoughts of what could happen at night in the kitchen.

The front room was crammed with a couple of sofas, a chair and a dark wood dresser. Opposite the dresser was an open fireplace where a pile of wood and kindling lay, unlit. Through the window, Jack could see the dark hood of the cave and the far slopes of the Deepfold Valley. Amongst the far hills would be Grindle village. He thought he could just make out the church spire.

Jack turned to the dresser and traced his fingers over the immaculately carved scrolling, running his eyes over the miscellany of plates, ornaments and books that jumbled its shelves. He noticed letters carved ornately in intertwined vines at the top of the dresser, a small 'v' and a larger 'H'.

'Who's vH?' he asked, noticing now a keyhole in the back of the woodwork, below the shelves. 'It must be someone's name; their initials.'

Leila shrugged. 'It's not our name. My mum's family are from here, from High Wicton; they've lived here forever, as good as. But their name's Higgins. She told me that this dresser was bought ages ago when the contents of the mill were sold. Long before she was born.'

'The mill?' Jack leant forwards but couldn't see a drawer, so what was the keyhole for?

'Wicton Mill, down in the valley.' Leila nodded through the window. 'Mum says this dresser's been in our family for as long as we've been living here, which is as long as anyone knows. We've had it for generations. As for "vH",' Leila looked up at the carved initials. 'He must be someone foreign. Been dead centuries. Dead and forgotten.'

Jack nodded, but right now his interest wasn't in vH. 'Where's the drawer?' he asked.

Leila shrugged. 'There must be a secret drawer,' she replied, matter of fact. 'I gave up looking for it years ago.'

'A secret drawer!' Jack scanned the dresser as if he might suddenly have developed X-ray vision. He tapped the wood up and down the casing. 'You can't just *give up* looking for a secret drawer.'

'I didn't just give up,' retorted Leila. 'I looked for ages. Then I gave up. And you won't find it now.'

'Beginner's luck,' suggested Jack, giving the dresser a sturdy nudge.

'It's not going to *fall* out,' observed Leila as the dresser rocked.

But something did fall. A book that had been lodged high on the dresser slid free. It landed on the top of the dresser cupboards with a thud like the slam of a crypt door. A cloud of dust billowed out. The dust was so thick that Jack was sure he could hear it fall, as if the book itself had sighed.

He took a step towards the ancient volume. It was bound in hard chestnut leather with black lettering stamped into the spine in gothic script.

'*The Key of Solomon*,' he read aloud. He hesitated, then picked it up. It was heavy and furred with cobwebs and dust. Jack turned back brittle flyleaves until he came to the yellowing first page on which there was printed,

Of the seventy-two Spirits
Imprisoned
by King Solomon the Wise,
of their Powers and Dominions
and of their
Summoning.

Jack read this aloud too. He riffled through the pages which coughed out yet more dust, wrinkling his nose at the finely engraved diagrams and the symbols interspersed with dense text. It was like a book of geometry: a book of very strange geometry.

'What *is* this?' murmured Jack.

'Mum and Dad were hippies,' said Leila.

'Hippies?' Jack knew the word but wasn't sure he knew what it meant.

'It was ages ago, in the 1970s. Summat like that. Mum and Dad were old when they had me. But when they were young, they were into stuff. Experimenting. That's what hippies did; they'd try anything different. Even magic.' Leila's dark eyes rested on the volume Jack was holding. 'That's a book for summoning demons,' she said. 'If you believe that can happen.'

'Your mum and dad were into some really weird stuff,' commented Jack. Leila looked at him so seriously that he had to ask, 'Do you believe that can happen? That you can summon demons?'

'Why not?' she replied.

In the waiting silence that followed, Jack could have sworn that the cold intensified and the light dimmed. Maybe it was just the gloomy coolness of the cottage. But he shut the book with a sharp *clop* and placed it back on the dresser.

Spooked by a book? Jack accused himself. Well, not just by a book. The ride that awaited him back across the Deepfold was on his mind, although it wouldn't be dark for hours. But as afternoon had lengthened into early evening, Leila's fear for her father began to take on flesh and blood.

'I guess you'll have to get back for your tea?'

Could she read his mind? Jack didn't want Leila to think he *wanted* to go.

'Yeah,' he agreed. Inwardly, he kicked himself. *Could I sound any lamer?*

He followed Leila out of the house and into the garden. Mrs Jones waved at him from where she was working amongst the runner beans. 'Nice to meet you, Jack. Maybe we'll see you again during the holidays?'

'I hope so,' replied Jack. He kicked himself again. *Now I sound desperate.*

He left Mrs Jones within the beans and Mr Jones within the tomatoes and emerged from the side of the house to where Paddy Rakhman was waiting. He had planted himself in the road, sitting on his bike which was small enough for both his feet to be square on the tarmac. The sleeves of his school shirt had been rolled up and his thick forearms were crossed over his chest.

'Leaving already? After such a rush to get here?' He didn't sneer. His eyes were deadly serious and burned like coals.

'I'm off. For my tea,' explained Jack. *Pathetic.*

Rakhman was below them but to Jack's eyes he filled the road.

'Don't let me stop you,' he said, and then, to Leila, 'I'm

not in such a hurry to get home. I'm riding down to the mill. Want to come?'

Leila shook her head.

A muscle in Rakhman's jaw hardened. 'I see,' was all he said.

Jack felt that to speak at this point would be to interrupt some private conversation that was taking place between Rakhman and Leila. But he wasn't going to stand there, feebly listening to their silence.

'Maybe I'll come over at the weekend,' he announced.

'OK,' said Leila. 'Good.'

'I've got a better idea,' said Rakhman.

By the way the moment stopped and the heat hummed too close, Jack knew he was going to hate this idea.

'We can *both* come over at the weekend. You and me, Jolly.' He turned his face away from Jack and towards Tor Cave. 'We can take a walk up there, together. A night walk. We can see what's out there.'

So this was it: a challenge.

It was crazy, obviously. Nobody would go walking through these woods after dark. Not now. Not unless they were armed. Rakhman had picked the most insane challenge imaginable and Jack knew why.

Leila.

But Rakhman kept looking at the cave, his long black hair towards Jack. 'Well? We can meet in the churchyard. Two a.m. Sunday morning.'

Nobody would go into these woods after dark, Jack told himself. *Nobody would go up to the cave.*

Nobody . . . unless they were Paddy Rakhman.

'You, me and whatever's out there.' Rakhman looked at Jack now, eyes blistering hot. 'Or would you rather stay at home?'

1.25 a.m.

Jack's alarm was set for 1.40 but he wouldn't need it. He'd lain awake ever since he had come to bed, listening to the thickening darkness that was broken only by the cries of the owls and the hourly clang of the church bell. 2 a.m. was waiting for him, heavy and hopeless as a gravestone.

'Don't go, Jack.'

That's what Leila had said as the three of them had stood in the road outside her house. It was the worst thing she could have said. Jack couldn't let Leila make excuses for him. So he'd had no choice. He'd had to agree to Rakhman's challenge. For three days now Jack had tried to occupy his mind with other things and, for three days, the night walk to Tor Cave had loomed over them all.

He had hoped that whatever was out there would be hunted down. But all the trackers, the police marksmen, even the cave divers had found nothing. And now they had moved on. So tonight, Jack and Paddy Rakhman would be the only people out there.

Well, Jack, Paddy Rakhman and whatever it was that had torn Tom Moore to shreds.

2 a.m. approached Jack like a leaden hangman.

Jack was so desperate to kill time that he'd even agreed to accompany his mother to the evening's meeting in the village hall where the Reverend Dorothy Weagg had been giving a lecture on 'Druid Relics of Ancient Grindle'. Mrs Jolly's passion for the rural life had extended even to its history, and the Reverend Weagg was an expert in local history. Jack had spent nearly two hours looking at slides of standing stones, withered oak groves and limestone caves. But all he could see was the horrific mess that had been lying in the back room of the same village hall three days ago.

1.30 a.m.

Jack slipped out of bed, feeling tired for the first time that night, yawning even. He didn't turn his light on, he didn't need to; he'd already left what he needed under a rug on his chair: a torch, a penknife and a BB gun. He stuffed the torch and the penknife into his pockets, but the BB gun he had to jam between the small of his back and the back of his jeans.

Would the BB gun be any use? Jack didn't know but he was taking no chances.

The one benefit of living in a house that creaked when it didn't need to was that when *you* made it creak, nobody noticed. So Jack was able to pad down from his attic room, cross the landing and descend the stairs past the accusing glare of the stuffed hawk, undisturbed. The house creaked and slept without a trace of his passing. Only when he was by the broad front door did he put on his trainers and then slip out and into the night.

Jack shivered, even though the air was still warm. The night was sweet with meadow grass. A gibbous moon cast a pale glow through slow-drifting banks of cloud, onto the treetops and over the road. Jack scuffed down the lanes to All Souls Church. About him, the cottages slumbered, curtains drawn, walls draped with creepers that clustered under the eaves and spidered over the crooked rooftops. His solitary footfalls were the only sound to disturb the thick night.

All Souls bobbed out of the darkness like a stone ship, its walls washed white in the moonlight. A breath of wind ruffled the beech trees which surrounded the church and its small graveyard. The toes of Jack's trainers grew wet from crossing grass. He came to a wooden bench with its back to the church wall, so he sat there to wait for Rakhman.

Perhaps Rakhman wouldn't come.

The night deepened. Out on the moor above the village, a vixen barked but Jack didn't know what it was. The bray screech had him scanning the silvered darkness for movement, had his ears aching with the effort of listening for the faintest footfall.

Silence. Nothing moved. Grindle slept.

The bell tolled in the spire, the heavy chimes reverberating through the stones before rolling into the night.

2 a.m.

A shape at the churchyard gate. Rakhman was here.

Paddy Rakhman moved silently. His T-shirt was lighter than the dark skin of his face and arms, but his eyes were bright. His long hair was tucked into a beanie hat and he stopped in front of Jack with his hands in his pockets.

Jack jumped up. He'd meant to stand slowly, coolly.

'What kept you, Rakhman?' was the ready line. But jumping up, the BB gun caught against a slat in the back of the bench, was flipped out of Jack's jeans and hit the old flagstones with a clatter which was followed by a loud *pop* and then a sharp smash of glass from not very far away.

Jack's ready line died on his lips.

Rakhman sighed and shook his head before peering into the darkness to their right. 'You missed the church but I think you hit the vicarage.' Then he looked down at where Jack was clambering under the bench to retrieve the gun.

'Leave it. We'll both be safer that way. You can fetch it afterwards.' He eyed Jack suspiciously as Jack emerged from beneath the bench, empty-handed. 'Have you brought any more . . . equipment?'

'A torch,' admitted Jack.

'Don't bother. A torch is no good for walking and it destroys night vision. Leave it.'

Why am I doing what he says? Jack snapped at himself as he did what Rakhman told him to.

'And a penknife,' he mumbled, standing up from where he had just rolled the torch.

Rakhman nodded. 'Fine. Just don't open it.' He turned and led the way out of the churchyard.

They walked side by side through the village. Passing through the moon-dappled night, they could have been mistaken for a pair of ramblers, strolling in companionable silence. But as far as Jack was concerned, he might as well have been walking alone. Rakhman's brooding silence warned him to say nothing, even though talking would have felt better. Maybe he could have joked into their *not* having to go to Tor Cave. But glancing sidelong, Jack could see that Rakhman's face was stone, his brows dark, and he knew there was no chance of Rakhman backing out: which meant there was no way *he* could back out.

They came to the edge of the village and to an old wooden fingerpost that leant out of the earth like a relic. It pointed across the fields and down to the Deepfold: the way Jack hadn't yet been. The fields were brushed by the light of the low moon, but where the hillside dropped into the valley, where the cliffs and trees followed the way of the river, it was black. And even the high fields faded from view as a hook of cloud pitched up from the east.

Rakhman didn't say 'This way' or 'C'mon.' He just set off, following the track which appeared as a narrow strip, darker than the grass of the meadow and uneven to walk on. It took them along the top of the sloping field a little way, before turning right and leading downwards.

The earth was dry now which meant that the deep ruts made walking treacherous for ankles. What with the warm air and the concentration required not to stumble, Jack was sweating and swearing and swearing and sweating in no time at all. Rakhman moved a couple of metres ahead, smoothly, silently, a silhouette darker than the rest of the night.

What am I doing here? Now that he was drawing close to where the trees began, the dull fear that had haunted Jack for the past three days became an electric terror that crept in at the back of his neck and drilled through his nerves. And with nothing but darkness to look at, Jack's inner eye returned to Tom Moore on that steel table, and that hanging eye. A low voice made Jack jump.

'*Here*,' repeated Rakhman gruffly, and Jack realized that he had wandered off the path.

They came to a wicket gate set in a high hedge. It squeaked as first Rakhman and then Jack pushed it open. Then they crossed the final patch of field where a solitary cow crunched grass in the darkness. And then they were into the trees.

Jack couldn't stop himself from talking now. 'It's so

dark.' If he'd just jumped into freezing water, his voice couldn't have been more shaky.

'It's night and this is the countryside,' stated Rakhman, a little way ahead. He didn't have to add, 'You idiot.'

Keep him talking, thought Jack. He needed to know he wasn't alone.

'Were you born here?' The 'here' wobbled, high-pitched, and Jack tripped on hard mud. His flailing arm caught hold of a tree that he couldn't see and he stayed upright.

'I've lived here all my life. With my dad.'

Jack had seen Fergus Rakhman only once but he'd heard about him. Rumours. Gossip. That he was mad, that he kept an axe under the counter in The Gallows, that he received travellers in the deepest reaches of the night.

'I was born in Dublin.' They tramped downhill as Rakhman spoke. 'In Ireland. My dad came here with me after my mum died.' And then, bluntly, 'She died when I was born.'

'Oh,' was all Jack said, but he thought about Paddy Rakhman growing up in The January Gallows, with only his mad-eyed, flame-haired father for company.

'I've got a brother,' said Jack. 'He's at university. Studying archaeology.' He didn't need Rakhman's silence to tell him how useless this information was. Then Jack swore as his feet splashed into cold water, sank into mud where a stream crossed the footpath. He had heard water trickling without realizing what it was; he'd been too occupied with the sound of his own voice.

Not being country-born, Jack didn't know that in the darkness, sound, smell and touch can help you see. But he was a quick learner, so now he kept quiet and listened, and the woods seemed to listen back.

The air grew cold as Jack approached the bottom of the slope. He could see patches of grey where the trees thinned out below and suddenly, he was out of the trees and crossing the track that followed the course of the Deepfold river. But when he looked down, Jack couldn't see the track; he couldn't even see his feet. They were hidden by a pearl fog that drifted along the valley bottom, curling over the great boulders of the dry riverbed and winding amongst the low trees.

'What's that?' Jack coughed as the chill fog hit his lungs, and he heard the noise again: a distant rush of water, as if echoing through caverns from far away.

'The river,' replied Rakhman, who was already on a small footbridge which spanned the foggy riverbed. 'It flows underground after the mill. Unless it floods.'

Their voices were muffled as they spoke to one another. Jack hurried over to Paddy Rakhman, his legs ghosting through the thick vapours, feet scraping dully on earth.

Once on the bridge he looked up. Trees or cliffs, the valley sides were black and featureless walls, but above them, the sky was indigo and sprayed with stars. And jutting into this sky, like a vicious rip, darker than the night, was Tor Cave. The moonlight fell weakly on its crest which jutted over the valley wall.

'The path goes up there, up through the woods and up to High Wicton.' Rakhman's voice was cool, quiet. 'But there's a track that breaks off, halfway up. That's the way we go. Up to the cave.'

Or we could just go back, Jack said, in his head. This was ridiculous. It wasn't a game. It was dangerous in these woods. *Really* dangerous.

Paddy Rakhman was looking at him, poker-faced, waiting for him to back out.

Jack knew that Leila wouldn't blame him if he did. But she was what this was all about.

A church bell tolled from over the hilltops, back the way they had come.

3 a.m.

Don't back down, Jack told himself.

Silence. Deep, fog-filled, moon-etched silence. And then a shrill shriek jarred Jack's teeth. Something brushed the front of his face and the air was full of flapping wings, followed by an explosion of undergrowth from somewhere on the riverbank. Then silence again.

An owl? It had to be an owl, hunting.

'I hate this place,' gasped Jack.

'I grew up here,' was Rakhman's blunt reply. He crossed over the bridge and Jack followed. He didn't want to go to the cave, he was terrified of going to the cave, but more than that, he didn't want to let Rakhman beat him.

The fog-chill was driven out by the steepness of the track. The heat and smells of the summer night returned. They climbed in blackness, Jack following Rakhman's noise, trusting him to find the way. And listening out for Rakhman as he was, Jack's ears were acutely tuned in to any other sound. So when there was a scrape and fall of earth somewhere to their right, Jack stopped dead.

Rakhman kept climbing.

'Paddy!' hissed Jack.

'What?' from the darkness.

'I heard something . . . I think.' It sounded pathetic but Jack's pulse was thumping so hard he could hear it in his ears.

There was a long pause before Paddy Rakhman said, 'Me too. It'll be an animal hunting.'

'What *kind* of animal?' quavered Jack. He was too frightened to pretend to be anything else. His eyes scanned the darkness so hard he could feel them bulging out of the front of his head.

Rakhman's voice was calm. Steady. 'Just up here we turn right off the main track.' He had dropped down the path so that he was closer to Jack. 'It's a ten-minute climb to the cave.'

Ten minutes? *Ten minutes?* Anything could happen in ten minutes.

Deep in the woods, the leaves stirred as if brushed by the wind. But there was no wind. Jack said nothing; didn't move.

'I'm going to the cave, whatever you do,' stated Rakhman, and he walked on.

Jack realized that Paddy was now locked in a battle with himself; he was hell-bent on going to the cave whatever Jack did. It was madness. But sticking with Rakhman was better than being alone.

The darkness below swirled up at him and a wave of darkness rolled down from above. Panting loudly enough to blot out any other sound, Jack scrambled after Rakhman.

He led Jack onto a path that was narrower, more rocky than the one they had been following. Jack climbed it in a fevered heat, sensing the steepening drop to his right where he knew sheer faces of limestone plunged down through the tangled wood and into the valley bottom. What little strength the hard climb left in his limbs was sucked out by raw fear. Then he saw Paddy Rakhman, up ahead, where the trees were not so thick. Moonlight filtered through the treetops, outlining his head and shoulders.

Jack stumbled over to him. Now the slope was gentle, sweeping up to the great mouth of the cave, which towered above them like a fortress gate. Up here, the stars looked even clearer. They certainly looked closer.

Through the lattice of sparse trees, Jack could see the silvered valley below and, looking the other way, he could see where the open fields dropped down to High Wicton. He thought he could pick out the narrow row of cottages, maybe half a mile away. A trail of smoke curled up from one chimney, dusty grey against the night sky. Was it Leila's cottage?

Jack sat down to catch his breath. The ground was hard rock covered by a meagre layer of earth. Rakhman was watching him.

'We've got here and we're still alive,' joked Jack.

Rakhman pointed up to the cave. 'The walk ends up *there*.'

'Come on,' reasoned Jack, whose ears were filling with the night sounds now that his lungs had stopped working like bellows. And he *could* detect sounds: small sounds, scraping sounds, coming from below them, from the way they had come. And almost silent, almost without trace, movement.

He stood. 'We don't need to go any further.'

Rakhman began to walk away, to walk towards the cave. 'You can back out any time you like,' he said.

Something was moving closer, Jack knew it. He hurried after Rakhman, drawing level with him. 'We've come far enough . . .' he began, but choked on his words as his right foot slipped into air.

'Careful,' warned Rakhman, pulling Jack away from

the edge. 'There's more space than earth up here.' His face was close to Jack's. 'The trees end suddenly and then . . .' he whistled quietly, '. . . you hit the bottom hard.'

Jack looked down, over the edge of the slope. The tree canopy began another ten metres below. But even this wasn't as sheer as the cliff which formed the outer wall of the cave a little further along. It was the rock wall he could see from his bedroom and his stomach turned as his eyes travelled up the huge escarpment.

'It's called Witch's Drop,' said Paddy Rakhman. 'There's a crack in the wall inside the cave. It leads out to that cliff.'

'I'll take your word for it,' Jack managed to say, realizing that his teeth really were chattering. He stepped away from the edge. 'Let's just get this done.'

Rakhman must have seen Jack start at a noise close by because he said, 'Calm down, OK? This place is full of animals.'

'That's meant to make me feel better?' muttered Jack as they both turned towards the cave. Then the stillness burst with a loud tumbling of stones beyond the closest trees. Jack's skin electrified and his wide eyes turned to Rakhman.

'OK,' whispered Paddy Rakhman. 'That's no animal.' Both of them stared at the ranks of gnarled trunks.

Earth ran. That was how it sounded to Jack: a rush of soil and stone within the trees and then the trees shook as if wrenched, branches groaning, leaves thrashing.

Jack couldn't speak. He gasped automatically, took a step back, stepped back again and then took one final backwards step at which his foot found . . . nothing.

'Paddy!' yelled Jack before his chest hit the rocky lip of the edge. He flung his arms forwards, fingers slipping over loose earth and stone, failing to take hold.

Falling.

'OK.' Paddy's hands clamped Jack's wrists. 'It's OK.' He was kneeling at the edge. 'Stop wriggling. Get your toes into the rock and push up. I'll pull.'

Jack gulped air. He couldn't find the strength to push. But that wasn't because the fall had winded him, it was because he could see what Paddy couldn't.

'Behind you,' he gasped.

The earth was moving, the surface crawling, running across the rock from all directions to a place behind where Paddy was kneeling. Mixed with the streaming earth were stone, splinters of rock, and wood and leaves that spiralled out of the trees as if torn by a whirlwind.

'Behind you!' cried Jack, arms weakening.

'Don't let go,' hissed Paddy, teeth gritted, eyes fixed on Jack's.

But Jack's eyes were fixed on what was forming behind Paddy Rakhman: a huge shadow rising, drawing into itself soil and stone. It began to take shape with wood and rock for bone, fleshing its vast skeleton with chunks of earth, cloaking itself in leaves and bark. Head and shoulders already blotting out the sky, Jack could now see arms, long arms tugging free of the ground, and at the end of each arm, skeletal hands. Hands of stone. Long-fingered. Clawed. Sharp. The claws raked across rock, scarring it. The long stone fingers clicked like shells as they curled and uncurled, bone-white in the moonlight.

The figure loomed high over Paddy, over both of them, its hooded cloak of bark and leaf merging with its giant, crooked skeleton and its withered earth-flesh. One long arm lifted, reaching forwards.

Paddy didn't take his eyes off Jack's. 'Don't . . . let . . . go.'

The claws of stone came for Jack's face.

Jack let go.

Jack's ears filled with rushing air. He was falling. A gaping skull of rock swooped after him followed by a spinning trail of earth and leaves. Claws whipped out of the darkness and he felt something tear his cheek. Then his ears were full of the noise of snapping wood. He hit the ground and the breath burst from him.

Alive! I'm alive.

Head spinning, limbs numb, Jack scrambled up and began to run, to get away from whatever was after him. The trees had broken his fall but they wouldn't stop the thing that had come out of the dark.

His legs took him downhill but his muscles were jelly. Jack was running and stumbling, stumbling and tumbling, slamming into trees, crashing through dense brush, hooking himself on crooked boughs and catching his feet in snaking roots. Desperate to get away, he was hurtling downwards without any thought of where he was going. In an explosion of earth and leaves, he burst out of the trees and cartwheeled down a short slope and onto the riverbed.

The cool air hit him as suddenly as the lumps of rock. Groaning, Jack rolled onto his back. He was lying in a sea of fog. He winced as a sharp stone dug into his shoulder but he could move his arms and legs so he didn't think he'd broken anything. He staggered to his feet, fog clinging to him like ribbons of weed. Dazed, he loped along the dry course of the river. He hurt so much he felt like throwing up, his muscles were shaking and his breath came in snatches but he had to keep going.

The fog can't hide you from that . . . that thing, Jack told himself as he hobbled over the rocks, wondering which way to go to find the bridge.

By the time his heart had stopped hammering out of his chest and his lungs had stopped bursting, he knew that the thing had gone. The only sound in all this night was the relentless murmur of the waters flowing deep beneath the rocks where he stood. Jack was alone. But as the sweat began to chill on his brow and the blood crusted on his hands, he began to wonder what had happened to Paddy.

Get help. You have to get help.

That was when Jack smelt smoke. Maybe he had caught the wood-tang before but now he really noticed it. He stopped and sniffed and the darkness lapped close to him. The drift of smoke was strong enough to taste at the back of his throat. Jack coughed, lungs still sore from running so hard.

Smoke meant people and people meant help. It seemed to be coming from the way he'd been heading so, setting his jaw against the pain, Jack loped towards the source of the smoke.

The fog was peeling from the riverbed and a pre-dawn haze of grey silhouetted the treetops up on his left as Jack heard the sound of metal striking metal: a distant clink at first and then a clanging as he drew closer. Then silence. Then again, iron ringing, the clamour blunted by the dense woods of the Deepfold.

Now, a little ahead of where he crouched, Jack could see where the trees narrowed so that the pale course of the boulders and stones vanished beneath black, arched boughs. And up on the bank to his right, where the woodland track ended and the trees took over, there was a low stone building with a high chimney stack. Smoke curled up from the chimney and into the sky in a charcoal smudge.

The hammering began again and Jack used the noise to mask his own footsteps as he scrambled over the boulders and up onto the path. Then he scurried to the end of the building where the chimney stood, to see what place this was and to decide if it was safe to ask for help.

Peering round the corner, he saw that at the far end there was a longhouse with a low flagstone roof. But closer to him and adjoining the longhouse there was a barn with a wide arched entrance. Jack was hiding at the end of this building. From within the arch there came a ruddy glow and the smell of hot metal. Inching along the wall, Jack could spy into the barn and he realized that it wasn't a barn at all; it was a forge. And inside the forge he saw a hulk of a man. A blacksmith.

Coals flared, blasting out a scorching glow, and the blacksmith was illuminated flaming red. His features were deep, his nose was hooked, his shoulders thick and hunched as a gargoyle. His eyes were like the coals themselves, and his hair and beard were ebony. For a moment he loomed out of the red heat like a spirit summoned from another realm and then the flames diminished and his huge torso was human again, his features still deep and powerful but on Jack's side of the spirit world. He creased his broad brow in measured contemplation as he hefted the mighty hammer, then struck down at the anvil.

A shower of sparks fountained from where metal struck metal and Jack stepped out from the wall.

'Sir?' he asked. He wasn't sure of the correct form of address for a blacksmith. Calling the man 'sir' seemed the best option.

The hammer hammered down again and Jack flinched as the metal rang. Then the smith turned his head and studied Jack, from his sweat-matted hair to his battered trainers. With the hand that wasn't holding the hammer, he lifted a double-bladed battleaxe from the anvil and plunged it into a barrel of water. Steam hissed upwards.

'Come in.' The blacksmith nodded his swarthy head at a low bench inside the wall. 'Sit down.'

Jack entered the red heat and iron air of the forge and sat in the flame-streaked darkness.

'My name,' said the blacksmith, in a voice as deep and resonant as yawning timber, 'is Weland.'

'My name's Jack,' said Jack, and then, deciding it was best to come to the point, he added, 'I need help.'

'Wait,' came the gruff command.

But Jack wasn't sure that there was time to wait. Anything could have happened to Paddy. 'There's something out there, something terrible,' he gabbled, noticing how wobbly his voice was, 'and my . . . my . . .' he hesitated to use the word, but he couldn't forget how Paddy had tried to save him from falling, '. . . my friend is out there too.'

'Wait,' repeated Weland, clanging the axe head back onto the anvil and levelling the hammer in his right fist. 'Your friend is coming here,' and, for a moment, Weland looked out of the mouth of the forge as if he could see through stone, through wood, through night itself.

Instinctively, Jack looked where the smith's furnace eyes had looked but he saw only darkness brushed by early dawn. Tiredness pulsed through his limbs and he leant back against the wall and watched the blacksmith at work, the rhythmic might with which he mastered the metal: hammer, sparks, steam, fire. He observed how

Weland moved unevenly on his feet and realized that tall and powerful as he was, he was lame in one leg. But his arms were strong as oaks and his eyes intense as an eagle's.

Jack's own stinging eyes wandered the inside of the forge, noticing the glint of armour, the lustre of blades, and, amongst those blades, one double-handed sword more mighty than the rest, propped in a corner, wrapped in sacking and bound with leather straps.

That was when Leila entered the forge. She hesitated just inside the entrance, her slender form dark against the blank pearl of early dawn.

'Jack?'

Weland nodded towards the bench where Jack sat, slumped.

'Jack!' Leila hurried over the earthen floor. 'What happened?' She was breathless, as if she'd been running.

'Leila?' croaked Jack in a tumble of emotions: shocked to see her, glad to see her, surprised to see her so flustered when usually she was so calm, bemused by everything that had happened to him and wishing that his voice didn't sound so feeble. He cleared his throat. 'I'm OK, but Paddy . . . I don't know what's happened to Paddy.'

'He's all right,' replied Leila.

'All right?' Jack was as amazed as he was relieved. How could Paddy have escaped the thing in the woods?

'Paddy's OK. He came to the house, banging on our door. He said you'd fallen.' Her words came in a torrent.

'He said he'd gone after you, tried to find you. He looked for you until daybreak and then he came to us.'

Paddy Rakhman did that? Risked himself to help me?

I owe you, Paddy, Jack said to himself.

'He was meant to be coming with me,' continued Leila with a back-glance to where she'd come in, as if Paddy might be standing there now. 'But I didn't wait. I . . . couldn't wait.'

The silence that followed was hot. Jack swallowed and looked at the beaten floor.

'Did he say *why* I'd fallen?' he asked.

'A creature.' Leila's voice dropped. 'He said that there was a creature that came out of the woods. A thing with claws.'

Her eyes narrowed and she raised a hand to touch Jack's cheek.

Jack didn't move although it burned where she touched. Leila leant forwards, her face close to his, her breath grazing the wound as her dark eyes studied it intently. Even with the gashes in his face, even with the image of the thing with the claws still sharp in his mind, everything vanished except Leila.

Jack cleared his throat in a business-like fashion. 'So, how did you know I was here?'

'I knew you'd either be dead, or you'd make it home, or you'd find your way here. I ran out to look for you before Mum could stop me. I hoped you'd be here so you'd be OK . . . so I'd find you.'

Jack felt a heat in his face that wasn't from the forge. 'Is it *very* bad?' he asked, turning his left cheek to Leila.

'I can't see the bone.' Her voice was clinical but her eyes told him it wasn't pretty. 'You've bled a lot. There's three gashes and they look deep.'

'They *feel* deep.' Jack touched the throbbing wound and felt the crusted strips of torn flesh. Looking down, he noticed the streaks of blood on the chest of his T-shirt, the spatters on his jeans. This wouldn't be easy to explain when he got home.

'Here.' Weland stood over the two of them and thrust a wooden mug towards Jack.

'Thanks.' Jack peered inside the mug.

'It's only water,' Leila reassured him. She shook her head when the smith offered to fetch her a drink and he turned away

'You know him?' whispered Jack.

'I live here, I walk in these woods. Of course I know him.'

Weland strode unevenly to a barrel of water at the far side of the forge into which he plunged a flagon. Water cascading from his arm, he poured the contents of the flagon down his throat, then slammed the wooden beaker onto a trestle table before wiping his hands across the chest of his leather apron. Then he looked directly at Jack.

'These woods are alive,' he said.

'Alive?' echoed Jack.

The smith clenched his fists, walnut knuckles cracking. 'Alive with death.'

Unblinking, eyes locked with Weland's, Jack put the mug to his lips and gulped water, spilling most of it over his chin and down his T-shirt. Then he put the mug on the floor and brushed dribble from his chin. 'Alive with death?' he repeated.

'A spirit.' The blacksmith returned to his hammer.

'Did it kill Tom Moore?' asked Leila.

Weland nodded and thrust the axe head into the bright orange coals before clanging it back on the anvil.

'What kind of spirit is it?' asked Jack.

The smith balanced the hammer in his grip. 'A revenant.' Up went the hammer. Down it slammed. Sparks cascaded. 'A spirit bound to this place, now released from its grave, wandering these woods, embodied in earth and tree and stone.'

CLANG!

'Released?' asked Jack. 'How?'

'A burial place at the bottom of the valley, below the cave . . .' The hammer arced high, swung down.

CLANG!

'. . . disturbed by the summer floods that washed away tree and root and rock, releasing the spirit from where it had been imprisoned.'

Imprisoned. So now Jack knew that there was a history to this; that somewhere, sometime, someone had encountered the spirit before. Encountered it and imprisoned it.

'Why?' asked Jack, voice husky, quiet. Outside the forge all was grey and still but instinctively he didn't want anything out there to hear what was being said. 'Why had it been imprisoned?'

'For practising witchcraft,' replied Weland, and the hammer banged down like a verdict.

Jack looked at Leila and spoke slowly, as if thinking aloud. 'So the *thing* is the *ghost* of a *witch?*' He shook his head in disbelief.

'You saw it,' Leila reminded him. But Jack needed no reminding. If he closed his eyes he could see the giant, ragged body, the skull of stone, the long arms, the claws.

'Yeah,' he sighed, slumping forwards, elbows on bloodied knees. 'I saw it.'

Death had come very close to him and Paddy: a ripping, tearing, shredding death.

'So why's it here?' asked Leila. 'Why is the spirit in the Deepfold?'

The answer from the smith was uncompromising as a blow from his hammer. 'Revenge.'

After a pause, Leila murmured, 'Don't see why anyone would want revenge on Old Tom Moore.'

Weland was focused on his work again and a succession of clangs punctuated the forge.

'How does he know all this?' Jack whispered to Leila with a nod towards Weland.

'He's a blacksmith,' she whispered back.

'Oh, right,' hissed Jack, beneath the singing iron. 'That explains everything. Ghosts, witches and blacksmiths: all part of the countryside experience.'

Leila looked at him quizzically, as if she was gauging how ignorant he really was. 'There's a lot you don't know,' she said.

'It's what comes of leading a *normal* life,' retorted Jack. 'Up to now.'

Leila spoke patiently. 'Blacksmiths work with earth and air and fire and water. They're part of *everything*; part of this world and the other world.'

'The *other* world?' repeated Jack, slowly.

'Yes, Jack, the other world.' Leila pointed to where the half-hidden armour and weaponry lay beneath its sacking. 'Who do you think he makes all of that for? Who do you think brings trade this far into the woods?'

I just thought he was mad, Jack felt like saying, but he settled for, 'Really, Leila? Fairy folk?'

'Really, Jack? A witch?' Leila's eyes were as fiery as Weland's. 'What came for you in the woods, Jack? What cut you? What nearly killed you?'

She was right. Twelve hours ago, he would have thought she was crazy. But now . . . now he had the gashes on his face to prove she wasn't.

Jack sighed and raked his hands through his thatch of blood-matted hair. 'Is it safe, now?' he asked loudly enough for Weland to hear. 'Is it safe out there?'

'Daylight is safe,' stated Weland, resting his hammer. 'The spirit cannot walk by day, nor can it cross running water.'

'So we're safe on this side of the river,' observed Jack, 'so long as underground rivers count.'

Leila looked at him coolly. '*You're* safe, on *your* side of the river.'

'Under the earth or over, it is a river,' stated the smith. 'But the spirit will grow stronger.'

'Great,' muttered Jack. As if things weren't bad enough with the spirit as it already was.

The blacksmith hobbled to the arched entrance in the side of the forge and rested one shovel of a hand against the wall. 'With each life it takes, the spirit will grow stronger.'

With each life it takes? How many lives would it take? 'So someone has to stop it,' announced Jack, heroically.

Weland said nothing. Leila raised an eyebrow at him before turning and heading outside.

'Just an idea,' he shrugged, before getting up and following Leila. He squinted in the brightening morning. 'Can it be stopped?' he asked the smith. 'Can it be killed?'

'By nothing mortal,' came the reply.

Of course not. How silly of me to ask. That would be too easy. Aloud, Jack said, 'Thanks. Thanks for your help and for explaining, about the spirit . . . the witch . . . why it's here . . . how it can't be killed . . . all that stuff.' He trailed off. Lamely.

Weland nodded, face tanned as his leather apron, hair and beard thick and wild as moss. 'You've nothing to fear so long as day rules the sky.'

'Great,' said Jack. 'Cheers.' He gave the smith a thumbs-up which made him feel even more silly than before. Then he hurried after Leila.

'So long as day rules the sky,' grumbled Jack. 'So nothing to fear then, apart from when it's *night*.' He kicked a stone and winced as he stubbed the toe of his battered trainers.

'There's no need for you to fear anything,' said Leila, and in the blank light of morning, her face was paler than ever. 'You're on the right side of the river.'

Jack said nothing to that because if Weland knew what he was talking about, and if the underground river did count as running water, then Leila was right. Up in Grindle, it was safe. But not on the other side of the river; not in High Wicton, maybe not in the forestry, where Leila's father worked. Leila didn't have to say how frightened she was; Jack had come face to face with what stalked these woods.

'I hate this place,' he said, not for himself but for Leila.

But Leila just sighed briskly and said, 'There'll be a way of sorting this out.' Then she smiled and her smile hit Jack as bright as the morning sun. 'You'll think of something.'

'I will?' Was she teasing him?

'Yeah. You're brainy. Smart.'

'I'm not that brainy and I'm not that smart,' said Jack.

If I was that *smart, I wouldn't be walking home with a chunk of my face missing.*

'Yeah you are. And you're brave.'

Jack laughed. He wasn't brave. He knew that.

Leila stopped walking. 'You are,' she insisted. 'No one ever takes Paddy Rakhman on, but you did.'

'All I did was go on a stupid walk with him. And to be honest, I was terrified the whole way.'

'That's what was brave of you,' stated Leila.

I didn't go on that walk because I was brave, thought Jack. *I went on that walk because of you.*

'Do you know what that is?' asked Leila.

'Huh?' grunted Jack, thoughts a million miles from where she was pointing.

'Up there,' she said.

Jack looked towards the wooded escarpments on the other side of the valley. Leila had screwed up her eyes because the sun was rising, its heat and wash-yellow touch breaking the dark crest of trees. Jack squinted too, then shielded his eyes.

'There,' her voice as definite as her pointing finger.

Jack saw the shape swoop up, then cut across the face of the trees before it hung in the sky, gliding in ever-widening circles.

'A bird?' he suggested.

'A buzzard,' said Leila. 'Hunting. Using the glare of the sun for cover.' She grinned at Jack. 'Picking off last night's stragglers.'

'Better walk quickly then,' said Jack, watching the slow drift of the raptor. 'Does it live in those trees?'

Leila nodded, a gentle aimlessness to their footsteps now, a fine mist of grit in their wake. "Those trees are rowans,' she said. 'Mountain ash they're sometimes called. But on this side of the valley it's mostly oak. Hazel too. Good for making walking sticks.'

They scuffed along the path, past sharp-scented elders, by dense beds of ragwort, saw a thrush cracking snail shells and the places where last night's owls had hunted and all the while, Jack absorbed the warmth: the warmth of the singing air, the warmth of the early-morning sun, the warmth of Leila's voice as she named the things they saw. But all the time, behind the warmth, there was the chill knowledge of what would be here when darkness fell. And Jack knew that although Leila was talking to share the country with him, there was another reason. He knew that she wanted to stop herself from thinking too much: from thinking about the spirit and the darkness and what might happen to her father who would have to go out in it.

Six chimes of a church bell rolled dully over the fields and valleys and Jack realized that they must have ambled past the footbridge he had crossed hours ago with Paddy.

'It's Sunday morning,' Leila reassured him. 'Everybody will be in bed. Apart from farmers doing the milking. Your parents aren't farmers. It's OK.'

OK? thought Jack. *How can anything be OK after what I saw in these woods last night? How can you be OK, Leila; you live on the wrong side of the river?* But he knew that Leila was trying to keep her mind off what Weland had told them.

A burst of raucous cawing snatched Jack's attention. Shielding his eyes from the morning, he squinted at the black specks circling over the brow of the hills across the river. Crows screeching as they flew, round and round above the trees, squabbling and diving and squabbling again.

'Look.' Leila was pointing directly ahead.

Jack peered through a screen of elders and saw a wide ribbon of peaty water that glinted with sunlight. It flowed towards them in a lazy drift that seemed too leisurely for the churning he could hear.

The Deepfold river.

A little farther on and Jack saw why the river was so loud. There was a mouth in the riverbed, a rock-toothed gap. It was no wider than the length of Jack's arm but it split the bed and the river water poured into it relentlessly. On one side of the chasm flowed the river and on the other continued the dry rock bed. Here was the place where the Deepfold river vanished beneath the earth.

'Into the very pit of hell,' announced Jack dramatically, immediately wishing he hadn't. After what he had seen last night, the words seemed too real.

'When it rains heavily,' explained Leila, 'the whole river fills but the water becomes a whirlpool there. It's called the Cauldron.' She paused thoughtfully before adding, 'There's people been sucked down in the floods.'

'Great,' said Jack, glumly. 'Witches and cauldrons: this is a lovely place.' But now his attention had been caught by something else, by a shadowy mass about fifty metres upriver from the Cauldron. He knelt and parted a cluster of hazel switches to get a better view.

On the other bank of the river there was a tumbledown building, old stone walls patched with moss, heavy timbers elbowing out of the sagging roof.

'That's the mill,' whispered Leila.

'Wicton Mill?' asked Jack.

She nodded.

The mill slumped on the riverbank at the foot of the woods, untouched by the morning sun.

'Have you been there?'

'Why are you whispering?' laughed Leila.

'You started it,' Jack laughed back, relieved to lighten the gloom of the mill. 'It looks so creepy.'

'It's not creepy.' Leila pushed through the saplings so that she was standing right by the river. 'There's a road comes down from High Wicton.' She waved her arm at the far hill, but whatever was there was hidden behind hedgerows. 'We go down the mill to swim. Come here.'

Jack did as she said. Leila knelt, scooped up some water,

then dampened the hem of her black T-shirt before using it to dab Jack's wounded face. Jack didn't move an inch. The sun was in his eyes and his skin stung and he could feel the heat from Leila's body.

'It looks bad,' she murmured.

'It feels bad,' admitted Jack, beginning to register the aches in his arms and ribs where the trees that had broken his fall had nearly broken him. But none of those sensations matched the pulse of Leila's closeness.

'Anyway,' he said, gruffly, 'it could have been loads worse.'

And it could have been: darkness, a skull-face of stone, claws.

A creature that couldn't be killed by anything mortal.

How can you kill something like that? Jack asked himself. But what he said was, 'Have you been in there?'

'In where?'

'Inside the mill.'

Leila sucked her lip as she finished dabbing Jack's face. 'Yeah. But not in the cellars. They're built into the riverbank and there's grating over them so you can't get down.'

'Like you'd really want to?'

'It's always been OK here,' said Leila, defensively. 'Until now.'

Jack looked to the hilltops, saw the crows circling and saw one speck that broke away. Two or three specks seemed to give chase before wheeling back to the others.

But the single crow continued its flight, arrowing towards the river with hard wingbeats.

'We're OK by day,' considered Jack, watching the crow. There had to be a way of thinking this through.

'But at night?' insisted Leila. 'Over there, on my side of the river? What happens then? You saw it. You saw the creature, Jack: you and Paddy. But no one will believe us; no one will do anything. They've all gone. We're on our own.'

The cawing of the crows, the treetops murmuring in the light wind, the listening hills.

Leila's hand was on his forearm. 'What'll happen at night, up there, in High Wicton? What'll happen to us? To my dad?'

'We'll think of something.'

But what? Jack knew that nothing mortal could help them.

'We'll think of *something*,' he repeated under his breath, but this time to convince himself.

'What is it?' Leila wasn't asking about what he might think of. She had noticed that his attention was fixed on the small black shape that was winging its way towards the river. Towards them. 'What are you staring at?'

'Just wondering what that bird's got in its mouth,' whispered Jack.

'In its *beak*,' Leila corrected him.

The black bird banked and dropped down suddenly,

landing square on a flat-backed slab of stone not more than ten metres from the tray-sized leaves of butterbur that screened Jack and Leila. It strutted back and forth, head jerking. In its beak was a stub. A small piece of wood, thought Jack. A twig. But there was something in its bead of an eye to suggest that if this was a twig, it was a twig that the bird prized jealously.

The crow shook its head, keeping a firm grip on the stub, biting on it. And now Jack could see just how thick it was, how red . . . how raw.

'Oh, God,' he gulped.

Leila spoke very quietly. 'It's a finger.'

The crow dropped its prize to the stone and jabbed hard at the choice morsel with its beak. Jack's gaze shot to the black specks that were circling above the hilltop: circling like vultures.

'What's happened up there?'

But Leila had already burst from the thicket. She was running towards the place where the river poured itself into the earth. The crow screamed at her, grabbed the torn finger in its beak and flapped clear of the ground, wingbeats sharp as cracking sailcloth.

Just to the right of where the waters gurgled into darkness, Jack bounded from rock to rock. Leila remained a couple of leaps in front, her feet accustomed to the ankle-snapping terrain. Once they had scrambled out of the riverbed, they were running through a deep meadow where goose grass snared Jack's shins. Leila was pulling ahead, quick as a deer.

'Slow down,' shouted Jack with as much breath as he had. After the tumult of last night, his legs and feet had been aching even before he had started to run. He wasn't sure of where he was, he wasn't sure of where they were going and judging by what the crow had in its beak, getting there fast would make no difference.

'Leila!' The surrounding woods killed his cry but Leila stopped. She turned, arms at chest height as if she had been frozen while running.

Jack shook his head. 'There's no point running,' he gasped.

Leila frowned.

'It's OK for you,' he panted, drawing level with her. 'You didn't spend last night being chased by the ghost-witch thing.' He sucked in more air. 'Can we slow down? Please?'

Leila's eyes flicked towards the wound in his face. 'OK. But we walk quickly.' Then, looking up at the hills where the crows circled, she said, 'Paddy was meant to be with me.'

'It won't be Paddy,' Jack assured her.

'How do you know that?'

Jack pushed past her and ploughed into the next thicket. 'Because it won't be.'

But Paddy *had* vanished, Jack knew that.

They skirted the field where Wicton Mill mouldered amongst ancient brambles and stunted blackthorns, then dived into the cool shade that pooled beneath the oaks on the hill. Here the air was sweet with mulched earth, warming in the dawn, pungent as tobacco. Toadstools clustered on rotting boughs, neat as skullcaps here, sprawling like leathery yellow ears there and, in the gloomiest places of all, waiting monkish and solitary, red hoods pricked white and full of bitterness.

'It must be up this hill, or the next,' panted Jack.

Leila was working her way through the undergrowth with hands and feet, as if she were climbing through a net. 'It's between the hills,' she rasped. A spar of sunlight pierced the dense oaks, striping her T-shirt and catching the sweat that beaded her skin. 'It'll be up at Wicton Slaughter.'

'Wicton Slaughter?' Jack swore. 'It's no wonder this place has ghosts and stuff with names like that.'

'It's where they used to take animals for the killing,' explained Leila in short bursts, panting as she climbed over the carcass of an old tree trunk. 'There's a farm there now.'

Jack stopped, leant back against an upright trunk and caught his breath. 'People *live* there?'

Out of sight and above the trees, the crows were screeching.

'They *did*,' replied Leila, darkly, before continuing up the hill.

A finger in the beak. Food for the crows! Jack thought. Then, *Why do I talk to myself like that? As if this place isn't bad enough without my own thoughts turning on me.*

But that always seemed to be the way. When he most wanted not to think of frightening things, his mind was most devious at coming up with them. And there was no stopping the questions: who was food for the crows? The people at Wicton Slaughter? Paddy?

It couldn't be Paddy. No way.

But it didn't matter who. All that mattered was that the black-hooded messengers above cried that something terrible had happened.

It was a tough climb. By the time he saw light break between the ranks of trees up ahead, his hands and legs were killing him. But light in the trees meant they were near the top. Jack pressed on.

Leila was there before him. She knelt by a weathered oak that leant the way two centuries of wind had dragged it. Jack knelt beside her, limbs drained and face burning from where the sweat had run into the gash down his cheek. He wiped sweat from his forehead and pushed the tongues of straw hair out of his face.

The ground sloped gently down to a farmstead that was spread across a break in the trees. Then the ground rose again, out of the woods and up to the moors.

'The forestry's out that way.' Leila pointed. It was bleak by day; Jack could feel the tide of darkness that would roll across the moors at nightfall.

'Your dad goes out there at night?' Jack imagined the silent loneliness of that walk across the moors.

'He has to,' was all Leila said.

The crows cawed high above the farm buildings that

were spread in a jumble across the opening in the woods. There was a small grey farmhouse, and outbuildings whose whitewashed stonework was striped orange from the rusty roofs of corrugated iron. Stacks of railings were propped against walls, old pallets were half-buried in the dried mud, clumps of dirty straw littered the mouths of the low barns and a broken tractor was forgotten behind a collapsed wall, glass cracked and mottled with lichen.

'Down there.' Leila's finger had switched from the moors to a long wooden building set at one end of the farm. Jack looked at her finger, blinked the hungry crow out of his mind, then looked where Leila was pointing. For the first time he registered the disgruntled lowing of cattle and an electric hum. Both came from the place where Leila was pointing.

'The milking shed,' she said.

The crows were densest over the long wooden shed, wheeling in an unruly circle, their racket rattling over the farm and surrounding treetops. Even as Jack watched, one of the birds dived to the open door, then strutted brazenly onto the concrete floor and vanished within.

'What's happened?' whispered Jack.

Now that they were here, Jack wasn't sure about going down *there*: down to the milking shed at the edge of the farm. It wasn't that he was frightened of what might happen to them: Jack knew that the sun wouldn't let the creature walk the Deepfold by day. But he was frightened of what they would find. He was frightened of what had happened in the shed. The finger must have come from somewhere, from somebody. Leila didn't know what to expect, but Jack did.

Look what it did to me, croaked Old Tom Moore.

Jack blinked the image away. His mouth was bone dry.

'No, no, no,' Leila was chanting under her breath as she started down the shallow slope.

'I don't think it's a good idea . . .' started Jack.

Leila cut him dead. 'We're here now, Jack. We have to know.'

Know? Know what?

'It could be Paddy. It could be them,' she thumbed towards the farmhouse with its drawn curtains. 'It could be someone from . . . from *home*.'

Jack understood. It could be Leila next, it could be her dad, it could be anyone. Leila needed to know what had happened, what *might* happen. And more than that, she wanted to believe that she could help: that by seeing what was down there she might actually discover something that would help her to stop it from happening again.

But Jack knew how hopeless this was. The witch could kill savagely, *would* kill savagely, and nothing could stop it. Nothing mortal. What options did that leave?

Where do I find something that isn't mortal?

'Come on, then,' he muttered, joining Leila, 'but we take this slowly, OK? And if you want to turn back, we turn back.'

'We won't be turning back,' stated Leila before wading into the bracken at the edge of the wood.

Jack walked by her side and together they drew closer to the milking shed.

They hugged the fringe of the wood, skirting the perimeter of the farm and although they said nothing to one another, Jack knew why. There was a watchfulness to this place, as if eyes were hiding behind the wooden slats of the shed. They didn't want to cross the open ground between the trees and the shed until they had to.

When they came to where the open strip of land was most narrow, Leila darted to the end of the shed. Jack sprinted after her and into the lee of the rickety wall, heart pounding. They pressed close to the green-speckled timber.

As they edged round towards the front of the building, Jack looked for a knot-hole that might allow them to peer into the gloom on the other side. The murmur of cattle and shuffle of hooves were inches away. The machinery continued to hum, oblivious to whatever had happened inside, but there was no hole in the wood. At the corner they stopped, knowing that once they rounded it they would be into the mouth of the shed.

Jack faced Leila. 'OK?'

Leila nodded.

OK, said Jack to himself, *time for my next act of reckless stupidity.*

Jack stepped out.

He walked into a body.

'Whoa!' he yelped, leaping back.

'Paddy!' gasped Leila.

Paddy held up his palms in a gesture of calm. 'I knew someone was sneaking around,' he said.

'Sneaking around!' retorted Jack. 'We were looking for *you*,' which wasn't strictly true because, more than anything else, Jack had been hoping that the one person they *wouldn't* find was Paddy. Now that Paddy was standing right in front of them, Jack's thoughts returned to the milking shed.

Paddy must have seen where he glanced. 'It's bad.'

He looked tired. His jeans were streaked with dirt and his palms and knuckles were caked with dry blood.

'What happened?' asked Jack.

'I went for Leila.' Paddy leant back against the wall of the shed. The crows grated the sky with their cawing. 'Leila went after you. I was slow; I was tired. I'd been looking for *you*.'

Even with the sapping certainty that there was something horrific in the milking shed, Jack felt a surge of strength from knowing that Paddy had been there to help him, and that Paddy was here now.

'Thanks,' was all Jack said. He knew that the two of them had faced something that could have killed them both. But it hadn't. They'd faced the witch and survived.

They'd done it together, and there was nothing left to prove to one another.

'You came looking for me,' observed Paddy. 'I guess we're quits.'

'Hardly quits,' said Jack. 'You saved my life.'

Paddy shrugged as if it were nothing, but Jack knew that whatever was going on out here, he had a new friend.

Friends, with Paddy Rakhman. All it had taken was a near-death experience.

'I was heading down to the fields, below the cave,' continued Paddy, 'then . . . I heard screaming . . . or maybe just one scream.' His olive face hardened as he described the cry. 'I knew that it wasn't an animal. An animal doesn't sound that desperate.'

Inside the shed, the machines hummed calmly.

'I didn't think it was either of you because it came from out this way.' Paddy cast his eyes across the tatty farm. 'Got here eventually and found his mum just where we're standing now. Out here, in the dirt, shaking and bawling. She'd found him, you see.' Paddy gritted his teeth. 'Found her son, in there. What was left of him.'

'Ray?' asked Leila quietly. 'Ray Hulme?'

Paddy nodded. 'She's in the house now. I got her inside, eventually. I've rung for the police. Not that they can do anything. Not now.' Paddy looked at the open door of the milking shed.

Leila started forwards, towards the doorway. Paddy

grabbed her arm. Jack could see her skin whiten where his fingers dug in. 'No.'

Leila tugged her arm free. She marched into the shed.

Jack and Paddy waited, looking at one another, saying nothing.

There was almost no sound from Leila. *Almost* no sound. But Jack thought he heard her draw breath sharply, then gasp again. When she emerged from the shed she walked slowly, hesitantly, as if blinded by the sunlight. Her head was down and her heels scuffed the dusty earth. She made it as far as the nearest stone wall, then slumped to a sitting position, elbows on knees, head in her hands.

At least I'd been wrapped in a bag when you saw me, said Old Tom Moore.

Jack knew that what Leila had just seen must have been spread about the inside of the milking shed.

'He worked the farm with his mum,' muttered Paddy, 'just the two of them. He'd gone out to do the milking before first light.' Paddy kicked a stone across the hard mud.

Nothing mortal, Jack thought. *Nothing mortal can kill it. But I'd better come up with something.*

He tried not to look into the shed as he walked over to Leila. But the fringe of sunlight revealed crimson streaks across the concrete floor, as if someone had dashed a bucket of paint across it.

Jack knelt by Leila. Her palms were pressed into her

face. He went to place his hand on her short black hair. It shone soft in the sun. He hesitated awkwardly, then dropped his hand to his side. He opened his mouth to speak, could think of nothing to say, closed it again.

Around them, the farm crouched in the hot sun.

Jack knew that this was witchcraft. Witchcraft as old as these hills. Witchcraft full of ancient places, buried under earth and stone and moss.

But earth and stone and moss were silent: a silence full of secrets.

'What do we do, Jack?'

Lost in his thoughts, Jack hardly heard Leila at first. Then he saw that she was looking at him with clear, hot eyes. No tears, but he could see fear. 'What do we do? It can't carry on, Jack. This can't go on happening.'

'Paddy's called the police . . .' he began.

'The police!' Leila's voice shook. 'What are they going to do? Arrest a ghost?'

'Someone will think of something,' floundered Jack, awarding himself first prize for feeble suggestions.

'They won't.' Leila ground her heel hard against the dry mud. 'They won't because they can't. How do they stop *that*?' and she pointed to the open door of the shed as if accusing it.

Nothing mortal, Weland had said.

OK, said Jack to himself, *so where do I find something that isn't mortal?*

'Who's next?' Leila spoke quickly and quietly, and sharp as a needle. 'You? Me? Paddy? My mum. My *dad?*' Her eyes filmed with tears.

Oh, no, she's about to cry. I have to think of something.

And it was then that the idea slipped into Jack's mind, stealthy as a thief. Maybe Leila's mention of her father triggered the association, maybe it was his own thoughts of witchcraft and magic. But where the thought came from didn't matter. It was the thought itself that mattered: the way it slipped into his mind and from there, irresistibly, into his mouth.

'We could summon a demon,' he said.

Leila looked at him solemnly. 'A demon?'

'Yeah. Nothing mortal can destroy the witch, right? But I bet a demon could. We could summon a demon from that book your mum and dad have.' Then Jack laughed, unconvinced by his own suggestion. He'd made it without thinking and already he realized that amongst his bad ideas this was one of the worst; one of the most pointless. You couldn't summon a demon. There were no such things as demons. Jack was sure of that.

But Leila didn't laugh. She stared at him, intense, a frown deepening. Then, thoughtfully, she nodded. 'We could. Why not? It might work. We summon a demon to destroy the witch!' Her eyes brightened as the idea took hold. 'It makes perfect sense.'

Jack liked Leila's eyes, really liked them, but he didn't like *this*.

'It's just a joke, Leila,' he said, slowly.

But Leila's breathing had quickened. 'It's not just a joke. It's a good idea.' Then her eyes narrowed. 'Don't back out of your own idea, Jack.'

Oh, no, she's as crazy as Rakhman. 'Look,' he reasoned, 'we don't even know whether demons exist.'

Leila's stony glance bounced his words back at him.

'OK, OK,' he admitted, 'they probably do. Everything else seems to exist out here. But if they *do* exist, right, if there really are demons, *think*. Think how bad a demon would be: how dangerous. It'd be worse than the witch.'

'Exactly,' Leila fired back. 'That's the point.'

And that *was* the point. 'There has to be something else . . .' began Jack.

A police siren wailed, distant but drawing closer.

'No.' Leila was definite. 'There isn't anything else, Jack. There's a witch on my side of the river and it kills people. And nothing mortal can kill *it*.' Her eyes were hot as the sun. 'I don't care how dangerous it is; we're going to summon a demon.'

The old scarecrow pointed at Jack, ragged as a robber's corpse on a gibbet. A rook sat on the outstretched arm and cawed at him brazenly before flapping across the fallow field.

'Even he thinks you're stupid,' observed Paddy as the two of them cycled, shoulder to shoulder. Taking the Deepfold road out of Grindle, they were heading for High Wicton. Up here, the road ran flat between sun-hazed fields, but only a short way ahead it dived down, zigzagging into the woods.

'Are you frightened?' Jack pedalled harder.

'No,' replied Paddy, keeping level with Jack. 'Just not stupid.' He looked across. 'Nice hat, by the way.'

Jack knew that the hat he was wearing was very like the beanie hat Paddy sometimes wore. 'It was cold this morning,' he panted, sweat prickling his brow from the effort of cycling fast in the mid-afternoon heat. He whipped off the hat and stuffed it in the back of his jeans, front wheel wobbling precariously as he did so.

'What time did Leila say to meet her?' asked Paddy.

'Half past two.' They were approaching the point where the road roller-coastered down. 'She said her parents would be out, shopping. She said there'd be enough time to pick a demon.'

Their legs pumped the pedals in unison.

'You really reckon this demon can be summoned from a book?' asked Paddy.

'Maybe,' panted Jack.

The road tipped downwards. Neither Jack nor Paddy slowed; they began to pick up speed.

'How much do you know about demons, Jack?'

'Nothing. How much do you know?'

'About the same as you. But I have this feeling that they can be a lot of trouble.'

'So can a homicidal ghost-witch,' observed Jack, raising his voice against the rush of air.

'We met the witch,' shouted Paddy, 'and *lived*.'

Fair point, Jack admitted to himself, hair thrashing round his face. 'Why *didn't* the witch kill us?'

'Because we were lucky?' shouted Paddy. 'Because it wasn't hungry? Because it didn't expect *you to* fall off a cliff? I dunno. But just because the witch didn't get us last time, it doesn't mean we go looking for something that will finish the job now.'

'If we don't summon the demon, more people will die,' yelled Jack. 'Maybe Leila. Maybe her dad. You. Me.

Anyone.' He squinted as sunlight strobed through the tangled canopy.

'I don't like demons,' Paddy yelled back at him, brakes squealing as he whipped round a hairpin bend. Then he pulled ahead. 'I don't trust them.'

Jack raced level with him. 'Nothing mortal can stop the witch, Paddy. *Nothing*.'

They hurtled down and over the high bridge that spanned the dry valley bottom, front wheels spitting stones.

Then began the leg-burning climb out of the depths of the woods.

Nothing mortal had stopped the witch. Nothing. After the emergency services had been to Wicton Slaughter, after what was left of Ray Hulme had been scraped from the milking shed floor and walls and put in a bag, and after Mrs Hulme had been taken away, there had followed two days of police dogs and police helicopters and people searching the woods and farms and they had found . . . nothing: no savage beast hiding in the hills, no murderous axe man in the woods. So the people who had come to help had gone and only questions remained, questions that drilled the nerves of the villagers and hooked their tongues. Questions, and the knowledge that out in the Deepfold there lurked something terrible.

Fear haunted the woods and the darkling lanes.

Jack and Paddy and Leila had said nothing about what

they knew. How could they say anything? Who the hell would believe a story about the ghost of a witch?

Jack swore as the strain of pedalling uphill stabbed into his thighs, sharp as the guilt that came with saying nothing: sharp as the guilt that came with knowing what would happen if the witch wasn't stopped. So it was up to them to stop it. Leila was ready to do anything and Jack didn't blame her. He was ready to do anything to help her.

'If we don't do something, there'll be more killings,' gasped Jack.

'As the witch seeks revenge?' grunted Paddy.

Jack grunted back in agreement. That morning he'd told Paddy about what the blacksmith had told him, and Paddy had listened to it all in silence: a silence that doubted nothing.

Panting, sweat streaming, they stood on the pedals to drive up through the bends of the woodland road.

'Your dad still thinks you fell off your bike?' asked Paddy.

'My dad . . . never . . . thought I fell off my bike.' Jack snatched the words between lungfuls of air.

Of course his dad hadn't swallowed the story about falling off a bike; Dr Jolly was a pathologist, he specialized in dissecting the evidence. Jack's story about crashing into a dry-stone wall wasn't supported by the evidence: no damage to the frame of the bike, no reason for the damage to his trainers, no explanation for the parallel clawings across his face.

'Couldn't tell them what really happened,' gasped Jack. 'But they know I'm hiding something.'

And that felt bad. His parents were worried; they were frightened, just like everyone else. And maybe, just maybe, thought Jack, his dad had seen something in his wounds that reminded him of Old Tom Moore.

Eyes stinging with sweat, thighs flaming, Jack cycled out of the shadow of the woods and into the blazing heat of the afternoon.

'You should have thought of something other than a demon,' stated Paddy.

Can't believe he can still talk, thought Jack, barely able to think. He gulped air and it felt like none was going down.

'Just . . . came into my head,' he managed to say.

Rakhman grunted. 'I'm worried about the inside of your head. Weird stuff happens there.' He wiped a thick forearm over his sodden fringe of black hair. 'Seems like I've finally met someone as crazy as me,' and he laughed quietly as if he were pleased to have done so.

I think, Jack decided through a head that was swimming with heat, *that that was a compliment.*

Their bikes crunched to a halt in front of Leila's cottage.

Leila was sitting on the front lawn in faded jeans and a black T-shirt. Her bare feet were buried in the cool grass and she wrinkled her nose as she looked up at them, shielding her eyes against the sun. 'They're out,' she said, confirming that no one else was at home.

Jack stopped, felt the blood rush back into his leg muscles and caught his breath as he took in the green backs of the fields, the steel-blue sky, the dark hood of the cave. The air was hot and still.

'The book's in the garden,' said Leila. 'I've put it on the table.'

Paddy strode up the path, as if they hadn't just cycled hard uphill for twenty minutes.

Leila waited until Jack had propped his bike and drawn level with her. Then she sprung to her feet and gave his ribs a gentle pinch. Her touch made him jump, but not because it hurt.

'Sorry.' She laughed as gently as her touch. 'You still in a bad way?'

'No,' insisted Jack. 'I mean, I've forgotten what oxygen is, but otherwise I'm fine.'

Leila's face was close to his as she studied the claw wounds. Her coal eyes, immune to the blazing sun, darkened. 'It looks painful.'

'It's nothing.'

Leila touched the wound. When her fingers grazed his face, Jack was as still as if it had been a Medusa-touch. 'Your dad put the stitches in?' she asked.

Jack nodded.

'Ouch!'

'It didn't hurt,' said Jack. But lying to him had.

Leila patted his face. 'Come on,' she whispered. 'Let's pick a demon.'

The book lay on a small metal table set beside the bean patch. The dark brown leather looked almost black in the sunlight. Paddy stood over the table looking down at the volume, arms folded.

'This is your brainwave, Jack. You open it. You pick the demon.' Paddy placed both his hands on the edge of the table. His long black hair hung past his face as he leant forwards. He looked up at Jack darkly.

'It's only a book,' said Jack. But it felt like much more than a book. It felt like something that was *waiting*. He read out the gothic lettering that was stamped down the leather spine. '"The Key of Solomon".'

Reaching forwards, he touched the edge of the front cover, flipped it open, flicked through the first few pages, then shuffled through the rest of the volume. The pages were thick and the print was so deep that he could trace how the letters and symbols had been stamped into the paper.

There were so many symbols, symbols that were mysterious: pentagrams, circles, unfathomable diagrams, weird shapes that meant nothing to him, letters in alphabets that he had never seen before. Some parts of the manuscript he could read and some he couldn't.

Leila's eyes were flitting between the pages of the book and his face. Paddy just stared down, his gaze drilling into the book as if he had a private dispute with it.

'OK.' Jack closed the front cover for the time being.

It actually felt a relief to do so. He looked up and both Paddy and Leila stared at him. 'It's in two parts, I think. The first part is general instructions, or history, stuff like that. And the second part . . . I think that part is where it lists the demons: seventy-two of them, according to the first page. Seventy-two demons that were imprisoned by King Solomon.'

'Someone must have let them out if they're available now.' Paddy pushed back a clutch of black locks.

'It lists their names,' continued Jack. "Their symbols. What they do. So,' he sighed and shrugged, 'I guess we pick our demon and then work out how to summon him.'

'Or her,' added Leila.

'Do you get female demons?' wondered Jack.

'Does it matter?' asked Paddy. 'A demon's a demon.'

Jack looked at the antique tome. 'It's only a book . . . but I'm still not sure . . .'

Leila was. 'Pick one.'

'Just remember, we don't know what we're doing.' The warning note in Paddy's voice made Jack feel even worse.

'I don't want to be killed by that witch-thing. I don't want anybody else to be killed by it.' Leila was glaring down at the book. '*I'll* pick one.'

But Leila didn't have to. Before her hand had reached the front cover there came a wind: a chill wind that flew with a whispering hiss from across the fields, flipping open the cover and riffling through the pages in a whirring arc.

Then the wind had passed and on the table before them, the book lay open.

Jack looked at Paddy, who looked at Leila, who looked at him.

'Read it,' she said.

'OK.' Jack looked down and warily read aloud what was there. '"Ashgaroth. A Prince of the East. He appears as a blond boy with the body of a locust and the tail of a serpent. His armour is black. He talks with the twelve winds and sees things past and present."'

'But not the future,' observed Paddy.

'"His service is in three parts."' Jack looked up and commented, 'OK. This is the bit where it tells us what he does.' He continued reading from the book. '"For the first part, he will hunt what you would seek. For the second, he will destroy what you would end. As to the third part, it is wiser not to ask, for desire begets despair."'

Jack turned the book round so that Leila and Paddy could see what was printed beneath the text.

'His sign. *There*,' and he pointed.

'Perfect.' Leila's voice was hoarse. 'He hunts. He destroys.'

'And there's that bit about despair,' commented Paddy. 'Do either of you understand what that bit means?'

Jack and Leila shook their heads.

With cool superiority, Paddy said, 'Don't sign up to something you don't understand.'

'But he's *perfect* for what we need,' insisted Leila.

Jack wasn't so sure. 'Do we need a prince? I mean, a *prince*? It sounds a bit powerful. He might be difficult to handle. There's loads of others. We could look for one a bit further down the scale. Couldn't we look for a demon who's a servant?'

'Try again.' Paddy gestured at the book. 'Close it, then choose another.'

'You just want to see if *that* happens again,' complained Jack, looking about as if it were possible to see approaching wind.

'Yes,' admitted Paddy, bluntly, 'I do.'

Jack slammed the book shut and then went to open it.

This time the wind came with such a slice of cold that Jack gasped and sprang back from the table. The air thrashed through the book and slammed it back open. Jack approached the table gingerly and saw the name and the sign.

'He *wants* to be summoned,' whispered Leila.

'But I'm not even sure how we're meant to summon him,' remonstrated Jack. 'Whoa!' he yelped as the pages of the book flew open in a hiss of wind.

Only Paddy remained at the table, arms folded, black hair whipping about his face. When the freezing wind had passed they all looked at the page that lay open.

'It's like he's already here,' whispered Leila, 'wanting to help us.'

'Wanting to *eat* us, possibly. Wanting to help us, no.' Paddy pointed at the page. 'It says "The Rite of Summoning".' He glanced at Jack. 'Are you really going to do this?'

'Yes,' said Leila before Jack could say otherwise.

Jack brushed back a lick of straw hair and approached the book. He studied the instructions on the open page. 'These are the instructions for summoning a demon prince.'

A demon prince? Either he was half-mad or he was standing at the edge of something that was crazily dangerous. Perhaps he was both.

'I don't think you want to go any further,' warned Paddy.

Was Paddy mocking him? Or was he as serious as he looked?

'Of course I do,' insisted Jack, before Leila could say it for him. 'I think it's you who wants to back out. I'm fine with this.'

Fine? With summoning a demon prince?

It was a blazing afternoon and he was trying not to

shiver. He heard the rumble of a tractor engine and the far lowing of a cow, but the sounds might as well have been coming from a universe away.

'Back *out?*' laughed Paddy, humourlessly. 'I never said I was *in*.'

Jack ignored him. He read the text swiftly. The steps to be taken were described in sequence and there were diagrams.

'Most of this is about how to be protected when the demon is summoned,' he explained, pausing from reading.

Paddy nodded. 'What d'you expect? Playing with demons is dangerous.'

'It's not playing!' snapped Leila and when Paddy glanced across at her she added, 'It's necessary.'

Jack was absorbed by the intricate diagrams. 'This is called the Pentagram of Solomon.' He indicated a five-pointed star within a double circle. Inside the boundary of the double circle were various words and symbols that meant nothing to him but which had to be drawn perfectly if the pentagram were to protect them. 'We have to be inside the star when we do the summoning.'

Is this for real? Jack asked himself. Paddy had said it was madness and he was probably right, but Leila wanted to do this and Jack knew he couldn't argue with that. He had seen what was in the woods. He knew what it did. He knew that only something extraordinary could destroy it. And, more than that, if Leila needed help, he wanted to help her.

Looking up, he realized that both Paddy and Leila were waiting for him to speak, for him to say what they should do next.

Why me?

'OK.' Jack cleared his throat, tried to make it sound as if this were very straightforward, as if he weren't dreading what might happen if they succeeded in raising the demon prince. 'According to the book, the rite has to be performed between nine in the morning and noon. And it has to be done in a secret chamber. We need chalk to draw the pentagram: the Pentagram of Solomon, it's called. We need a sword. And . . .' he looked down again to remind himself, '. . . we're going to need salt to seal the doors and windows.'

'And the blood of a cockerel,' read Paddy. He pointed at the page of instructions. 'It says salt *and* the blood of a cockerel, to seal all openings to the chamber.' He looked at Jack. 'Have you got any cockerel blood knocking about?'

Inspiration struck. 'I think I can sort the blood,' said Jack, 'and the salt.'

'And I can get a sword,' said Leila. No one asked from where but Jack thought he knew.

'I'll get the chalk,' volunteered Paddy. 'There's always chalk by the dartboard in the lounge bar, for keeping score.'

There remained the question of where they would perform the rite. 'Any suggestions?' enquired Jack.

'The mill?' proposed Leila.

Jack was quick to stamp on that. 'Summon a demon in that creepy ruin? No way.'

'You're summoning a *demon*, Jack,' Paddy scoffed drily. 'The venue is the least of your worries.'

'We're not doing this in the mill,' insisted Jack, 'and what d'you mean, *I'm* summoning the demon?'

Paddy glanced over Jack's shoulder, as if he could see someone behind him.

'What?' asked Jack, unnerved and looking where Paddy had looked.

Paddy shrugged. 'I don't see a big queue of volunteers.'

Leila stepped closer to Jack. '*We're* summoning the demon,' she said. 'Both of us. You don't have to help if you don't want to, Paddy.'

Paddy closed the book firmly and left his hand on the cover as if to keep it shut. He sighed. 'OK. There's an attic room in The Gallows. An empty room, used for nothing. It's right under the roof. You can do it there. My dad sleeps in the mornings so he won't disturb you, and no one turns up at the pub at that time. I'll keep watch.'

He slapped Jack on the shoulder. 'Cheer up, Jack. It'll be your finest moment. I'll make sure nothing interrupts. It'll just be you, Leila and the demon.'

Paddy had to shoulder the door to get it open. It gave way with a creaking yawn. The room was long and narrow with low beams and a couple of small windows at knee height along one wall. Dust lay on the parched floorboards, thick as fur, and it rose in a mist, speckling the shafts of sunlight that lanced the gloom.

Only yesterday we opened the book, thought Jack*, and now we're* here.

He was the first to enter the attic and he stooped to avoid the rafters. A plastic shopping bag hung in his hand. He brushed a cobweb from his face.

'It certainly feels secret.' His voice was hushed.

'You won't be disturbed,' Paddy assured him. 'Dad's flat out.'

It was so quiet that Jack thought he could hear the dust drop. And with the sun beating on the roof just above his head, it was hot. He'd reached the centre of the long room before he realized that Paddy had remained behind. 'What?'

Paddy's solid form filled the doorway. He leant against the frame. 'I know how you feel about Leila.'

'How *do* I feel about Leila?' Jack's face suddenly felt as hot as the sun-scorched roof.

'Willing to do *this* for her.'

Sometimes Paddy's coolness made Jack want to lose his altogether. But as calmly as he could he said, 'Someone has to do something. The witch won't just go away.'

'Yeah, but *you* don't have to do this.'

'You're not going to, are you?' retorted Jack.

Paddy stared at him a long time before shaking his head and conceding, 'I guess not.'

But Jack realized that this wasn't just about Leila. He realized that Paddy really didn't like what they were about to do, and not because he was frightened; Paddy Rakhman didn't get frightened.

Jack scratched his head. 'Why not?'

Paddy shrugged his solid shoulders. 'It feels wrong. It feels . . . worse than the witch. We didn't make the witch happen. But this? This is a mistake we could avoid.'

Maybe Paddy was right about that, but Jack wasn't going to turn back now. 'You wouldn't say that if you were Leila,' he replied.

With a sly grin, Paddy said, 'There you go again, Jack. Leila, Leila, Leila. *Catch*,' and before Jack could say anything else, he tossed him a stick of chalk. Jack caught it.

From outside there came a faint roll of tyres on tarmac. Paddy bent forwards to see out of the nearest window. 'Here she comes.'

Jack knelt to look out. He had to press his face right up to the pane to see down to where Leila had propped her bike against the front of the pub. In her hand she held a tatty satchel and on her back was . . .

'A sword.' Paddy Rakhman whistled softly, impressed. 'She's cycled from High Wicton to Grindle with a sword on her back.'

'It's all wrapped up,' observed Jack. Even from this lofty angle he recognized the shape, the sacking and the leather bindings from the forge.

'Weland said we could borrow it,' panted Leila after she had run up to the attic. The satchel was fat with its contents and she placed it on the floor before unlooping the sword from her shoulder.

'Did you tell him what we're going to do?' asked Jack.

Leila knelt, her knees visible through jeans that were torn because they were old. Dust settled on her black T-shirt. She tugged at the leather thongs to loosen them.

'He didn't ask. I didn't tell him.' She paused to wipe a rivulet of sweat from her face with the back of her hand. A streak of dust smudged her forehead. 'It's heavy,' she muttered, methodically unravelling the sacking. The sword thudded against the wooden floor.

Jack glanced at Paddy.

'Don't worry. Dad won't wake,' Paddy reassured him. 'Just try to keep the noise down when your demon shows up.'

'Done!' Leila threw the bindings and the sacking into a corner and stood holding the pommel of the sword uppermost. With the tip of the scabbard on the floor, the pommel came to just below her chin.

Paddy stepped into the room now, grasped the handle with two hands and pulled the sword free. There was a hiss and then the air rang as if cut by the gleaming blade. Jack and Leila stepped away and the scabbard hit the floor like a deadweight.

'Whoa! Careful,' gasped Jack as Paddy held the sword out, then swung it. The huge steel blade hummed, slicing the sunlight.

Paddy nodded. 'It feels good.' He let the point rest on the floor before taking a look at the crimson ruby, fat as a coal, that was set in the pommel. He tilted the sword back and forth, allowing the jewel to catch the light. It flickered as if it were burning.

'Weland made it.' Leila took the sword from Paddy and gently laid it on the floorboards. Instantly, the room seemed less busy; as if in being released, the sword was resting once more.

'It's called Gram,' said Leila.

'The sword has a name?' Paddy scratched his chin.

'Yeah.' Leila sounded as if nothing could be more natural. 'It's a magic sword.'

'Magic?' began Jack, but before he could say any more, he thought he heard a sigh, thought he saw an ember pulse deep within the ruby.

Paddy asked Leila what the magic did.

'Weland said that it would protect us,' she answered.

'That's good enough for me,' said Jack.

Am I going mad? he asked himself, because he actually felt that the sword *could* protect them.

'The book's over there,' said Leila with a nod towards the satchel. She looked at Jack. 'Salt?'

He nodded and raised the plastic bag he'd been holding. 'In here.'

'Cockerel blood?' enquired Paddy. He didn't have to smirk to make it sound ridiculous.

'Well,' commenced Jack, 'there was no chance I could get an actual cockerel. So . . . I got this . . .' He reached into the bag.

'Chicken thighs?' Leila scowled at the shrink-wrapped portions.

'Funnily enough the supermarket didn't sell cockerels,' Jack snapped back. 'They don't have a "sacrifice" section.'

'But Jack,' Paddy was trying not to laugh, 'the rite said *blood*, not chicken thighs. You can't spread chicken thighs over the doors and windows.'

'There *is* blood, see?' Jack held the clutch of cellophane packages aloft. 'There's always blood off chicken portions. It's revolting, but it's blood.'

'Well,' said Leila truculently, 'I hope they're male thighs.' Then she flipped open the satchel and pulled out the book. 'Let's start.'

Silence fell.

'I'll wait down there,' Paddy motioned towards the bottom of the stairwell that led up to the attic, 'to make sure no one comes up here. And I'm around in case you need help from outside this room.'

Leila squatted beside the sword. Her fingers traced the windings of the handle. 'We won't need help. We just do what the book says. And then we destroy the witch.' She looked at Paddy, then Jack, eyes defiant.

'I'll be waiting for you.' Paddy pulled the door shut behind him.

This won't work, Jack told himself. *You can't just summon a demon. OK, I've seen a ghost-witch, I've met a blacksmith who makes magic swords, but summoning a demon? No way. It won't work.*

And yet, alongside the disbelief, Jack could feel a tightening knot of fear.

Supposing this *did* work?

Leila had placed the book on the floor in the centre of the room. She opened it. 'It's no different from following a recipe.'

'You follow some weird recipes.' Jack knelt beside her. The sun shone through the low windows in dusty beams. 'OK. The most important thing is to get all the protection in place. We work from the outside in. Windows and doors first, then the outer circles and all these markings. The last thing we do is close the pentagon; the star.'

'Chicken blood round the doors and windows?' confirmed Leila.

'Yup. All along the gaps. Then the salt.' Jack laid the bag of salt and the portions of chicken on the floor. 'There's stuff that has to be read out at the same time.'

'I'll do the reading while you do the sealing,' suggested Leila.

'This bit's in Latin,' Jack pointed out.

'I don't have to understand it.' Leila looked carefully at what was written. 'I just have to say it.'

And so, as Jack dipped his fingers in the blood, then rubbed it about the door and windows, Leila recited the words of sealing, and even though the day was hot and Jack didn't understand a word of what she said, the nape of his neck prickled like ice.

When he had finished with the blood and the salt, he left them by the wall and joined Leila in the centre of the room. From outside there drifted the scoffing squawk of a crow.

'Now we draw the Pentagram of Solomon.' Jack had hold of the chalk. 'How's your art?'

'OK,' said Leila.

'Mine's not.' He handed over the chalk. 'It has to be exactly like the diagram. *Exactly*.'

'All right. Keep your knickers on, Mr Jumpy.'

'It's hardly surprising if I'm a bit jumpy,' grumbled Jack.

Leila hesitated, then took hold of his hand. It was so unexpected, Jack's heart nearly bolted into his throat.

'Thank you.' Leila's eyes held his eyes as steadily as her hand held his. 'You don't have to do this, I know that. Thank you,' and she kissed him lightly on his wounded cheek.

It was only a kiss, but Jack felt as if his veins had been filled with fire.

Jack Jolly, Witch Hunter. Master of Demons.

One kiss could change everything.

'Let's do this,' said Jack, heroic, even though he was only holding the book open for Leila to copy from.

Leila worked back and forth, studying the diagram before chalking precisely what she saw over the dry old floorboards. First she drew the outer circle, then she marked the eldritch symbols and strange words that ran around the inside of the circle. She moved in a trance of concentration, silent but for the chalk tapping and scraping over the wood.

It took her three attempts and a lot of rubbing-out with a wetted finger before the inner circle had been drawn perfectly.

'Now for the star,' she said.

'Make sure you keep plenty of space in the middle for both of us and the sword.' Jack pulled the sword close.

'It's called Gram,' Leila reminded him.

Jack was going to say that it was only a sword, that calling it by the right name didn't matter. But maybe it did.

Leila drew the chalk across the floor steadily, leaving straight white lines in its wake, never lifting it from the boards until it came back to the place where it had started: a five-pointed star, with her, Jack, the book and most of the sword inside the central pentagram.

'I don't suppose it matters that the sword . . . that Gram is sticking out a bit?' considered Jack.

'I don't suppose it does,' agreed Leila. She took the book from him and held it open at the Rite of Summoning.

Jack read through what he would have to say and what he would have to do.

'"Take the sword. Face east, then south, then west, then north, then east again, and each time draw the symbol of the demon in the air with the sword, saying . . ."' He stopped. 'We haven't got a compass! How do we know which way's east?'

'We don't need a compass.' Leila pointed through the nearest window. 'The sun rises on the other side of the valley. On my side. So that way's east.'

Jack glanced out at the far hills and woods. He made every effort not to look at Tor Cave; he felt unsettled enough without that black mouth gaping back at him. But the cave was impossible to avoid.

'OK.' He made a mental note of where the compass points lay before facing the book again. Leila was standing beside him with the pages open across her chest. She reminded him of a winged lectern, the kind he had seen in churches.

'I draw the demon's symbol in the air with the sword and each time say "Spirit, I summon thee". Then, when I get back to east I say it three more times.'

'Do you draw the symbol on each of those times too?' enquired Leila.

'I don't know,' huffed Jack. 'It doesn't say so.'

'Then you don't,' she decided. 'We just follow the recipe.'

'I wish you'd stop calling it a recipe,' complained Jack. He bent closer to check what happened next. 'When the demon appears, I hold out the sword, point it directly at the spirit and say, "Obey your master, or I will destroy you in the fire unquenchable."' Jack repeated the words in an effort to lodge them in his memory. '"Obey your master, or I will destroy you in the fire unquenchable."'

'That's a bit of a mouthful,' commented Leila.

'Hmm. You don't get many recipes with that instruction,' observed Jack, glumly. 'Then I guess we tell the demon what we want it to do.'

Leila nodded. 'I guess we do. We tell it what we want it to hunt, what we want it to destroy.'

As to the third part, it is wiser not to ask, for desire begets despair.

What that meant remained a mystery to Jack. He reached down, took hold of Gram and raised it with the handle in both hands. 'It's lighter than I thought.'

It hadn't just been Paddy's strength that had allowed him to wield the huge sword with such ease. It was the sword itself.

It moves with me, Jack realized. *Like it's alive.*

Leila humphed. 'It was heavy enough when I cycled over.'

'Just keep the book open. I'm going to have to keep checking what I'm meant to be doing.'

Leila nodded.

'Right.' Jack grinned but he knew how feeble that grin must have looked. 'Here goes.'

Standing in the centre of the pentagram that had been drawn on the floor of the attic room in The January Gallows, Jack turned towards the windows. Towards the east.

He closed his eyes. Focused. Visualized Ashgaroth's sign.

'Will it really look like a locust,' interrupted Leila, 'with a human head?'

'How should I know?' Jack was exasperated. 'That's what the book says.'

'Sorry. I just wondered. Carry on.'

Jack held Gram in both hands with the mighty blade pointing east. He drew the sign of Ashgaroth with the tip of the sword, imagining it in the air before him.

'Spirit, I summon thee.' His voice sounded weak in the dry heat of the attic room.

He turned to face south. He moved the sword and this time the sword moved with even greater ease, as if it knew what was expected of it.

'Spirit, I summon thee.' Jack felt his brow prickle with sweat. The heat hummed in his ears.

Twice more he repeated this part of the summoning and then he turned to face east for the final part of the rite. His back was towards Leila but he could feel the intensity of her stare. Before him was a low window through which he could see the rooftops and crooked chimneys of Grindle village, the meadows, the dark belt of the Deepfold woods, the black mouth of Tor Cave. The sky was a blistering blue. He blinked sweat out of his eyes.

'Spirit, I summon thee.'

Behind him, Leila was whispering, 'Find the witch; kill the witch. Find the witch; kill the witch.'

Louder this time. 'Spirit, I summon thee.'

Gram's steel blade glinted like silver and the ruby burned.

'Spirit, I summon thee!'

From where would Ashgaroth appear? Jack braced himself and waited for the demon prince.

Nothing.

Did I say it three times?

Then he heard Leila moving and he guessed she was turning to look about the room, looking for any sign of the demon. Sword grasped in both hands, blade still elevated, Jack looked about the room too.

No sign of a demon. No sign of a boy with the body of a locust. Not even a fly.

'It had to work.' Leila's knuckles were white where she held the book. 'It *had* to.'

Jack let out a long sigh and lowered the sword and in that instant, from outside The January Gallows, there came an explosive *BANG*.

Leila's eyes opened wide. Jack realized that his jaw had dropped and his pulse had kick-started into overdrive. They looked at one another for a moment and then, forgetting about the chalk pentacle and the protection it was there to give them, they ran to the window and looked outside.

A car was coasting off the high road and into the village: a long, black car, old and dusty with a bonnet like the nose of a shark. It pulled left and with a final backfire blast from the exhaust, it crunched to a halt outside The January Gallows.

A galloping up the stairs, the door flew open and Paddy burst into the attic. He looked at where Jack had dropped Gram, just inside the circle, next to where Leila had dropped the book. Then he looked to where Jack and Leila were kneeling at the low window.

'Just as we finished the rite,' whispered Leila.

Paddy knelt beside her to look out.

Jack rubbed the window clear where his breath had fogged it.

The driver's door squealed open. Out came a long leg, then another and then, jerkily, the rest of the driver appeared. He was dressed all in black: black trousers on his gangly legs, a black, three-quarter-length coat around his narrow body and, in his hand, a broad-brimmed, slightly battered, black fedora hat.

The driver had his back to the pub. He straightened up, drew a hand through his long white hair, smacked the hat into shape and placed it on his head. He surveyed the view over the village to the Deepfold and appeared to sniff the air with a nose that even from the attic window was notable for its length.

Is this the demon? thought Jack. There *was* something of the goblin about this tall and crooked stranger who had appeared spinning mystery in his long black coat and battered hat. That was when the stranger turned and, with his long nose leading the rest of his face, looked up.

Jack, Paddy and Leila bolted back from the low window.

'Did he see us?' gulped Jack.

'Don't think so,' replied Paddy. 'No reason for him to be looking for us.'

Jack paused before asking the next question. The obvious question. 'Is it *him*? Is it . . . Ashgaroth?'

'He doesn't look like Ashgaroth.' Paddy crawled forwards, back to the window. 'He looks like one of those old gunslingers. You know? Like from a cowboy film.'

Jack didn't say what he thought about goblins, but he did say, 'It is a coincidence, though, isn't it? Him turning up at the very moment . . .'

'There's no such thing as coincidence,' snapped Leila.

Paddy caught Jack's eye. It wasn't like Leila to be so curt.

Jack raised his eyebrows. 'Was it something I said?'

he mouthed. Then all three of them looked out of the window again but the stranger had vanished.

'Where . . .' gasped Jack.

There came a hollow knocking that seemed to echo from the bottom to the top of the old pub. Silence, and then it was repeated.

'He wants to come in,' said Paddy.

'He wants to *come in*?' whispered Jack, hoarsely.

'Yes, Jack.' Paddy stood. 'This is a pub and he wants to come in. It's what customers do.' He headed for the door.

'And you're going to *let* him in?' queried Jack in disbelief.

'Yes, Jack. It's what people who own pubs do.'

Leila leapt to her feet. 'Wait.'

'Wait?' Paddy frowned.

'Maybe he'll go away.' She spoke quickly. 'If he's safe, it's only one customer you're losing. And if he's not safe, it's better not to let him in.'

'You're the one who wanted to summon a demon,' commented Paddy. Jack knew that Paddy might as well have shouted, 'I TOLD YOU SO.'

'Yeah, Paddy, but none of us are inside the circle,' replied Leila, archly.

Both Paddy and Jack looked down at where they stood, as if there could be any doubt about it. Leila was right.

Three more raps on the front door.

'Why won't he just go away?' hissed Leila.

Then, from far below, voices. Talking.

Paddy closed his eyes and sighed in dismay. 'Dad.'

Only a couple of seconds later there was a roar of, 'Paddy! Paddy, where are you, you spit-blooded wastrel of a goat?'

'He doesn't like being woken up,' muttered Paddy, apologetic. 'Not before midday.'

'Paddy!' roared the voice.

'I've got to go,' said Paddy.

'We're coming with you,' stated Jack, and before Paddy could say otherwise, all three of them were running down the narrow stairs.

The stranger was framed inside the old doorway to the pub. His long limbs were all elbows and knees and his broad hat sat at an angle. His silhouette jerked, spiky against the bright rectangle of day.

'Greetings.' He doffed his hat and bowed towards Jack, Paddy and Leila. Replacing his hat, he took a step forwards and now Jack could see his face: gaunt cheeks with deep wrinkles and bright blue eyes that twinkled as if the stranger were enjoying a joke that only he knew. And that nose . . . thinner and longer than an ordinary nose should be.

Perfect for sniffing things out, thought Jack.

In a rusty voice with a twist of old Yankee, the man said, 'Ezekiel Creek.' He smiled and eyed them keenly as if inspecting their thoughts. 'Delighted to make your acquaintance.' He smiled again and Jack shuffled uncomfortably.

'Help Mr Creek with his luggage,' barked the short, stout, red-haired, red-bearded, bow-legged, goggle-eyed man who stood between Ezekiel Creek and Jack: Fergus Ben-Nazim Rakhman. Voice as broad and bray as a Dublin trawlerman's. In one hand he held a pen and, in the other, what Jack guessed was a cosh.

'Perfect for smacking sense into the brains of the unruly,' gargled Fergus Rakhman, one eye rolling in Jack's direction while the other remained riveted on Ezekiel Creek. He brandished the cosh. 'When the door starts knocking out of hours, you can be bound it'll be some dog of a journeyman spewing his wares, or a butt-notching blodger hell-bent on burglary.'

'Mr Rakhman,' protested Ezekiel Creek in a pained voice.

'Or exceptionally, and on this occasion,' backtracked the landlord, 'a gentleman of calibre.' He offered the pen to the tall stranger and motioned to a dark oak dresser that stood against the wall of the entrance lobby. An old cane salmon rod hung above the dresser, festooned with spider webs. 'Mr Creek, if you would be so good as to sign the visitors' book.'

Then he eyed Jack, Paddy and Leila in different directions and all at once. 'And you three whelps can help the gentleman with his luggage before I mistake you for a troop of slack-gobbed jobbernowls and beat the sauce from your viperous spleens.'

He swung the cosh. Jack was nearest and, had he not ducked in time, he could have sworn it would have cracked his skull. He scarpered after Paddy and Leila who had already darted outside.

'I'm sorry,' muttered Paddy, dark-eyed. 'You can see why it's better when he's asleep.'

Jack could see a lot. He could see why The January Gallows had so few customers, he could see why the villagers called the landlord mad and he could see why Paddy Rakhman was afraid of nothing. Living with Fergus Ben-Nazim Rakhman, it must have been a choice between that or living like a mouse.

'Never a dull moment,' joked Jack.

'Never a sane one.' Paddy walked to the rear of the car.

Jack walked round the front, touching the long shark-nose of the bonnet. 'I think it's an old Citroën,' he said.

'It looks as weird as Coincidence Creek,' commented Leila, who was following him.

Jack turned to her. 'Do you think there *is* a connection, between him and the rite? I mean, there must be, mustn't there? He can't have just turned up, out of the blue, at that moment, by *chance*.'

Leila's eyes narrowed. 'I think we need to watch him. Closely.'

Paddy pulled open the boot of the estate car. 'How much luggage?' He whistled under his breath.

By the time the three of them had heaved and sweated

between the pub and the car, the entrance hall had been filled with two trunks, a leather suitcase, one long silver briefcase and a stone urn that was almost as tall as Leila. Its wide mouth was covered by a steel lid and in its neck was set a dial that reminded Jack of the kind of dial used to lock a safe. All about the urn and over its lid were wrapped so many chains that it appeared to have been bound in a metal vine with padlocks for fruit.

'Something tells me he doesn't want anyone to get in,' observed Jack. He noticed that directly above the dial there was a small glass bulb that glowed green.

Paddy tugged at one of the chains. It barely moved. 'Or anything to get out,' he said.

Rakhman senior stamped up the stone-floored passage and thrust a key at Paddy. 'Room 3,' he snapped. 'Get it up there. All of it.' Then he stomped into a small panelled parlour where Ezekiel Creek sat at a table with his hat on the bench beside him. His long white hair straggled over his shoulders.

'Landlord,' Jack heard him say, 'I have been on the road a long while and would greatly appreciate a plate of bacon and eggs, if you please.' The landlord grunted. 'And a cup of coffee.'

Do demons drink coffee? Jack asked himself.

'And perhaps a small glass of wine?'

That was more like it.

'Can't see any locust legs,' Paddy whispered in his ear.

'Let's shift it all,' said Leila. 'Then we can go.'

With a great deal of sweating and swearing and rattling of chains, they manoeuvred the luggage up the rickety staircase of The January Gallows and into the large guest room at the front of the premises.

'He has a good view over the whole of the village,' observed Leila, wiping perspiration from her face with the front of her T-shirt.

That is very distracting, thought Jack, catching sight of the tight white flesh of her belly.

She strode to the broad bay window and leant forwards to look out, palms on the sill. Her short black hair was spiky from the sweat and dust of all the morning's work. 'He can see out over the Deepfold too.'

Jack stood by her: partly to see out of the window and partly just to be standing by her. Leila pointed and her finger touched the pane. 'See there? That's High Wicton. From up here he can see *everything*.' Jack could feel her mind turning this over. 'What does he want?' she pondered. 'Why is he here?'

'It can't be the sumptuous accommodation,' he commented. He looked about, at the yellowing walls, the dark beams, the threadbare carpet, the cracked and blotchy mirror and the sunken four-poster bed where Paddy lay with his hands behind his head.

'And what has he got all this luggage for?' Leila had wandered across to where they'd dumped the cases and trunks and the huge stone urn.

'I thought you were in a hurry to go,' murmured Paddy, but Leila ignored him.

Jack watched her move amongst the items, touching them, running her fingers over the surfaces gently, moving as smoothly and slowly as a cat. She stopped in front of the urn and studied the dial.

'Put your tongue back in, Jolly,' whispered Paddy, one eye open.

Angrily, Jack mouthed, 'Shut up.' He pulled a face that meant Paddy was being an idiot. That was when he noticed Leila watching him. Hoping to hide his exchange with Paddy, he continued to pull extraordinary faces. He rubbed his forehead too.

'Jack, what are you doing?' asked Leila.

'I've got a headache.' Jack huffed and pinched the bridge of his nose in what he hoped was a continuing display of discomfort. 'Maybe it's sunstroke.'

'We're indoors, Jack,' Leila pointed out. 'We've been indoors for over two hours.'

'Delayed effect,' groaned Jack. 'Just hitting me now.'

Leila shook her head and knelt by the long silver briefcase. Idly, she ran a finger over the clasp. 'Combination lock.' Then she approached the tall urn, its grey stone bound by the web of interlinking chains. 'Taking no risks, is he?' She tugged at one of the chunky padlocks.

Jack noticed that she had leant forwards to inspect the neck of the urn. 'Look here.' Her voice was hushed.

'Marks in the stone.' He joined her and looked where she indicated. 'Notice anything familiar about them?'

The marks ran round the neck, a little below where the lid sealed it. They had been etched into the stone and were so worn and so faded that for the first time, Jack realized how old the urn must have been. But time-blurred though they were, there was no mistaking the marks. In miniature, each one was a perfect replica of the diagram Leila had drawn on the floor of the attic room only an hour ago.

Jack swallowed, and it felt as if his throat had been filled with sawdust. The smell of bacon frying wafted up the stairs.

'What's Creek got locked in his jar?' whispered Leila.

'Whatever it is,' came Paddy's smooth voice, 'it's best *kept* locked in his jar.'

'Paddy!' A yell from downstairs. 'Paddy! Get down here. You're waiting on.'

Paddy swung his legs from the bed but remained sitting on the mattress, watching Leila.

Reading her, thought Jack.

From downstairs, 'Paddy! What's keeping you, you epizoon sloth-spawn?'

Leila eye's flashed at Paddy. 'Keep Creek busy. Keep him downstairs.'

Paddy's voice had a warning edge. 'Don't do anything stupid, Leila.'

'We have to find out a bit more about him,' replied Leila, all innocence. 'We need to know what we're dealing with.'

She was right, of course, but Jack sensed where Leila's thoughts were heading and he didn't like it.

'Jack'll be here to keep an eye on me. Won't you, Jack?'

Great. Anyone plans to do something stupid and they rope me in. Going on a night walk to find a homicidal witch-ghost? Jack will come too. Summon a demon prince? Count Jack in. Play the detective with Ezekiel Creek's bizarre belongings? Jack can't wait to start.

Sometimes, Jack told himself, *you just have to say NO!*

'Sure, I'll stay with you,' he replied, mildly.

You are putty, he accused himself.

Paddy shook his head. 'You're as crazy as she is.' He headed for the door. 'It was very dull before you turned up, Jack.' The door closed with a soft thud.

Jack refused to be taken in by Leila's blameless pout. 'What?'

Leila idled back to the urn and her hand came to rest on its classic neck, just below the dial. The dial and the tight-fitting steel lid looked starkly technological alongside the ancient stone and the old-fashioned chains.

'The bulb is green,' considered Leila. She looked at Jack. 'Green for locked, I suppose.'

'I guess so,' replied Jack, who had the strongest sense that green was good.

Leila's nose wrinkled thoughtfully. 'Anyway, with all these chains, I don't suppose the lid can come off.'

The chains were lashed tight round about the huge urn and over the broad steel plate of a lid, but Jack wasn't keen to put them to the test. He plucked up the courage to say, 'I think we should leave it alone, Leila.'

Strange how much courage it took to back out of something, to refuse to do it. He hadn't had the courage to face down Paddy's invitation to the night walk and that had nearly got him killed. Automatically, his hand rose to his left cheek and his fingers traced the swollen wounds.

Leila sighed. 'You're probably right,' she conceded. 'We shouldn't mess with what we don't understand.' She looked at him intensely and Jack could see that she was biting back fear. Desperate fear. 'I'm sorry, Jack,' she gasped, as if surfacing from freezing water. 'I can't stop thinking about the witch. I just want this to be something that can help us. Creek can't have turned up out of the blue for nothing. We were asking for help and . . . and he appeared. I just want to know what he's here for. I *need* to know.'

Now I seem heartless, thought Jack. 'I know, OK? I understand. But we have to be careful, Leila. And I don't see how doing anything with that dial will change anything. In fact,' he pointed out, 'unless you know the combination, how to turn it, you won't be able to open it anyway.'

Salvation! A good reason for not even trying to work the dial and it didn't make him look heartless.

But his spirits sank as Leila said, 'If you listen carefully, you can hear the dial click when you turn it the right way.'

'In films,' Jack was quick to point out.

Leila shrugged. 'It's worth a try.'

'But what about all those chains?' Jack waved a hand at the ironmongery that lashed the urn from top to bottom. 'We can't exactly take the lid off.'

A little smile crept at the corner of Leila's mouth. 'No. But we might be able to peep inside.' The smile crept away again and Leila said, 'Let's see if we can find out what Creek keeps in his pot. It might show us what he's here for. We have to find out.'

'You shouldn't mess with it, Leila,' insisted Jack, a final warning.

Leila shrugged. 'I can't help myself.'

What am I meant to do? Jack asked himself. *Wrestle her to the floor?*

'I'm going,' he snapped, feet rooted to the spot.

'Stay,' gasped Leila. 'Please, stay.'

'Give me one *good* reason why.'

Leila's hand was raised towards the urn but she paused. 'Because it feels better when you're with me,' she said, dark eyes bright, unblinking. '*Everything* feels better.'

Then she turned the dial.

The dial clicked as it turned in Leila's fingers: little clicks like the ticking of a clock, clicking and ticking as rapidly as it was turned. Leila's ear was against it, her dust-smudged face as focused as a professional safe-breaker's.

The minutes passed and the dial turned and nothing happened.

Inwardly, Jack relaxed. However determined Leila was to discover the contents of the urn, they would remain a mystery. So, when her face turned to his and a grin broke through the grime and she said, 'Got one!' it felt as if it was his guts that were being twisted rather than the dial.

'Got . . . one . . . what?' he stuttered.

'One bolt. One piece of the combination. I heard it opening.'

'Oh,' gulped Jack. 'Great.'

Leila focused back on the dial, ear pressed hard against it.

Jack cleared his throat.

'Sh!' hissed Leila, testily.

'How many do you think there are?' Even her scowls looked good, he thought.

'How many *what*?'

'How many bolts?'

'How should I know?'

Leila turned her face back to the dial.

But there was no missing the next bolt opening because after more full turns and half turns, one way and then the other, there was a loud *CLICK*.

'I think we must be nearly there,' whispered Leila.

'Really?' *You whimpered*, Jack told himself. *That was a whimper*. He cleared his throat brusquely. 'How can you tell?'

'I just can.' Leila wiggled her fingers, made a fist of them then stretched them wide. 'Here goes.' She continued to work the dial.

The room felt hot, the air too thick to breathe, and sweat prickled Jack's brow. Slowly the dial turned, clockwise, anti-clockwise, clockwise, each click counting out time.

Click . . . click . . . CLICK.

'Bingo!' announced Leila and she shot a smile at Jack before stepping back from the urn and standing alongside him.

The green light began to flash red. Then the flashing stopped; the red was constant.

BANG.

With a gasp, both Jack and Leila took a step back.

It sounded as if a heavy piece of iron had been slammed against another heavy piece of iron inside the urn. In its wake, there was a reverberating echo.

Jack could hear Leila breathing shallowly beside him. His pulse was thumping. Then, from within the huge urn there came a metallic cacophony of slams and bangs and rattles and clanks, as if a whole railway station had been flung down a gargantuan flight of stairs. Jack had to press his palms into his ears to force out the noise: the tsunami of sound was deafening at first although the urn didn't move a fraction. But the noise diminished until Jack had to listen hard to detect the final, distant clangs, like iron bars a long way off, closing. Or opening.

Arms hanging limp by their sides, Jack and Leila stared dead ahead: mute, unblinking, barely breathing.

A long, low hiss, almost an exhalation, and from all around the rim of the steel plate that covered the mouth of the urn, there came a rolling blanket of vapour. It unfurled down the curving walls of stone like a fall of fog, drifting into nothingness as it whorled onto the wooden floor of the room.

'You've opened it,' whispered Jack, hoarsely.

Almost as soon as the vapour had ceased to pour out of the loosened lid there came the first cry: a long, agonizing shriek that seemed to come from inside the urn, yet from a very great distance away. A pause and then it was answered by another. This one sounded much closer.

'Leila,' gasped Jack, 'what have you done?'

Leila bit her lip. 'I'm sorry, Jack. I'm sorry.'

And then the screaming burst from the mouth of the great stone jar without stopping: a yowling, caterwauling bedlam of screeches and roars. It grew louder and louder as if it was coming closer and closer; as if it had started deep within the urn and was now hurtling towards the loosened lid.

Wide-eyed, Jack stared at the web of chains studded with heavy padlocks. Could they really hold back the pandemonium that was storming their way?

He grabbed Leila's wrist. 'You have to close it.'

'Close it?' Leila didn't move.

'Lock it again,' insisted Jack. 'Turn the dial, Leila. Close the lid. Quick!'

Leila made as if to move but her feet remained rooted to where they were.

CRASH!

Something had smashed into the underside of the steel lid, driving it upwards so hard that every chain on the urn strained to keep it shut. Fine dust burst from the stone where the chains crashed against it.

'Leila!' shouted Jack. 'Close it!'

Another crash followed by a volley of crashes, thundering up and into the lid as if something inside was determined to smash it off. And all the time there was a tumultuous shrieking and screaming. The chains shook and strained, the padlocks squealed and the air was full of shattering stone.

'Leila!' Jack's cry was lost within the chaos. He pulled her forwards.

Leila stumbled towards the urn, shards of stone coating her hair and shoulders. Her fingers scrabbled at the dial. She spun it one way, then the other.

'I don't know how,' she yelled.

'You opened it,' Jack yelled back.

'Closing it's different,' screamed Leila in desperation.

With a snap and a boom, one great chain burst loose, flinging a padlock the size of a shoebox at Leila's head. Jack dived at Leila, taking her to the floor, his body covering hers as the great chunk of metal hummed past his face. It smashed through one of the bedroom windows in a detonation of glass. The tentacle of chain uncoiled hard enough to splinter the floor. It missed them both by a breath.

Through the storm of wood splinters and stone dust, Jack saw the bedroom door fly open and then Ezekiel Creek was standing within the maelstrom, his long coat whirling and his white hair whipping as if he had been conjured from the chaos itself. He took three long steps to the urn, dropped to one knee by the dial and spun it in his long, stick-fingers. Fingers and dial moved in a blur and then . . .

CLUNK.

The steel lid clamped down fast. The chains hung loose and limp. The screaming had stopped. All was silent, all was still, save for the gentle patter of stone dust, falling like ash.

And Ezekiel Creek, chuckling.

He stood over Jack and Leila, crooked legs so narrow it looked like his black trousers had been bandaged about them. His black shoes were inches from Jack's face. They were long and pointy. Jack had a perfect view up the nostrils of the poking nose, over which bright blue eyes twinkled down, one silver eyebrow raised, arch as a conjuror.

Jack rolled off Leila.

'Whose idea was that?' enquired Ezekiel Creek.

Jack bit back the word 'hers'.

'Mine,' murmured Leila.

Creek squatted down so that the tip of his nose was millimetres from hers. He inspected her like a collector of rare insects. 'That is *most* interesting, young lady,' he drawled.

She stared back at him, unflinching, and Jack was surprised at the venomous hostility in her eyes.

'I think I know who you are.' Ezekiel Creek spoke quietly. 'And I will be watching you very carefully.'

Jack was sure that if Leila could have growled at him she would have done. But before she had time to do anything, Ezekiel Creek was standing upright again. 'I have yet to finish my breakfast.' He brushed specks of stone from the shoulders of his black coat. 'If you would be so kind as to excuse me, I shall return to it.'

His shoes crunched over grit as he walked to the doorway, where he stopped. His back was to them but Jack could picture the smile on his goblin face. 'I take it that you have seen what you wanted to see?' He laughed, dry and wintry. 'I most certainly have.'

Jack saw Leila the following afternoon. But in between the bedlam of that morning in The January Gallows and next seeing Leila, he was busy. Mostly, he was busy doing nothing, but that was crucial. Jack knew that he had to be seen doing nothing if he was going to cool his parents' suspicions about his recent activities. And Jack's parents, like everybody else, were full of suspicions.

Fear lay thick over the Deepfold now, silent as midwinter snow and just as lonely. It swirled through the villages, fingering its way under cottage doors, blowing round the wainscots, slipping down the chimneys. Even in the middle of the day, the people of Grindle and High Wicton felt its chill. When they met in twos and threes they spoke in hushed voices as if they might be overheard and when they hurried the lonesome roads home, they stopped from time to time, listening for footsteps behind but not daring to look back for fear of what might be following.

That was by day. By night, nobody walked the cobbled streets and only cars that had taken a wrong turn off the high road swished down the empty lanes. Doors were locked and windows shut tight, despite the summer's heat. Sealed within their homes, the villagers left the bare roads, the misty fields, the high moors and the murmuring woods to the owl and the fox and the terror that walked the Deepfold.

Jack made no mention of Paddy or Leila or where he might go or what he might do. He said nothing about the fear or what he knew about it. Any suggestion of that and his parents would probably have locked him in his room and barred the windows, if only to protect him from his obvious madness. So he did his best to be bored and disinterested and this seemed to reassure his mother and father greatly.

But that first evening, having found a battered telescope during his aimless explorations of The Old School House, Jack had climbed up to the loft and, pushing open a skylight, had wriggled his head and shoulders though the gap. Up there, beneath a dusk sky striped with a smoke of purple cloud, Jack had surveyed the village.

From the high roof with its neat clay tiles, the view over the cottages and the crooked lanes was like looking into a map. And as Jack accustomed himself to the telescope, he noticed that across this map there travelled the narrow black figure of Ezekiel Creek. What business did The January Gallows' unexpected visitor have with the village of Grindle?

Ignoring a heron that perched on the ridge tiles above him, Jack had kept the telescope focused on Ezekiel Creek's battered black hat. Back and forth went the hat: vanishing behind a wall here, emerging around a gable end there and disappearing altogether below the crabbed boughs of the hollow lanes. Back and forth went the telescope.

'What are you looking for?' Jack had murmured, for, most plainly, Ezekiel Creek was in the business of looking for something. And Jack couldn't fail to notice that at an hour when the people of Grindle had deserted the village streets, Creek had emerged from his lodgings and was at his most industrious, his black, stick figure scuttling up and down and across the village and his battered hat weaving through the long grass of the surrounding fields.

Jack had spied from his rooftop eyrie until night was so thick that all he could see were chinks of lamplight in the houses below, and a big yellow moon amidst the spray of stars that arched over the blackness of the far hills and the jutting crag of Tor Cave. Then he'd shut the telescope with a *clop* so sharp it had startled the heron who flapped its wings in his face before ghosting into the darkness.

Now it was the following evening and Jack was using his T-shirt to wipe the blood from where Leila had grazed her ankle. A sliver of slate at the edge of her small front lawn had cut her as the two of them had gone to sit on the grass after tea. It was just the two of them there. Paddy was being kept busy by his father, hauling barrels of beer and cleaning tables in The Gallows.

'He's busier than usual,' Jack had explained when he'd arrived at Leila's, 'as punishment, for the damage to the room.'

Leila had bitten her lip, knowing full well that that had been no fault of Paddy's.

'So, we know two things about Creek,' Jack was now saying. 'We know that he's looking for something, or someone. And we know that you don't like him.'

'Was it obvious?' asked Leila, who was looking at Jack rather than where he was dabbing.

Jack laughed under his breath. 'Just a bit.' In truth, he had been taken aback by Leila's poisonous glare when Creek had come into the room, but he wasn't sure that she realized she had even looked at him like that.

'It's like a kind of instinct.' She was very definite. 'He gives me the creeps. He did the second I saw him.' She pulled her foot back now that Jack had finished. 'Sorry, about your T-shirt.'

Jack crossed his legs where he sat and looked at where the green cotton was stained dark brown and shrugged. 'It'll wash out. Mine did.'

'But what's he doing?' asked Leila, returning to what

they had been talking about since Jack had cycled over to her house that afternoon. 'What *is* he? He can't have just turned up when he did by chance,' she insisted. 'He turned up right as we were summoning . . .'

'Yeah, I know,' interjected Jack, before she could say the name. It was evening and just saying the demon's name felt a risky thing to do.

What time in the evening? It's hard to tell in high summer, thought Jack. He had cycled over and been here for hours and the time had passed in a blink. He should have gone before now but he couldn't peel himself from the grass and say goodbye. Not yet. He remembered how Leila had kissed him when they had been in the attic. That kiss, lightly given, had set itself in Jack's mind like a branding iron.

'And what did he mean about seeing what he'd wanted to see?' continued Leila.

I take it that you have seen what you wanted to see? I most certainly have.

What *had* Creek wanted to see?

Jack wasn't even sure what *he* had seen. Or heard. What do you call a giant stone jar wrapped in chains that is full of screams and crashes? But he knew that something terrible was being kept in The January Gallows: being kept there by Ezekiel Creek.

He let out a long breath and flicked a buttercup through the air. 'Maybe he wanted to see how stupid we were?' he suggested.

'Is Ezekiel Creek the demon?'

The obvious question.

Leila repeated it. 'Is he the demon, Jack?'

Jack stared at the grass. 'How can we know if Creek is the demon? We don't even know if demons exist.'

A sniff from Leila made it clear that to her the matter was beyond doubt.

'And if he is a demon, he hasn't done anything demonic,' Jack pointed out.

'Not *yet*,' observed Leila. 'Maybe he's picking the right time. Maybe that's why he was creeping round the village last night like you saw. Maybe he's getting *ready* to do something.' Her eyes were suddenly wide, hopeful.

'You *want* him to be the demon!'

'That *was* the point of summoning him!' Leila snapped back. She bit her lip.

Jack could see how her eyes now glistened and he realized that she was struggling not to cry. He knew that Leila was the sort of person who would do anything not to cry in front of other people.

'The witch is out there, Jack.' The fear was building within her; her voice was tight, urgent. 'You don't live here, but at night it is *so* dark. There aren't any street lights.' Leila's hand grasped his. 'When I look out of my window, when the moon is hidden by clouds and I look out there, out to the woods and the valley, the darkness is blacker than it should be. And it drifts, like there's a shadow moving across the face of the night. Blacker than black. I see it, Jack. I see it and it feels like it's . . . it's *waiting*.'

A little further down the lane stood the little girl, Liza. She was singing, her voice aimless, mixing with the buzzing of the flies.

Jack knew that Leila had to believe that something was going to stop the witch. 'Maybe Creek *is* the answer,' he said, because maybe Creek was and because he wanted to make Leila feel better.

'Part of me wants him to be,' said Leila, digging her fingers into the grass, 'and part of me . . . hates him.'

Jack was rocked by her vehemence. '*Hates* him? You don't even know him.'

'Part of me hates him and I don't know why.' She tore out a handful of turf.

'OK, listen. I don't know whether Creek is the demon, although he turned up bang on cue, but there is something . . . something else.' Jack had told Leila all about what he had seen from the roof of The Old School House, but there was more: there was what he had seen this afternoon, before he had come to Leila's house. What he had *heard*. He hadn't been sure whether to tell her about it or not; what he had heard might upset her even more. But now he felt that she needed to know everything about Creek, and he felt that he would be cheating her if he kept the information to himself.

'Go on.' Leila rolled onto her belly, ready to listen intently to what Jack had to tell her.

And so, Jack told her . . .

He had been riding up the village to the road that led to High Wicton, when he had seen the most unexpected thing: Ezekiel Creek, clad in black, his hat pressed hard to his head, riding a bicycle that Jack could have sworn belonged to Paddy Rakhman. Creek looked too long for the bicycle, his pointy elbows and knees sticking out in all directions, heels nearly scraping the ground and his black coat flapping behind him. The wheels squeaked as he pedalled and his neck stuck out so far over the handlebars that it looked as if body and bicycle were working energetically merely to keep up with the tip of his curious nose.

Jack had followed at a distance. This was the way he had been heading to go to Leila's, but he didn't want to be seen. He cycled across the high meadows once Creek had vanished into the Deepfold and there, looking down through the trees that engulfed the steep woodland road, he caught sight of the wild-caped cyclist flitting through the gaps below.

Down to the bottom of the valley Jack had gone. He had left his bike where Creek had left Paddy's, in the trees before the bridge that spanned the dry valley of rocks. Flattened grass and snapped bracken revealed the place where Ezekiel Creek had plunged into the woods. Jack had left the road, as Creek must have done, and tracked a deer path that picked the only way along a moss-filled gully. The gully was scraped out of the sheer banks above the riverbed, a stone-filled riverbed that gurgled with the rush of hidden waters.

Even in the middle of the day, it had been dark down there, the gnarled canopy of boughs shouldering out the sun. Only Jack's clumsy scrambling had disturbed the heavy silence. He could have turned back. He admitted to Leila that he'd wanted to turn back. But he'd also wanted to know what had drawn Ezekiel Creek down here, down to the depths of the woods. He'd *really* wanted to know.

Jack had been a long time clambering through ragged oak and dense wild thickets of hazel and blackthorn. He hadn't realized where he was until he spotted a high chimney twisting out of what he had taken to be a rock fall up ahead. He drew closer and the rock fall took shape, became a long stone building buried amidst root and oak and boulder, and *then* Jack had smelt smoke, heard the muted clang of iron on iron and known that Ezekiel Creek must have been paying a visit to the blacksmith. He had come to the forge.

'But the entrance would have been on the other side,' observed Leila.

'I knew that. So I climbed higher, so I could look down into the forge.'

Leila laughed and flicked a blade of grass at him.

Yes, Jack admitted to himself, *I was pretty daring: master of the woods, seeing all yet unseen, cunning as a fox. At least, that's how I felt at first.*

'What did you see?' asked Leila.

It had been the strangest sight. On one side of the great anvil stood Weland, leather apron wrapped about his thick body, hefting the hammer in mighty blows. On the other side of the anvil, Ezekiel Creek was sitting on a tall barrel. He leant forwards with his knees drawn to his chin, his long pointy shoes sticking up and his long pointy nose sticking forwards so symmetrically that he looked like a black crescent moon. His hat sat on the barrel beside him. His white hair straggled over his shoulders. He had a cigar between his teeth and in his hands he nursed a mug, brim-full of steaming liquid. The two of them were illuminated with the crimson glow thrown out by the furnace, their features charcoaled by deep shadow.

Jack had been too far away to hear much of what they said, but he'd heard a little.

'You know Leila?' Ezekiel Creek had asked the smith.

'Yes.' The hammer banged down.

'And her spirit? Is it strong? Is it tough?'

BANG. 'Yes.'

Creek had leant even further forwards then, perched atop the barrel like a gargoyle. 'How long will she last?' He chuckled. 'That is the question, Mr Weland. How long will she last?'

And then, quick as a lizard, his head had turned to look out of the forge and up towards where Jack was hiding. Camouflaged behind bracken and rowans, Jack hadn't moved. He hadn't even breathed.

Creek had uncurled his long legs from the barrel, patted his hat back on his head and strode out of the forge, cigar still between his teeth and the mug of what must have been tea still in his hand.

'Mr Weland,' he drawled. 'I have the sense that we are not alone. Do you possess such a thing as a rifle?'

The blacksmith remained by his anvil but he had looked straight at Jack.

OK, 'master of the woods' might have been overstating it. At the time, Jack had struggled to be master of his own heart, which had found its way into the back of his throat.

When the smith spoke, his voice was deep and louder than it needed to be. 'It will be a small woodland creature. Weak and nervous. It will pass by. No need for a rifle. There has been enough death in these woods.'

Ezekiel Creek had remained out on the path, looking in Jack's direction as he'd replied, 'Oh, there will be more, Mr Weland. Mark my words. There will be more.'

And as soon as the back of the black coat had swirled behind Creek, Jack had retreated from the hillside and crept back to where he had left his bike.

'He *looked* a bit like a demon when I saw him sitting there, by the furnace,' laughed Jack. 'The red fire gave him a kind of hellish glow.' But this attempt to lighten the mood didn't work.

'What was he asking about my spirit for?' demanded Leila, fiery as the furnace.

'Maybe he wanted to check that you could cope with everything that's going on.' Jack didn't really expect Leila to accept that, and she didn't.

'Creek couldn't care less about me,' she snapped. 'And that stuff about how long will I last? That's about the witch, isn't it? That's Creek guessing whether I'll be next.' She tore out another handful of grass. 'And we still don't know what he's doing here.'

I knew it was a bad idea to tell her about the forge.

Jack tried to think of how to change the subject from Ezekiel Creek, but he didn't have to. Maybe it was mentioning the witch that prompted her, but suddenly, Leila sat up. 'Jack, it's getting late.'

Liza and her singing had long since gone. The sun was sinking in a smudge of orange and mauve and a yellow moon was creeping out of the hills to the east. Jack had been lost in closeness with Leila as they had lain side by side on the cooling grass. But now day was failing.

'You can stay,' she suggested.

It was a suggestion that Jack found hard to resist. But despite the temptation of spending more time with Leila, and whatever the dangers of the woods, Jack knew there were other perils if he failed to get home.

'Mum and Dad will kill me if I don't get back,' he muttered.

OK. It isn't night yet. I only have to get over the bridge. And it's downhill all the way.

Leila sighed. 'Well, if you're going, you'd better go now.'

Her disappointment was so obvious, Jack felt all the more like staying. But he was already walking down to where his bike was propped against the wall.

Leila joined him. 'You'll be OK. It won't be properly dark for another half an hour.'

Jack nodded. 'No time to talk.' He grinned, hoping that his grin looked a lot more nonchalant than he felt.

'But there is time for this,' said Leila.

For what? Jack was going to ask, but he didn't get the chance. Leila's kiss was sudden, unexpected, and after he had begun to cycle away, he kept the feeling of that kiss on his lips. Not even the gloom beneath the trees could blot it out.

The bicycle wheels turned, the gears clicked, the road began to dip and faster now, Jack cycled into the throat of the Deepfold. But it wasn't night: not yet. And he had that kiss to keep him company. For a moment his thoughts drifted: drifted back to Leila's garden. Too late his eyes focused back on the road.

A piece of rock on the tarmac, a hard jolt and the pedals locked. The bike chain jammed in its cogs.

Jack stopped, his breathing loud in the falling darkness.

It wasn't night yet.

Not quite.

Alone and under the trees, Jack's fingers worked in a frenzy. But the chain was jammed fast. The moon rose over the woods, chasing the last light of day from the sky. The air grew cold and as Jack's eyes adjusted to the darkness, he picked out silver bars among the trees where the moonlight that washed the roof of the woods slipped through. Although it was pitch outside the moonlight, he knew that below him the road would steepen, then drop through the woods in a series of hairpin bends before bottoming out at the bridge. All he had to do was free the chain.

A noise. An owl?

God, I hope it was an owl.

Jack cast a glance back the way he'd come. Where the road entered the woods, there was a disc of moonlight.

SNAP.

Somewhere behind him. Was it movement through the trees?

Sing. I'll sing to myself; blot out what I don't want to hear.

'The Grand Old Duke of York . . .' Jack's voice was off-pitch.

'He had ten thousand men . . .' Once more he worked his fingertips into the chain and pulled.

'He took them up . . .'

What was that? Like something scuttling across the roof of trees, right over his head.

Jack's throat was in his mouth and his sweat was ice. He tugged harder and sang louder: 'He marched them up to the top of the hill and he marched them down again.' A shaking of boughs behind, as if something had just dropped through.

'And when they were up, they were up.'

Don't look up the road. Get the chain free.

'And when they were down they were down.'

Don't look back.

'And when they were only halfway up . . .'

DON'T LOOK BACK.

'They were neither up . . . nor . . .'

Jack looked back.

For a moment, the distant disc of moonlight was clear. Then, something rose up from the road, silhouetted against the pale light: something ragged and tall with long arms that stretched either side like great raven wings, long arms that ended in raking claws of stone.

For a moment, the thing hung in the moonlight. Then it swooped down the tunnel of trees, racing towards Jack.

'Down!' screeched Jack and in desperation he kicked the cogs. The chain went loose, free at last, and he leapt onto the saddle.

His legs exploded into a whir, driving the bike as fast as they could, down the road, which was already perilously steep. He didn't know how close the witch was but his back was so exposed it felt raw. And in the blur of cold air and night and silvered shadow, following the road became guesswork. Jack guessed the first hairpin right. In a squeal of brakes he guessed the second. But he missed the third.

With a face-whip of low branches, Jack was into the trees. The front of his bike hammered and skidded over loose earth and rock. One moment he was sliding side-on, the next he was coasting through air before hitting the ground in a bone-jarring thud.

But it would be worse than a bone-jarring thud if he hit a tree or came off a cliff.

He concentrated on heaving the front wheel downhill and keeping his balance and heading for the pools of unbroken light that showed him where there was space. But he didn't dare slow down. From behind there was a snapping and a shaking of branches and a tearing over the earth that let him know that the thing was following, coming after him. Drawing closer.

I am about to die.

Jack couldn't hear the air racing past his ears because

his ears were full of his own unbridled screaming. He was flung left and the witch crashed after him, he spun right and the witch crashed after him, he nose-dived between the trees and the witch came crashing after him. Jack's hair streaked behind his head, twigs and leaves slashed at his face and, open-mouthed, he screamed and scrambled his way through the trees and over the rocks.

He hit the road entirely by accident.

One instant he was bouncing across a boulder and the next there was a crystal silence as Jack, bike and spinning wheels arced out of the trees and through the air.

Had he seen that this would happen, had he thought about jumping like this, it would have ended in disaster. But driven by raw, reckless, unadulterated terror, and blinded by night, Jack didn't have time to think about anything. It just happened. He was out of the trees, sailing through the air and then there was a butt-jarring thud as the bicycle tyres touched down.

And the bridge was only fifty metres ahead of him.

Make it to the bridge.

In a sawmill of debris, the witch burst out of the trees behind him. Jack couldn't stop himself from snatching a backwards glance. The underworld light revealed an eel-dark shape whirl up the tunnel of trees. Hanging upside down from the boughs, like a bat, long arms dangling, stone claws dragging over the tarmac, the witch hurtled towards Jack.

Jack's legs pumped.

Thirty metres and the sound of raking claws was closing.

Make it to the bridge. Make it to the bridge.

His thighs burned. He couldn't breathe. Now he could pick out the low stone parapet and the dark line where the road began to climb again.

Nearly there.

Hissing, claws sliced the air by his ear and Jack screamed with the effort of cycling faster than he had ever cycled before.

Almost there.

Seconds.

The air was scythed again, but Jack had made the bridge. Stone hit stone as the great claws gouged the bridge wall in a spray of rock. Jack rocketed over the bridge . . . and straight at a body.

He slammed on the brakes, felt the bike judder to a stop beneath him, felt the handlebars pass beneath his somersaulting body and heard his bike clatter across the road as his own body hit the tarmac. He rolled to a halt at a pair of pointy-shoed feet.

'Hello, Jack,' said Ezekiel Creek.

Magnesium-bright specks of light ringed the shadows that pooled across Jack's eyes. He blinked, uncurled, looked up. 'What are you doing here?' he gasped.

'I might ask the same of you,' replied the parched voice.

Jack shuffled away from Ezekiel Creek on his elbows and all the time, Creek stood there, looking down at him, broad-brimmed hat and white hair just visible in the fog of night.

When he was sure that Creek wasn't about to strike, Jack got up, swaying, and glanced back at the bridge. All was still: no sign of the witch. Weland had been right about the running water.

'Did you see it?' panted Jack. His voice was so hoarse from screaming, it hurt to speak. 'Did you see it?'

'Why yes, Jack.' Dry laughter. 'I couldn't miss it. The two of you made quite a spectacle.'

'We summoned a demon to destroy the witch.' Jack threw the words down recklessly, like a challenge.

Go on, Creek. What are you? He half-expected a flash of sulphurous flame from where the crooked black figure was standing.

'It would appear that you haven't made a very good job of it,' was all the old man said, and he pointed a long, gnarled finger at the far side of the bridge. 'Destroying the witch, that is.' He took a step forwards. 'Why don't you go home, Jack?'

'That's where I'm going.' But Jack took a step back, towards the bridge. He peered beyond Ezekiel Creek, trying to see where his bicycle had ended up. He spotted Paddy's bike still propped against a nearby tree. The broad-brimmed hat came towards him and, retreating from it, Jack found himself back on the bridge. He wanted to leave, to leave now, but he remained on the bridge long enough to ask, 'What are *you* doing down here, Mr Creek?'

Creek's face drew close to his. Warm breath rasped against his scarred cheek and Jack smelt tobacco. 'I'm acquainting myself with the nature of the vicinity, Jack. I'm accustoming myself to the manner of the *darkness*.'

Jack drew away. He didn't like the way Ezekiel Creek had lingered over that last word and he knew why. He was still shaking, still in terror at what might be here, but Ezekiel Creek was as much at ease as if it had been broad daylight.

He likes *the dark*.

'There's worse than witches, Jack.' Creek's whisper crawled down Jack's collar and prickled his spine. 'But you have to get very close to the darkness to find it out.' Ezekiel Creek's face came even closer to Jack's until they were nose to nose. 'And the trouble is that when you get close to the darkness, the darkness gets close to *you*.'

Jack's legs were against the stone parapet of the bridge and he felt himself leaning backwards. Behind him there yawned the drop.

'How close dare you come, Jack?' whispered Ezekiel Creek. Then his arm shot out and he seemed to snatch something from the darkness itself.

'See?' Creek's fist was before Jack's eyes. Out of it there

came a shrill squeaking, almost too high-pitched to hear. Moonlight broke through the deep woods, patterning the arched bridge like pieces of a broken china plate. In a chink of light, Jack saw what Creek held in his hand: a tiny bat, wings clamped within Creek's long and knobbly fingers. Its mouth opened and closed as it squeaked.

'Come too close and the darkness gets you, Jack. It gets you and it squeezes.'

Creek leant forwards, pushing the squeaking bat right up to Jack's face. Jack arched backwards: much further and he would topple over the parapet. But he didn't slip away.

'Let it go,' he hissed, through gritted teeth.

'When you come face to face with the darkness, begging is a solution . . .' the bat wriggled and squeaked wildly, ' . . . to *nothing*.'

The fingers tightened. Jack shut his eyes. The squeaking reached a crescendo, then stopped. A coat sleeve brushed Jack's face as Creek extended his arm beyond the bridge, then opened his hand. Jack heard the soft *pat* of a tiny body landing on the rocks below.

'A word of advice, son: don't play with darkness.'

Jack pushed himself away from the parapet and recovered his bike from where it had come to rest on the safe side of the bridge. He started to pedal uphill, unsteadily.

'Goodnight, Jack,' chuckled Ezekiel Creek.

'He had your bike,' Jack was saying to Paddy. They were sitting on the swings at the small playground on Grindle village green and Leila was sitting opposite them on the roundabout. She was chewing on a long piece of grass and squinting in the broad sunlight. Jack had just finished telling them about what had happened in the woods last night.

'You shouldn't have gone.' Leila gouged a chunk of earth with a twist of her heel. 'I shouldn't have let you.'

'I had to go,' Jack assured her.

Paddy swung slowly, scuffing his heels over the worn grass. 'Jack just wanted to prove himself. Again.'

'Shuddup.' Jack sat motionless, arms hugging the chains of the swing.

'Nearly got yourself killed,' muttered Leila.

Jack looked at her, at her torn old jeans, her loose T-shirt, her battered trainers, and his eyes stayed looking. Crows wheeled and cawed overhead and the air was heavy with the scent of grass and elderflowers.

'What?' asked Leila.

Jack shook himself out of his thoughts. 'I reckon that Ezekiel Creek isn't the demon.'

'Try telling that to the bat,' growled Leila and she looked at Jack pointedly. 'I said there was something bad about him.'

'You said you hated him,' recalled Jack.

'I do.'

Paddy swung by. 'How d'you know he's not the demon?'

Jack explained. 'Demons wouldn't have to nick a bike to go down the Deepfold.'

'Says who?' asked Paddy on the return swing.

'And I think,' declared Jack in a fashion that ignored Paddy entirely, 'that Ezekiel Creek has nothing to do with the witch either.'

'Yeah? Why was he rooting about in the Deepfold then?' demanded Leila, hotly. 'Why did Creek the freak show up at all?'

Abruptly, Paddy stopped swinging, dust stirring where he had braked with his heels. 'Just a *little* aggressive, Leila,' he commented.

'Well, why *is* he here?' she snapped. 'What's he doing? What's he up to?'

Paddy starred at her, coolly. 'It's not like you to get so wound up,' he said.

'D'you know what gets me wound up?' shouted Leila. 'You saying things like *that* gets me wound up.' Her dark eyes flashed at Paddy.

History, thought Jack. *These two have known each other a long time. You're the new kid. Keep your mouth shut.* But Leila *was* acting strangely and in her eyes Jack saw the bitterness he'd noticed when she'd looked at Creek in The Gallows.

Paddy shrugged. 'He's a bit weird, Leila, but that's it.'

'He killed a bat. And you're sticking up for him just because he's a customer.' Leila twisted the blade of grass round her finger. 'You'll say anything if your dad wants you to.'

'Doesn't matter to me whether he's a customer or not. We're not *all* skint,' retorted Paddy, calmly.

Leila's eyes were smarting now. 'We're not all living in a lunatic asylum,' she shouted.

'Whoa, whoa, whoa!' cried Jack, hands raised as he jumped off the swing and stood between Paddy and Leila. 'Leave it. Both of you.'

Paddy was staring at Leila. 'What's wrong with you?' he asked, gently. 'You're . . . different.'

Leila looked away.

Jack sat on the roundabout by Leila. 'It's frightening in High Wicton,' he said. Leila said nothing. 'OK, it's frightening everywhere. And whatever we did in The Gallows, it hasn't made any difference to anything. Creek shows up. It can't be a coincidence; he must be connected with what's going on. But what he's doing here we don't know and he won't say. And we can't hang around waiting for something to happen. We can't wait for a demon that didn't show up to get rid of a witch that won't go. And we can't let the witch just carry on . . .'

'Killing?' volunteered Leila.

Jack shrugged, his shoulder brushing Leila's. 'So, I've been thinking, thinking what to do.'

'And?' asked Paddy.

'We need a different strategy.'

'Different?' Paddy raised his eyebrows.

'Yeah,' replied Jack. Leila's shoulder had come to rest against his. 'We need a change of approach.'

'Go on,' said Paddy.

Jack wondered whether, behind his straight face, Paddy Rakhman was laughing at him; it was always difficult to tell with Paddy. But the heavy silence that fell as Paddy and Leila waited for him to speak made him realize that they actually wanted to hear what he had to say, that they thought he might have come up with a good idea. It made him feel a bit uncomfortable, as if they were relying upon him to find a solution to all of this.

Relying on me? *Given what happened with the demon, or what* didn't *happen, this shows how desperate things have become.*

'OK.' Jack spoke cautiously, as if his words were footsteps in a minefield. 'When we were with Weland he said that the witch had been *imprisoned*.'

Apart from the cawing overhead, nothing interrupted him, so Jack continued.

'That was a long time ago, but the floods disturbed the grave which is why the witch has been released. But before that, it *had been* imprisoned. So,' Jack sucked in a breath, 'if it has been imprisoned once, it can be imprisoned again.'

He waited for Paddy to kick down his idea like it was made of matchsticks, but all Paddy did was purse his lips and then say, 'Fair enough. But how do we imprison a ghost?'

Leila said nothing. She didn't have to. Jack knew that she was desperate for anything that might rid them of the witch.

'We need to find out more.' Jack had already thought this through. 'We need to find out exactly what happened the first time.'

'How?' asked Paddy.

Jack's eyes turned from the playground to the high steeple of All Souls Church. The grey spire was sharp against the deep blue sky but Jack thought of witches, burnings, hangings. 'Local history,' he said.

The red-brick vicarage was engulfed in Virginia creeper. Jack led the way through a front gate with peeling paint and down an uneven path of crazy paving. The path was bordered by unkempt rose bushes whose trailing branches bristled with thorns.

'Sorry,' he heard Paddy murmur to Leila, behind him.

'Me too,' he heard Leila murmur back.

When all three of them were standing before the arched front door, Paddy grimaced sceptically.

'The Reverend Weagg knows about local history.' Jack's hand was on the bell chain. 'She might know about this.'

Paddy jutted out his chin and nodded. 'Go on, then. It can't be any worse than summoning demons.'

Jack pulled the chain. The door was answered by the Reverend Weagg: bountifully coiffured ash-blonde hair, spectacles on a chain over her pink cardigan, bright eyes and brilliant teeth.

'Charity collection or a lost football?' She beamed at them.

'Actually,' said Jack, coming straight to the point, 'we've come about local history.'

The Reverend Weagg put on her spectacles and looked at Jack, then Leila, then Paddy with as much curiosity as if *they* were items of local history. 'Extraordinary!'

There was a voice from somewhere within the cool depths of the vicarage.

'It's some children, darling,' she called over her shoulder to someone who Jack assumed must have been Mr Weagg. 'They've come about local history.' Her attention returned to the visitors. 'How can I assist?'

'We want to find out about a local witch,' said Jack.

'Dead, or alive?' Reverend Weagg clapped her hands and laughed joyfully at her quip.

'It's a bit difficult to say . . .' began Jack.

'Dead,' interrupted Paddy, dropping the word like a gravestone before Jack could say anything more.

'Hmm. Witches.' The vicar's brow furrowed. 'There was a dark period in the village's history . . .' Her voice trailed off thoughtfully and then, sharply, she said, 'It's a grim enquiry when we have come upon such dark times of our own.'

'You know about the witch?' asked Leila.

'I know there *was* a witch, centuries ago. There was a whole family of them. But as for the particulars . . .' She removed her spectacles, let them drop, pursed her lips as she sought to recall something. 'There are papers, I believe, within the archives. But it's dry, dusty stuff. I'm not sure you'd be all that interested.'

'Oh, we would,' insisted Jack.

'Definitely,' agreed Leila, enthusiastically.

The Reverend Weagg laughed like an amused headmistress. 'Such a passion for local history. How unexpected. Or is it a passion for *witches*?'

'We just want to know the history,' replied Jack, earnestly, 'and we'd be very grateful if you would help us.'

'Be careful what you wish for,' warned the Reverend Weagg. Jack felt her gaze intensify as she looked at him. 'What you desire most will cause you most trouble.'

He blinked back. It seemed a very serious thing to say and it made him feel guilty for no reason at all.

'We only want to look,' Leila assured her. 'I don't think it will cause any trouble.'

The Reverend raised her eyebrows and sighed. 'You'd be surprised where trouble lies.' Then she smiled kindly. 'Well, I don't suppose an interest in local history will cause any great upset. Come along.'

Jack, Leila and Paddy were led into a room that served as the Reverend Weagg's study. Glass-fronted bookcases lined two opposing walls. Between them stood a large walnut desk that looked through sash windows into the verdant depths of the back garden. On one side of the fireplace opposite there was a sofa, on the other there was an armchair and between them there was a low oval table.

'My name's Dorothy. Reverend Weagg is such a mouthful and I don't like Mrs. This is the room where I write my sermons, where I do my research,' she explained. She raised one of the sash windows a couple of inches. 'There: a little cool air. Forgive me for not opening it wider, but the other night,' she turned to face them, 'somebody shot, I say again, *shot*, one of the vicarage windows! And the following morning, outside the church, I found a small gun and a torch.' The glasses returned to the vicar's nose and Jack tried not to swallow loudly or shuffle suspiciously. 'I suspect foul play.'

'You should get the police to fingerprint the gun and the torch,' suggested Paddy, helpfully. 'I bet the criminal isn't very far away.'

Jack glared at Paddy. But he knew that he must have been blushing with guilt.

'Dark times,' mused Dorothy Weagg, hitching up her skirt and kneeling at a cupboard beneath one of the bookcases. 'You're the doctor's son, aren't you?' Her voice came from within the cupboard where her head and shoulders had disappeared.

'Yes,' replied Jack.

'And how are you and your family liking Grindle?' A loud rustling of papers.

'We love it,' Jack assured her.

'That's a nasty cut.'

Jack was perplexed. 'What is?'

'The cut. To your face. It's nasty.'

You should have seen what did it to me, thought Jack. 'Oh, you know,' he blathered, 'fell off my bike. One of those things.'

There was a muttering from within the cupboard and a displacement of faded paper files and old ledgers. 'And how is *your* father, Paddy?'

'Same as usual.'

'Indeed? Aha! At last. I knew it would be in the most awkward place.' Dorothy Weagg emerged from the depths of the cupboard cradling a sheaf of tatty papers within an age-mottled manila folder that had been tied up with string. She plonked them on the oval table and blew dust off the cover.

'*The Grindle Witches*,' she announced, still on her knees and reading the biro scrawl on the front of the folder. A cool late-afternoon breeze wafted in through the window. 'It's a collection of documents, relevant parish records and the like. Don't think I've ever actually read it.' She patted down her skirt. 'Shall we dive in?'

All four of them were kneeling about the table now.

'Please be careful,' warned the Reverend. 'The papers in this file will be very old: some of them hundreds of years, I dare say.' She tugged the string and opened the folder.

The collection of papers fell apart, exuding a whiff of age. The sheets were thick and when unfolded they were much longer than A4, and the writing was perfect: rolling copperplate in soot-black ink.

'They're *really* old.' Leila pointed to a date beneath one elaborate signature. 'Seventeenth of January *1697*.'

'Try not to maul them,' cautioned Dorothy Weagg. 'This is history. *Real* history. History is all about us.'

'I wish it would stay where it was buried,' Paddy muttered to Jack.

'What was that, Paddy?' enquired the Reverend, pulling free a sheet covered in a spidery scrawl.

'Do these say where it was buried?' interjected Jack, covering for Paddy. 'Where the witch was buried?'

Dorothy Weagg peered at him over her spectacles. 'You're not planning a spot of grave digging, are you?'

Grave digging?! We want to put something back in its grave, not take it out. With utter conviction, Jack said, 'That's the last thing we'd do.'

'There's nothing about witches yet anyway.' Leila was sifting through a sheaf she'd pulled to her edge of the table. 'It's all complaints.'

Paddy frowned. 'Complaints?'

'Yeah. Listen.' Leila picked up a sheet of paper, rust-brown with age, and read from it. '"Gwendolyn Lea, who did make complaint of the vanishing of her daughter, aged seven years and three months. Richard Mannings, who did make complaint . . ."' she paused as she deciphered the beautiful, ornate hand, '"who did make complaint of the vanishing of his eldest child. Mary Oakley, who did make complaint of the vanishing of three,"' Leila's voice was husky and low, '"of three of her children."' She fanned open the other sheets that were before her and looked across the table at Jack and Paddy. 'The lists go on and on: missing children.'

Dorothy Weagg bit her lip, pensively. 'Those are records of proceedings. Legal proceedings.' She inspected the papers spread before Leila. 'Trial proceedings.'

'I thought witches were tried for flying on broomsticks. For curses. Stuff like that.' Leila's voice was gruff.

The Reverend Weagg sighed sadly. 'When it comes to the worst crimes, people show very little originality. To the cruellest, children have always been irresistible.'

Only the dull buzz of a distant chainsaw broke the unhappy silence that followed.

Jack had been riffling through the papers and his fingers came upon a thick document, folded and heavy. He opened it with care; it unfolded with a crackle. The document was written in a dense gothic script and at its foot there was a seal of red wax, stamped with a coat of arms.

'This looks official,' he said.

Dorothy Weagg shuffled alongside him. 'Aha. This is more like it.'

'More like what?' asked Paddy.

'A report of what actually happened.' She hummed to herself as she cast her eyes over it. 'A mixture of Latin and English,' she muttered. 'Doubtless to prevent the uneducated from learning more than was good for them.'

'Like the demon book,' Leila whispered to Jack.

'Like the *what?*' enquired the Reverend Weagg with a piercing scowl in Jack's direction.

Great, groaned Jack, inwardly. *Every time someone puts their foot in it, Jolly has to dig it out.*

'Like the dreaming book,' choked Jack.

'*Dreaming* book?' Dorothy Weagg was not convinced.

'Yes,' insisted Leila. 'My mum and dad have a book about dreams.'

'And some of it's in Latin,' explained Jack.

The vicar shook her head. 'I thought you'd said something about demons.'

Jack and Leila both laughed: a little too desperately, thought Jack.

'What does it say?' asked Paddy, driving his forefinger hard onto the surface of the unopened document.

'Careful,' warned Dorothy Weagg, sharply. But her attention returned to what was written there. The study was silent but for their breathing. Birdsong slipped through the open window.

'It's signed by someone called Gilbert Fox-Bradley, an examining magistrate, signed on the twenty-fourth day of January 1697. See the date? There?' She pointed. Paddy, Jack and Leila nodded. Dorothy Weagg scanned the record, pointing to the writing where it revealed a matter of particular significance. 'At its head it says "Regarding Witches in the Village of Grindle".'

Stop-starting as she read it to herself, Dorothy Weagg explained what the document recorded. 'There was a whole family of witches, eleven in number . . . they lived in a farmhouse on the Grindle High Road and they "long practised witchcraft of a most maleficent nature": that's how Mr Fox-Bradley describes it.' She read on, words surfacing under her breath like air bubbles popping. 'Soldiers were sent . . . the witches were discovered in the cellars of the farmhouse . . . as were the remains . . .' Here she looked up and shook her head, '. . . the remains of twenty-seven children. The record says that their bodies had been used in the witches' rites.' She sighed. 'Poor souls.'

'Twenty-seven!' murmured Paddy in disbelief.

'The soldiers destroyed the farmhouse,' said the Reverend Weagg, and Jack's thoughts drifted from the vicarage to the moss-covered ruins that he cycled past on his journeys to and from the bus stop, how they now lay sleepily within the meadow grass and what horror they had once concealed.

Dorothy Weagg patted the pile of papers that Leila had been reading from. 'These are summaries of the statements taken from all the people who had lost children to the witches. And after the statements had been taken, a gallows was built at the western edge of the village and there the witches were hanged.'

'The January Gallows,' whispered Leila, lingering over

the name. Then she smiled at Paddy. 'You live right where the witches were executed.'

Paddy smiled back, emptily. 'Home sweet home.'

Dorothy Weagg read directly from the document. '"Ten bodies fed the crows before they were cut down and buried in unconsecrated ground, each with a stake of yew through the heart so that the accursed spirits might never rise again."' She sighed again. 'Well, it's nice to know that that was the witches out of the way.'

'If only,' muttered Leila.

'Ten?' Jack drew closer to the document. '*Ten* bodies? I thought it said that there were eleven witches?'

Outside, and for the first time in weeks, the day filled with shadow. Beyond the long garden, Jack saw that a bank of cloud had risen from the north.

'You know, I think it did,' agreed the Reverend Weagg. She adjusted her spectacles and cast her eyes over the record again. 'Ah, my Latin is not what it should be. There's a passage at the end, here, see? In Latin. I rather skipped over it, to avoid the tricky business of translation.'

'Can you read it?' asked Jack. Instinctively, he knew that this would be important: something that had been written so as to keep its meaning hidden from the curious. Why else would it appear at the end and in Latin?

'Listen.' Dorothy Weagg held up a hand. '"It is with grave sorrow that I record that one of the witches evaded capture."' Not even the summer warmth could prevent a chill from stealing through Jack's body. '"His whereabouts are, at this time, unknown. The gallows wait for him, but my work here is done."'

The Reverend Weagg folded up the document as if imprisoning the dark facts it contained.

'One of the witches got away.' Jack turned this fact over in his mind. 'It's a bit different from being imprisoned.'

The Reverend Weagg shook her head. 'You three say some strange things. I've given up asking why.'

The abrupt chime of the front doorbell distracted her. 'I think we've found out as much as we're going to.' She smiled. 'I'll see who that is and then see you off. Could you tidy up the papers while I'm gone?'

She breezed from the room.

'So, one of the witches escaped,' said Jack.

Escaped and has now come back, he thought, pushing a sheaf of papers into a small mound, trying not to bend the edges.

'But something must have happened to it,' observed Paddy.

'Something?' Leila shrugged. 'Like what?'

Paddy shrugged back. 'How should I know? But it was *imprisoned,* remember? So in between escaping and it being here now, somebody imprisoned it. That's what we need to know about: we need to find out how it was done.'

Paddy was right. But Jack's attention wasn't on Paddy.

It was on something his fingers had detected as he'd been scooping up papers. Something heavy, with a lopsided weight. He pushed the documents apart to see what his fingers had found.

A yellowed envelope.

Paddy and Leila watched him pick it up. 'There's something inside,' said Jack, shaking it gently. The envelope was unmarked but there was something long and hard within. He flipped it round.

'It's sealed.' Leila's nose was up close to it, her eyes shining with curiosity.

Jack hesitated.

'Go on,' urged Paddy.

Jack glanced toward the doorway, but there was no sound of the Reverend Weagg. As carefully as if it might be booby-trapped, he tugged the envelope open. In the silence that had fallen, the rips were unbearably loud. He dipped his thumb and forefinger inside the gap he'd made and pulled out . . .

'A key,' whispered Leila.

Jack turned the thick brown key in his palm. The handle was ornate: a finely wrought design of loops within a metal ring of entwined vines. He held it by its chunky teeth, raising it to the light to inspect it.

There was something familiar about the intricate decoration within the handle. 'It's like letters,' he whispered.

Leila's brow furrowed and she traced the design with

her fingertip. She sucked her lip and then, breathlessly, exclaimed, 'It's the same as the dresser! The dresser at my house!'

Jack saw it: the small 'v' wrought beside a larger 'H' within the pattern of the handle.

'The secret drawer!' he realized. He placed the envelope on the table and on top of it, the key. 'It'll open the drawer. It's bound to.' He paused in his excitement to push a flop of straw hair away from his eyes. 'Although what it's doing here, with all of this . . ?' He shrugged. 'Any ideas?'

Leila shrugged back.

Paddy rubbed his broad jaw. 'That key was put there, right? Someone put it in an envelope and bundled it up with a load of stuff about witches. So, it's got to be connected to the witches. And let's say it does fit the drawer in that old dresser at Leila's . . .' His eyes were keen in his olive-dark face. 'Witches? Secrets in a drawer in Leila's dresser? Isn't it a *worrying* connection?'

'I thought *nothing* worried you,' quipped Jack.

Paddy's reply was cool. 'I don't mean worrying for *me*.' He looked at Leila. But Leila was staring across the room and out of the window. 'What?'

'Someone's in the garden,' she said.

Paddy strode to the window and looked out.

'Nothing,' said Jack, joining him there. He rested his hands on the wooden sill and looked out. Deep shrubs in the borders, knotted old roses with stems as thick as his wrist and thorns like sharks' teeth, and bowing over them, tall trees, leaves darkened by the passage of summer.

At the far end of the garden there were mounds of rhododendrons, leaves thick and waxy, branches skeletal and black, motionless in the breeze which whispered across the lawn. And maybe, within the rhododendrons, there was a shadow: a shape within the shadow? Slight movement? Jack's head inched forwards until his nose was touching the windowpane.

'Jack!' from behind him, sudden and loud.

Jack's head nearly went through the glass with shock. He spun round, then slumped back against the window when he saw it was the Reverend Weagg standing in the doorway, one hand on the doorknob.

'Jack,' she smiled, 'your father's here. He's been looking for you and somebody said they'd seen you come here. No secrets in a village like this, I'm afraid.' She laughed lightly. 'He wants to speak to you. I told him you were engaged in historical research but I have to say he didn't look convinced.' She glanced to where the archive material lay spread across the low table and her eyebrows raised as if to indicate that Dr Jolly's suspicions were misplaced. 'Still,' she said, 'I think you'd better speak to him. And I'll tidy up the paperwork.'

'I'll help,' volunteered Leila.

It was not an easy meeting.

'Coming home in the dead of night . . . Serious injury to your face . . . Friends we've never met . . . We don't recognize you, Jack,' were just part of what his father had to say to him, too loudly, in the porch of the vicarage.

What am I meant to do? Explain that I was attacked by the ghost of a witch? That the witch is lurking in the woods below High Wicton? That we tried to summon a demon to get rid of it?

The truth wouldn't have helped at all, so Jack said nothing, and that made his father even angrier.

'I'll get things straight here and come home,' was Jack's sullen response at the end of his father's accusations. The air had become humid with the rising of the clouds.

'Before dark,' snapped Dr Jolly. 'I don't want to come out looking again. We've had enough, Jack.'

Jack knew that his parents were like this because they were worried for him, because what had happened to Tom Moore and Ray Hulme had crippled the villages with fear, because everyone knew that something terrible stalked the darkness.

'OK,' muttered Jack. 'But can you just go now, Dad? *Please.*' He lowered his voice. 'And stop embarrassing me.'

Dr Jolly shook his head and turned. Jack watched him walk away, head slightly bowed, shoulders slightly hunched. He watched until his father had vanished into the lane and the crunch of his footsteps had faded.

Dorothy Weagg placed a hand on his shoulder. 'Is everything all right, Jack?'

'Not a hundred per cent,' sighed Jack, still looking in the direction his father had gone.

'Just be kind to them, even if you can't tell them everything.'

'I wish . . . I wish . . .' began Jack, who was going to say that he wished he could tell his father what was really happening. But the Reverend Weagg interrupted him with a squeeze of his shoulder.

'Wishes, wishes,' she said. 'Remember, Jack, be careful what you wish for.'

'Yeah,' agreed Jack. *We wished for a demon to get rid of the witch. How careful was that?* He sighed. 'Thanks for the advice, and for the local history,' he said.

'You OK?' asked Paddy when he and Leila had joined Jack in the lane outside the vicarage.

'We heard quite a lot of that . . . what with your dad going on,' explained Leila.

'Yeah, I'm fine,' lied Jack, who felt awful. 'Just Dad being difficult.'

Paddy looked at him as if he'd just failed a basic IQ test before saying, 'You call *that* difficult?'

An image of the flame-haired, red-bearded, wild-eyed, curse-spitting Fergus Ben-Nazim Rakhman came to mind.

'Fair point,' said Jack. It was strange, but knowing that other people had weird home lives of their own made things feel better.

'Come on.' Leila led the way back towards the swings.

'It won't be dark for a couple of hours and we need to plan what we're doing next. Although I know anyway.'

Paddy and Jack exchanged expectant glances, but in fact they didn't get as far as the swings. Before they reached the small playground, Paddy halted.

'What's he doing now?' He pointed to a black figure that had slipped from the back of The January Gallows. It darted past where the shark-nosed Citroën was parked and vanished into the fields beyond. The tall grass would have hidden the figure from view entirely but for his hat and the long fishing rod he carried.

On their bellies, using the thick grass at the edge of the green for cover, Jack, Leila and Paddy followed the bobbing progress of the hat and the rod around the border of the field. The low, violet-bellied clouds made the evening darker than usual.

'That's the old cane salmon rod from The Gallows,' observed Paddy.

Jack pushed grass out of his nose. 'Is he going fishing?'

Paddy's eyes narrowed. 'He's going fishing for something, but I bet it's not salmon.'

The hat and the rod proceeded through the meadow grass, as if floating along under a power of their own. Then Ezekiel Creek surfaced, clambering a wooden stile quick as a beetle before vanishing into the fields on the other side of the graveyard. The hat and rod continued their disembodied progress until his stick figure emerged, secretive and with a whiff of skulduggery. He flitted into the trees before All Souls hid him from view altogether.

'What's the sly old snake doing?' hissed Leila to herself.

Jack caught a glimpse of the venom in her eyes. *He certainly brings out the worst in you,* he thought. But he wanted to follow Creek now, to see what he was up to. 'Come on. But not too close.' Jack remembered how Creek seemed to have sensed him when he had followed him to the forge. 'He's got a nose for spotting things.'

Paddy and Leila followed right behind Jack as he loped to the graveyard wall, climbed over it, then dashed to the nearest corner of the church.

'He's going round towards the vicarage,' whispered Leila. 'Towards the far end of the garden.' She slapped the church wall. 'I knew it. I knew there was someone in the garden.' She was as triumphant as you could be in a whisper.

Had Creek been there? Jack wondered. Had he been listening to them through the part-opened window? And if he had been hiding, why was he going back there now?

'There's nothing to fish for in the garden,' he pointed out.

'Who says he's fishing for something that's in the *garden*? Come on.' Now Paddy led the way, behind the church and round to the dense border of the vicarage lawn. Stealthily, inching through the hard mesh of branches, the three of them worked their way into the rhododendrons. Faces masked by the leaves, the deep shadow, the glooming evening, Jack, Paddy and Leila watched.

They watched Ezekiel Creek sneak his way up to the back of the vicarage, jerky as a stork stepping over hot coals. They watched as he backed into a huge bush that sprouted beside the part-open study window. They watched as the long cane fishing rod emerged from the bush and, with a hook dangling from its tip, slipped through the gap in the window and into the study.

From deep within the shrubbery, Ezekiel Creek was fishing for secrets.

Jack whispered. 'He was spying on us, listening to what was happening, and now . . .' The cogs in Jack's mind clicked into place. 'Now he's come back to sneak the key!' He looked at Leila. 'The key to the secret drawer in *your* dresser.'

'He won't sneak the key,' said Leila, sly as the salmon rod.

Paddy didn't take his eyes off Creek. 'Why not?' he murmured. 'He looks like he knows what he's doing.'

'He won't get it because *I've* got it.' Deep within the shadows of their hiding place, Jack saw the triumphal sparkle in her eyes. Then he saw the key, an inch in front of his face, as Leila displayed it.

'I took it, and tomorrow we'll see if it opens the drawer.' She tossed the key, caught it and pocketed it in her tatty jeans. 'See what's inside.' She laughed quietly, but there was a bitter edge to the laugh. 'Fish all you like, Creek,' said Leila. 'I'm one step ahead of you.'

Late afternoon, and having bolted down an early tea of ginger cake and orange juice, during which his mum was all the sweeter to compensate for yesterday's bitter words with his father, Jack left The Old School House and cycled up the village to meet Paddy. He hoped that by this time of the day, Paddy would have finished all the tasks conjured up for him by Fergus Rakhman.

Outside The January Gallows was Ezekiel Creek. He sat on a bench with his back to the stone wall, long legs stretched out before him, his hat on his head and a cheroot between his teeth. Jack felt the keenness of the old man's hooded gaze as he pedalled up the road.

'Good afternoon, Jack,' called Ezekiel Creek, without removing the slim cigar. If he knew that they had been spying on him the evening before, he showed no sign of it.

'Good afternoon, Mr Creek,' said Jack, coming to a halt before the black-clad wanderer. He sat astride his bike.

'It's a fine afternoon,' assessed Creek with a skyward squint from under the dented brim of his hat. 'But there's rain in the air.' The tip of the cheroot bobbed up and down in time with his dry, Yankee drawl.

'You've got a good nose for weather?' enquired Jack.

How can I have used that word? 'A good *sense* for the weather,' added Jack, hurriedly.

Creek chuckled and smoke slipped from between his lips. 'I have a good nose for most things, Jack.'

Jack glanced up at the sky: mostly blue but dabbed with cloud.

'Since you are not entering the inn, I take it that the purpose of your visit is to speak with me.'

Jack said nothing.

'Unless it is merely to stare, for which there is no charge.' Ezekiel Creek withdrew the cheroot and blew out a stream of aromatic smoke.

'I'm here to meet Paddy, actually.'

'Ah. Wrong again.' Creek flicked ash and replaced the cigar between his yellow teeth.

'But since I'm here, may I ask you a question?' ventured Jack. By daylight, Creek was a good deal less unsettling, but Jack hadn't forgotten about their meeting in the woods and the bat.

'Ask away.'

'What are you?'

'I'm a hunter.'

Jack did all he could to stop his eyes goggling from his head. As coolly as he was able, he enquired, 'Are you here to hunt the witch?'

Because if you are, you might be a demon.

Jack rested his foot back on the bike pedal, just in case.

'I'll be straight with you, Jack. As straight as I can be.' The crystal blue eyes were so much brighter, so much more full of life than the straggly white hair, the wrinkle-hatched skin, the funereal clothes. 'I am not here to hunt the witch. I am here to hunt something different. But as to what that is, I am not at liberty to say.'

'Jack. I didn't know you were here.' It was Paddy, standing in the doorway. 'I'll get my bike.'

Ezekiel Creek tipped his hat towards Jack. 'Off you go. And be careful.'

Careful? 'It isn't night yet,' Jack pointed out.

'It doesn't have to be, Jack. Darkness comes in many forms.' The old man drew on the cheroot and the tip glowed red.

'Come on.' Paddy pulled up, then kicked off towards the High Wicton road. Jack followed him.

'Careful with that front brake, Master Rakhman,' Ezekiel Creek called after them. 'It isn't so good.'

The ride to High Wicton left Jack sweating, and not just because of the memory of the ghost and the chunks of stone gouged from the bridge, which he showed to Paddy. The air had become thick, humid, and by the time they emerged from the Deepfold on the other side of the valley, the sky had already half-filled with cloud.

'There's a storm brewing,' said Paddy, weather-wise as a

farmer, as they leant their bikes by the wall at the foot of Leila's front garden. They went round the side of the cottage and Jack waved at the little girl who was watching from an upstairs window, two houses down. She waved back.

'What a hurry you two must have been in,' laughed Leila's mum, opening the back door to let them in. Jack was still a little breathless and sweating from the ride. The kitchen smelt of tea and bread.

'I've been baking,' she added, as if to explain the shreds of dough on her fingers and the dusting of flour down her jeans.

I don't believe it, thought Jack, recalling his own mother's newly discovered passion for baking. *It's like there's an epidemic.*

'Leila's in the front room.' Mrs Jones turned her attention to the oven and in an expert tone, observed, 'First two loaves nearly done.'

'Thanks.' Paddy headed for the front room. Jack politely mumbled something about a storm brewing and followed him.

'I waited for you. *All day.*' Leila was standing in front of the old dresser. The key was in her hand. Ready.

Jack was amazed she'd been able to wait. 'Haven't you even tried to see if it fits?'

'I don't need to.' Leila looked from the ornate handle of the key to the equally ornate carving over the top of the dresser. 'I know it will fit.'

'Have you found the drawer yet?' Paddy sat on the burst arm of a sofa.

Leila shook her head. 'Not a clue. I guess it'll reveal itself when unlocked.'

'Go on then,' urged Jack, standing beside her. He could sense the taut anticipation in her strong, slender body.

Leila required no further prompting. Key extended like a notched finger, she leant towards the hole in the woodwork, below the shelves.

'Slice of bread, anyone?' asked Leila's mum, popping her head round the door.

Jack and Leila spun round, backs to the dresser, hands crossed before them, innocent as a pair of choirboys.

'No thanks, Mum,' replied Leila.

'Jack? Paddy?'

'No, thank you, I've just had tea,' said Jack.

'Likewise,' echoed Paddy, poker-faced.

'OK.' She smiled brightly, then looked at each of them in turn, quizzically. 'Sorry to interrupt,' she whispered before leaving.

'That was close,' exhaled Jack.

Paddy sighed. 'You're only opening a drawer, not robbing a bank.'

'Yeah, but we don't know what's *in* the drawer,' replied Jack, striking a superior tone.

Paddy shrugged. 'We don't even know if there *is* a drawer.'

Leila turned the key.

A tray of wood shot from the base of the dresser, catching Jack's shins with an audible *crack*. Jack yelped with pain, then clenched his jaw to keep the noise down, hopping from one leg to the other.

Paddy nodded wisely. 'So there *is* a drawer.'

'Yes, Sherlock,' gasped Jack, rubbing his shins. 'There is a drawer.'

'Keep the noise down,' hissed Leila.

'Yeah, Jack,' added Paddy with a smirk. 'Stop squealing.'

'Shuddup,' groaned Jack.

Leila was kneeling where the thin wooden tray that had shot from the dresser now rested on the floor. 'It isn't much of a drawer.' She sounded disappointed.

'Containing one piece of paper.' Jack reached for the solitary sheet, ignoring the ache across his shins. He lifted it out and held it for the others to see. It wasn't as big as the page of a paperback book.

'That's a lot of secrecy for a small bit of paper,' added Leila, critically.

'What's on it?' asked Paddy.

Jack studied it. It was old; that was obvious from the yellow stains and elaborate lettering. 'Harfleets' was stamped across the top in bold, cursive print: lots of loops and flourishes.

'"Purveyors of fine wines and spirits"', read Leila.

'And someone's written out a list.' Jack pointed to the handwritten script, deciphering words like 'claret', 'sherry' and 'brandy'. 'And there's prices, see? In guineas.'

Leila's nose wrinkled. 'Guineas?'

'Money. Old money.' Jack sniffed the paper. 'It even smells old.'

'It's a receipt,' said Paddy. 'For the sale of alcohol.'

Leila frowned. 'And that's meant to be secret?'

'What's on the back?' asked Paddy.

'Not much,' replied Jack, who had noticed the faded scribbles and figures. 'Just workings-out, I think.'

Paddy reached down. 'Let's have a look.' He took the receipt from Jack and his dark face focused intensely on what was written. Jack looked out of the small window at clouds the colour of cannon smoke.

'It's not workings-out,' concluded Paddy, handing the receipt back to Jack. He brushed long black hair back from his face. 'It's directions.'

'*Directions?*' Jack scrutinized the scribbles. They were written in ink so old that it had turned pale brown, like washed blood. There were numbers written, then crossed out and below the numbers, words: words that were so faded, time had almost succeeded in erasing them altogether.

North of the centre.
Below the wine.
A loose stone.

Jack read this aloud, then looked up at Paddy. 'You're right,' he murmured.

'It happens,' Paddy murmured back.

Leila scowled at the note in frustration. 'What use is *that*? Below *what* wine? Where?'

Be logical, Jack told himself. *Think this through. This was written down to be helpful; that was why it was kept. And it was important; that's why it was kept secret.*

'It must have meant something to the person who wrote it,' he said. 'And it must have been intended to mean something to whoever read it afterwards. It's not meant to be impossible.'

'The fact that it's a receipt for booze must be relevant,' added Paddy.

'Yeah, there's a big alcohol theme,' agreed Jack. He weighed this up. 'Something has been put in a place where wine is stored: something to do with the witch, given that the key was with all those old papers.'

'Below the wine,' pondered Paddy. He nodded to himself. 'You keep wine in a cellar.' He leant forwards, muscular forearms draped over his thighs. 'So, we've got directions to find something in a wine cellar. But a wine cellar where?'

Silence. A silence as brooding as the storm sky that had gathered over the Deepfold. A silence that was broken by a click of Leila's finger and thumb.

'vH!' she announced, excitedly.

'vH?' queried Paddy.

'Yeah.' She pointed to the top of the dresser. 'Whoever

owned the dresser, and this key, whoever Mr vH was, he must have put the paper in the drawer.'

Paddy was mystified. 'How does that help us with a wine cellar?'

Jack's face fell as the facts clicked into place. 'You said your family bought the dresser generations ago.'

Leila nodded.

Jack swallowed. 'From the Mill.'

Leila nodded again. Jack knew that she had already worked out where they would have to go. His voice was husky and his throat was dry. 'Whatever we're looking for, it's under the cellars of Wicton Mill.'

Wicton Mill: rotting, tumbledown, its broken walls sunken within the wild woods of the Deepfold.

Leila's eyes smiled. '"North of the centre. Below the wine. A loose stone."'

A slap of Paddy's palms on his thighs made Jack jump. 'Let's go.' He was standing already.

'What? Now?' floundered Jack. Another chance to die and, as usual, one of his two friends was jumping at it. And dragging him with them.

'Would you prefer tonight?' asked Paddy. Then, to Leila, he said, 'We're going to need a torch and a compass.' He grabbed a poker from the fireplace. 'And we'll take this. The way down to the cellars is locked. We can use this to prise the locks off.'

Paddy had the poker hidden down the inside of his T-shirt when they left the cottage.

'Don't you need raincoats?' asked Mrs Jones, as they filed through the kitchen. But Jack and Paddy didn't have coats with them, and there was no way Leila was going to wear one if they weren't.

'Be careful, love,' she said to her daughter. 'Be back before dark.'

Jack could hear pleading in that voice and it made him shudder.

Leila fetched her bike from the lean-to. Her father leant out as she left. He waved to Jack and Paddy, his fingers speckled black with earth.

The little girl was sitting on her own front lawn beneath a sky of lead. 'Where you going, Leila?'

'Down the mill.'

'Can I come?'

'No, Liza.' Leila rattled her bike down the uneven stone steps.

'I aren't going back inside,' insisted the little girl, sullenly.

Without a glance up to where she sat, Leila said, 'Then you'll get wet.' Leila swung onto her bike. 'C'mon,' and she led the way down the lane.

Jack smiled and waved up to the little girl. She didn't wave back; she just watched him depart with an unblinking frown.

Leila was right about getting wet. As soon as they had started free-wheeling the narrow lane that elbowed down to the mill, the rain began to fall. The first rain in weeks.

It came with a rumble of distant thunder and a smell of dust and ozone: big, cold drops that smacked into the treetops and hit the ground like marbles. First there was a hesitant spatter and then it was pounding, drilling into the wild greenery and hissing across the road.

The trees closed over them so it was like cycling through a green tunnel. The rain crashed against the dense canopy which held it back for half a minute. Then it broke through, running down the tree trunks in black rivulets and tipping off the leaves in streams. The air was warm and the black tarmac steamed.

The lane steepened. Jack lost sight of the others and the sound of his squealing brakes competed with the racket of rain on the treetops. By the time he coasted out of the green tunnel, his hair was plastered to his head, his face was sopping and his clothes clung to him like sodden weeds. His bike shuddered to a halt. Here the tarmac ended and the way became lost amidst brambles and hawthorn thickets.

Leila and Paddy had dismounted already and were waiting for him. Leila's short, black hair was spikier than ever and in her dark jeans and T-shirt, she looked like a black slash, blurred in the coursing rain. Paddy's olive skin glistened and his arms were folded, poker in hand and bike propped against his side.

In silence they entered the thickets, wheeling their bikes and Leila leading the way. Beyond the high nettles and ferns, Jack could see the hills that led up to Wicton Slaughter and from beyond those hills came rolls of thunder. Then he became aware of another noise, a surging rush of water, and he knew they were close to the river. And now, through the tangle of hazel, hawthorn, bramble and fern, Jack saw the broken walls of Wicton Mill, engulfed in knotted greenery and sprouting broken beams and rotting rafters.

Leila bashed her way through the last stretch of undergrowth and, ducking beneath the low branches of the rowans, she came to the wall of the mill.

'Will the torch still work?' There wasn't one inch of Jack that wasn't drenched.

Leila grinned in the pouring rain and patted a bulge in her jeans pocket. 'Plastic bag.' Then she wiped water from her face. 'C'mon.'

Bikes left outside, the three of them entered the gloomy dampness of the ruin. Rain dripped from a broken roof, cracked with daylight. Jack started at a flurry of wings as a chain of rooks screeched raucously and bolted outside with a crazy flapping.

The mill was empty. Weeds choked between the stones of the bare walls and the floor was earth. Leila seemed to know where they were going because she picked her way purposefully through the rubble until she came to an iron grille that had been set in the floor. Without saying anything, Paddy strode up to the grille, identified the padlock that fastened it to a bracket set in the floor, rammed the poker into the lock and levered it up with a wrench.

There wasn't even a squeal of shearing metal. With barely a pop, the padlock cracked off. Paddy kicked it aside and took hold of the iron bars. They were set in a hinge and this did squeal as he pulled the gate open. He let it fall with a crash, then kicked away the earth to reveal a trapdoor.

'Give us a hand, Jack.' He laid the poker down and dug his fingers into the edge of the wood.

Jack knelt, felt for where wood met stone and, grasping as well as he could, he pulled. The trapdoor was heavier than he'd expected. With a creaking yawn, it opened wide.

There was a click from Leila and the fuzzy yellow beam of a torch poked into the low darkness. A flight of steps disappeared into the gloom of the cellars. Above them, the rain continued to fall.

Leila sucked in a lungful of air as if she were about to dive into water.

'I'll go first,' she said.

The dark swallowed Jack as his feet felt their way down the dust-crunchy steps. He couldn't see Leila at all. The only thing to break the murk was the feeble beam of the torch. He could hear Paddy's breathing behind him and he could hear Leila's careful footfalls immediately ahead. But for these sounds and the torchlight, all was blackness.

'There's more than one cellar,' said Leila. The beam of light probed left, then right, wobbling as it did so. Jack caught sight of brickwork, alcoves, low doorways. He imagined a skeleton manacled at the foot of a wall and then wished he hadn't.

'Hold it still,' snapped Paddy, pushing past. His voice reverberated around the walls and Jack realized that down here there was a lot more space than he could see. Now that his eyes were adjusting to the gloom, he realized also that the faintest glaze of daylight managed to leak through the open trapdoor above. He felt his shoulders ease a little as he began to pick out the walls and portals by the faint cast of distant day.

Paddy's solid form was directly in front of him. His broad shoulders turned from one archway to the next as he considered which one to take. He must have retrieved the poker from where it had been dropped because its iron length was back in his hand.

Suddenly, the poker pointed dead ahead. 'Wine racks.'

'Where?' Jack peered into the gloom. Seeing anything in this grainy darkness was made all the harder by the dancing torchlight. Then he glimpsed rows of shelving against a far wall, yellow and black in the unsteady beam.

Leila was already into the cellar, footfalls slapping over the cold stone floor. 'It's massive,' she announced, voice booming round the walls as the torch turned like a lighthouse lamp.

Instinctively, Jack drew closer to the torch. Looking about, he saw wine racks lining three of the walls. They sat above deep brick alcoves. Their empty wooden frames were strung with cobwebs.

Beyond the torchlight, Paddy paced the edge of the chamber. At one end, Jack heard him say, 'Hear that?'

Jack listened. The silence was thicker than the darkness, but then he heard it: the boom and rush of water, close by. 'The river,' he whispered. He'd seen how the old mill sat on the riverbank when he'd first walked here with Leila.

'It's flowing right outside, on the other side of this wall.' Paddy kicked at something. 'Let's have some light.'

Leila directed the beam towards him. 'OK?'

'Not on me,' complained Paddy. 'On the wall. There's something strange about it.'

'Whoa!' Jack was startled to see Paddy standing by a heap of rubble that reached to the ceiling. It had been piled precariously and Paddy had been kicking at its base. 'I'd stop kicking, unless you want to be crushed.'

There were no wine racks at that end of the cellar.

Paddy stepped back. 'Someone's blocked up an opening.'

'An opening for what?' asked Jack.

'It'll be from the mill wheel.' Leila played the torchlight over the column of loose stones. 'There isn't a wheel now but one of the old beams must have come in here from outside. It's blocked in now because it's derelict.'

'Doesn't look very safe,' muttered Jack before the torch was flicked away from the far wall, leaving Paddy in swimming darkness.

'Let's find the loose stone,' said Leila.

'We've found a whole pile of them here,' commented Jack.

'Yeah, well, it's not these stones,' grunted Paddy.

'OK, it's meant to be beneath the wine, right?' said Jack, trying to be helpful. 'There isn't any wine here but I guess beneath the wine *racks* comes to the same thing.'

Great! The alcoves. I knew this was going to end with us crawling about inside dark alcoves.

Leila pulled a small compass from her back pocket and angled it in the torchlight. Her face, neatly profiled against the blackness, nodded towards the racks against the wall opposite the entrance. 'Yup. You're right. That's north. So it'll be under those racks.' Then she sighed. 'It's a lot of racks.'

'North of the *centre*,' Jack reminded her. 'So I guess it'll be halfway along that wall.'

The cobwebs that draped the racks above the alcoves were thick and huge.

You know what big cobwebs mean? he asked himself. *Big cobwebs mean big spiders:* massive *ones.*

'Gloves,' murmured Jack.

Paddy's voice. 'What?'

'Just thinking,' explained Jack, 'next time we go grubbing about in dark, derelict wine cellars, we should wear gloves.'

'We'll start with the middle three and work outwards,' was all Paddy said. He headed for the centremost alcove.

Jack scratched his head, sure that something was already crawling across his scalp. 'I don't want to sound less than enthusiastic, right. I mean, I don't mind going first, OK? But seriously, don't we need three torches?'

Paddy was scornful. 'It's a loose stone, Jack. We have to *feel* for it, not look for it. We don't need the torch. We can take one of these alcoves each and keep going until we find the loose stone.'

'We have to *feel* for it,' Jack grumbled to himself, imitating Paddy's resolute voice. He dropped to his knees at the mouth of the alcove left of Paddy's. Paddy had already set to work; Jack could hear him scrabbling at the floor, rubbing it, testing the cold stones.

Jack took a glance back at the way they'd come in. The cellar entrance was a less-black arch in the rest of the blackness: a blackness that was disturbed only by the rush of the swollen river, the sound of hands rubbing over stone, a glow from inside the alcove that Leila was searching and the heavy rasp of his own breathing.

'Oh, God,' he muttered, gingerly inserting his head and shoulders into the space beneath the wine racks and half-closing his eyes against whatever might get into them.

The air was dank. Jack spread his fingers wide and pressed his palms to the floor. He felt the slightly curved faces of the stones and the specks of grit. Deeper he went, until he was in the alcove up to his waist. When something ran over the back of his hand he yelped, jerked his head up and away and then yelped more loudly as the back of his head banged into the roof of the alcove.

'Shuddup,' was all that Paddy muttered from the adjacent cavity.

'Why?' snapped Jack. 'We have to *feel* for it, not listen for it.'

Ha! Even at a time of darkness, my rapier wit is devastating.

'I am listening for it,' murmured Paddy. 'Listening and feeling for looseness.'

Listening *for looseness? Ridiculous.*

It was like exploring the inside of a coffin: barely enough space for shoulders and a feeling that at any moment the air might run out and the walls crush in. But teeth gritted, Jack worked across every stone in that piece of floor until he was sure that none of them were loose.

'Brilliant,' he groaned to himself. Now he would have to crawl into the next coffin.

So his relief was as great as Leila's when he heard her shout, 'Yes!'

Wiping sweat and dust from his face, he slid out of the hole and over to Leila. The torch was shining over a stone at the far end of her alcove. She was out of the alcove, but Paddy was already inside and on his belly, poker by his side, fingers in the gap between the stones.

'It's difficult to get it out,' he hissed between clenched teeth.

Jack saw the stone move slightly but slip back each time it was about to come free.

'Use this.' He stretched in and handed Paddy the poker.

'Cheers.' Paddy pushed the stone and rammed the tip of the poker into the gap. Then he was able to use both sets of fingers to prise the stone free. It came out of the floor with a scrape.

'What can you see?' asked Leila. There was no point

trying to crawl into the hole; it was already cramped with one body inside.

Jack heard Paddy blow away dirt and dust. Then there was a hollow knocking.

'Wood. There's something wooden down here, but it's covered by more stones. I'll need to get them loose.'

Paddy's black hair and dark brown skin were powdered with grit by the time he had dislodged another half-dozen stones. When he had finished, there was a jagged hole in the stone floor. Jack couldn't see what was inside the hole until Paddy carefully lifted clear a small casket. It was made of wood and studded with iron.

'Is it locked?' asked Leila.

'You don't need a lock . . .' gasped Paddy, worming backwards and out of the alcove with the casket in his hands, 'when you've buried it in stone.' He put it down and wiped his hands down his T-shirt. Even in the gloom, the web of old scars on the back of his left hand stood out waxy white.

'Nice work, Paddy,' said Jack.

Paddy grinned, eyes and teeth bright in his dirt-streaked face.

He was right: there was no lock. Jack turned this over in his mind: a key, a secret drawer and instructions that had led them to this casket. Not easy to get to, but not impossible so long as you knew where to look.

'This was *meant* to be found,' said Jack. 'But only by the right person.'

'Well, I'm going to be the right person,' said Leila, and handing the torch to Jack, she opened the lid.

A lustrous glow poured out.

Leila gasped. 'Gold!'

Jack saw that the small wooden box was full of gold coins. They caught the torchlight and cast it back at the cellar in a yellow haze. He uttered a low whistle.

Paddy swore with astonishment.

'Like pirate treasure,' whispered Leila, breathless, and she dipped her fingers into the coins which jangled as she stirred them. 'Can we sell it?' She looked up, eyes as shiny as the coins.

'We don't know whose it is,' Jack pointed out, gently. He didn't want to extinguish the brilliance of Leila's eyes.

'It isn't anybody's,' stated Paddy. 'It must have been here years . . . centuries.'

'Finders keepers,' stated Leila, grin lit by the golden halo of the casket. Then her face changed, questioning. 'There's something else in here.'

Jack frowned. 'Something else?'

She nodded, eyes narrowing. 'Yeah, under here. Under the coins.' Her fingers dug deeper within the clinking gold. Jack held the torch beam steady as a laser. When Leila pulled out her hand she was holding a scroll. It had been sealed with red wax and tied about it was a length of cord on which there hung a gold ring. She turned the ring so that its broad face was illuminated. The gold was engraved with intertwined letters, sharp in the torchlight.

'vH,' whispered Jack. 'Again.'

Paddy knelt down to inspect the wax. 'Sealed with the same ring, or the same letters. See?'

Impressed into the ruby seal were the letters Jack had seen on the dresser, the key and now the ring.

'It's his property,' concluded Jack. 'Whoever vH was. Hidden for safekeeping.'

'For the right person to find?' confirmed Leila, as if she were seeking Jack's reassurance. He nodded.

Paddy pulled the cord free of the scroll. The ring dropped onto the gold coins where it landed with a clunk. 'We want to find out about the witch, yeah?'

The witch. Jack felt his stomach tighten. The gold became less lustrous, the surrounding darkness darker.

'The key led us here,' continued Paddy, 'so this is what we're meant to find.' He shook the scroll. 'We're meant to read this now, to read what Mr vH wants to tell us.'

A message written centuries ago, but written for them. *A message from the dead,* thought Jack.

'Read it,' said Leila.

With his thumb, Paddy snapped open the seal. It crumbled into brittle specks of red that scattered over the gold.

'Like drops of blood,' considered Leila with a slow smile.

'Like you're getting weirder and weirder,' muttered Paddy, but what Jack noticed was how red Leila's lips were in the glow of the gold and the yellow torchlight.

'Concentrating?' enquired Paddy with an arch glance in Jack's direction.

'Waiting for you to start,' replied Jack, voice gruff.

The scroll unrolled stiffly, the parchment apparently wanting to roll up again. Paddy held it top and bottom like a town crier and Jack held the torch above his head like a lantern. All three of them clustered tight so they could see what was written there. Outside the circle of torchlight, the darkness pressed close.

The scroll had been written in a bold, flowing hand, full of loops and whorls. The ink was as black and vivid as the day it had been set down.

Paddy read out the words that headed the script.

'"The True History of the Grindle Witch by Johannes van Huygens, Sea Captain, written this 3rd day of April 1700."'

'At last,' whispered Leila, eyes bright.

'So this is vH,' whispered Jack. 'Johannes van Huygens.'

'Why are you whispering?' asked Paddy.

Jack shrugged. 'It feels . . . safer?'

Paddy shook his head, then continued to read from the scroll.

'"I write this history with the blood of the wretch still fresh on my hands and the memory of these events as alive as the wretch is dead."'

'Sounds promising,' observed Jack. Anything that dealt with the *death* of the witch was promising.

'Go on,' urged Leila, even though she was capable of reading it herself.

Beyond the far wall, the river whooshed and gurgled, its waters swollen with the rain. Paddy cleared his throat. '"For three years the village of High Wicton and the neighbouring hamlets have been plagued by the depredations" . . . whatever that means . . .'

'It's when something preys on something else,' said Leila with cool authority, eyes fixed on the scroll.

Jack noticed Paddy catch his eye but Jack ignored him. Why shouldn't Leila know that word, even if he and Paddy didn't?

Paddy shrugged and continued.

'". . . been plagued by the depredations of the solitary witch who did escape the justice of the Grindle hangings. For three years there has been sickness and the failure of crops and much affliction by death and the loss of small children, the bones of whom, from time to time, have been discovered within the Deepfold.

"The location of this evil having been identified as the Tor Cave, none have dared to venture into the woods or paths by day or by night, for fear of the magic and the violence of the witch."'

Of course it would be Tor Cave. I hate that place, thought Jack.

'"The witch having taken the children of Silas Longnor by creeping from the hills at dark and stealing into a bedchamber, this night I, and others from the village of High Wicton of a like resolve, have faced the Devil himself.

"Armed with a musket, swords and boar spears, we marched on the cave from my home at the mill, sure in the power and protection of the Almighty. The way was steep and the rain was hard."'

Jack closed his eyes, imagining the party of villagers clambering the wooded hills with a ramshackle cluster of weapons, flickering torches in hand, the rain pouring and the great mouth of the cave waiting for them.

'"The witch called down lightning, for the Deepfold was blasted by great bolts and forks that felled trees and broke rock, but we persevered. I led the way, my cutlass in one hand and my musket in the other.

"At the cave . . ."' Paddy paused as if it were he who was about to enter the vast stone gullet, '". . . at the cave we hesitated, for the darkness was deep and the witch was within. Then, with a cry, Silas Longnor led the way. How to describe that charnel house?"' Paddy hesitated. 'Charnel house?'

'That one's got me,' said Jack, as if 'depredations' hadn't.

'It means a place of the dead,' whispered Leila. 'Of dead bodies.'

Paddy scowled at her. 'How do you know that?'

'It just came to me,' she said with a shrug.

Paddy shook his head and continued. '"The floor was strewn with body and bone. Within the main chamber of the cave, a shape stirred, a great ragged shadow, a wretch with eyes of hate and a howling mouth. I levelled my musket to take my chance lest the witch close with us but he bolted to a crack in the wall of the cave."'

The crack Paddy told me about on our walk, guessed Jack. He swallowed drily.

'"While some pursued the witch, six of us made haste to where the hill climbs over the cave itself. The sky was wild and torn by lightning. Looking down, we saw the witch crawling up the cliff. The rest of the party were gathered on the narrow ledge below. Again, I raised my musket and this time there could be no escape. We remained like that, the witch and I, caught in the flashes between earth and sky. Even now, I see those eyes, burning with hate as the bony fingers slipped from the wet rocks. The witch had time to scream his final curse, which I set down here, though I have thought long before so doing –

I will bring death to the last of your line
As you bring death to the last of mine.

"And with that, he fell to the valley bottom, his body breaking upon the rocks."'

'Witch's Drop,' Leila said to herself. No mystery now why the sheer cliff of the cave had been given that name.

'"We buried him there, above the river, with a stake of yew through his heart. Pray God that the stake never be removed."'

But the stake that had imprisoned the witch within the earth had been dislodged by the summer floods and the spirit of the witch had been released, just as Weland had told them. Jack exhaled slowly, heart thumping as if he'd just witnessed the events himself, and re-living how close he had actually come to the terror that stalked the Deepfold once more.

'There's a list of names,' Leila pointed out.

'I'm coming to that,' said Paddy, tersely. He carried on from where he'd left off. '"And so I set down this history, as a record of things seen that should never have been and as a warning to those who come after us: that the descendants of the people of High Wicton who saw the witch fall might know who they are, that they might know themselves to be marked by the curse of the Grindle Witch."'

Jack read aloud the names that were listed in the flowing script. '"Silas Longnor, Adam Hulme, William Ipstone, Francis Onecote, Eli Moore, Captain Johannes van Huygens. May God protect our souls and the souls of those hereafter."'

His cracked voice faded in the darkness of the cellar. Inside his chest, his heart lurched.

'The names,' he whispered.

Tom Moore, descendant of Eli Moore.

Ray Hulme, descendant of Adam Hulme.

Was this the pattern of the witch's vengeance?

'That night in the woods, Paddy, you and me. The witch could have killed us, yeah?'

Paddy's voice was gruff. 'Yeah.'

'It could have killed us, but it didn't.'

'Maybe you were lucky,' suggested Leila.

'It wasn't luck, Leila. You don't stay alive if the witch wants you dead. It's the names.' Jack grabbed the scroll and pointed at the list. 'Rakhman? Jolly? We're not there.' He swallowed, and tried to keep his voice quiet and low. 'Weland said the witch was back: back for revenge.'

Leila nodded, eyes round as sovereigns.

'And now we know why, from this.' Jack shook the scroll.

'A curse,' whispered Leila, hoarse.

'A curse on those who destroyed the witch, all those years ago. A curse on their children. And this,' he shook the scroll again. 'This was a warning. Hidden to keep it safe for future generations.'

'But why did the witch come after you, then?' asked Paddy. 'That night, when you were on the bike?'

'I don't know,' admitted Jack.

'Oh, God,' gasped Leila. 'Liza!' She looked at Jack, face aghast.

'Who?' Jack asked.

'Eliza Onecote. The little girl who lives two down from me.'

'Always hanging around,' added Paddy.

'Her family are from Wicton,' continued Leila. 'Always have been, as far as I know. She might be next, Jack. She's in danger. We've got to warn her, warn her family; get her away from Wicton.'

'OK, OK,' Jack assured her. 'As soon as we're out of here we can warn them.'

Jack had felt the warmth of Leila's breath on his cheek when she spoke, each word touching his skin like a hot fingertip. In the cool gloom of the cellar, he was sure he could feel the heat from her slender body.

Wake up, Jolly, he told himself. *There's a homicidal witch-ghost on the loose and all you can think about is . . .*

Darkness.

It was very dark in the cellars of the old mill. Jack blinked as if he could blink the darkness out of his eyes. His thoughts came back to the question that had lurked behind them moments before.

Why did the witch come for me? Why? My name isn't on the list.

'Do you recognize any of the other names?' asked Jack. The sensation of Leila's body heat was fading, as he began to consider just how dark it was down here.

How dark it had become.

Paddy and Leila shook their heads.

Tom Moore: dead.

Ray Hulme: dead.

Eliza Onecote: in danger.

And that was it?

Data circled in Jack's mind: the letters vH, the old dresser and its secret drawer, the witch coming for him . . . coming for him . . . straight after he had left Leila's house . . . only moments after Leila had kissed him . . . after he'd spent the afternoon with her . . . after she'd cut her foot . . . after he'd wiped the blood from it.

Leila's blood on my clothing.

Blood that I carried into the Deepfold.

Oh, no!

'What was your name, your family name?' Jack choked the words out, trying to recall the name Leila had told him days ago. A name that sounded like . . .

'Jones?' stated Leila, blankly.

Jack shook his head. 'No. Your mum's name. Her family are from Wicton, right?'

Leila nodded, eyes solemn, luminous in the feeble torchlight.

'What was her family name?'

Suddenly, Leila's eyes widened as what Jack had realized now broke upon her. 'Higgins,' she whispered.

'Higgins . . . van Huygens.' Jack spoke rapidly. 'See? The name's the same, changed by time but that's all. That dresser wasn't bought in an old farm sale generations ago; it's been passed down through the generations, through *your* family.'

'It's a guess, Jack,' fired Paddy.

But Jack knew that Paddy was only saying that because he didn't want Jack to be right.

'It's not a guess,' Jack snapped back. 'The witch came for me, right? It came for me after I'd got Leila's blood on my T-shirt, from where she'd cut her foot. Only a few drops, Paddy. Only a few drops, but they were enough.'

A few drops of Leila's blood had summoned the witch from rock and tree and earth and had brought its tearing vengeance upon him.

'It makes horrible sense.' He turned to Leila. 'Johannes van Huygens was your ancestor. This mill was his home. And when he, or whoever it was, left the mill, they took the dresser with them, up to High Wicton. And the gold and the ring and the scroll were left here, forgotten. And with them was left the warning, which you've found, just as you were meant to.'

Leila was breathing swiftly, sharply. 'Found too late,' she whispered. 'We found it too late, Jack.'

'What time is it?' asked Paddy. His voice was calm; Paddy's voice was always calm. But the question was like a chasm opening.

Instantly, Jack knew why the darkness had been unsettling him, why it had been creeping under his skin and crawling along his nerves.

The archway into the cellar had vanished. Well, not really vanished, but it was no longer visible. Where, earlier, daylight had fingered through the broken roof of the mill and leaked down the stairs, rendering the low doorway a fuzzy arch of grey, now that doorway was as black as everything else.

And so Jack realized: outside the mill, night had fallen.

Jack, Paddy and Leila were silent. The rush of the coursing river water filled the darkness, that and their breathing. They were waiting, listening, instinctive as animals, gathered round the wavering beam of torchlight.

Then, from the floor above there came a rasp of stone scraping over stone and Jack sensed a shape, moving through the darkness, a shadow drawing closer to the open trapdoor that led down to the cellars.

'It's coming for me, Jack.' Leila's voice was shaking. 'The witch is coming for me.'

A low hiss of leaves, sweeping over the floor above. Then a moment of silence. But Jack knew that the witch was only pausing at the top of the stairs as it sensed its way, sensed its way close to them. Closer to Leila. Then, step by step, the thud of wood, the rattle of stone and the whisper of leaves as the spirit-body drew nearer, down the steps and into the cellars.

'Turn off the torch,' hissed Paddy.

A click and the pitch black swallowed them.

'We're trapped,' Jack managed to gulp, although his lungs seemed so far up his throat he could barely speak at all.

Stone claws scraped along the walls as the witch came closer; a shriek of rock that shrilled in Jack's ears.

Nearly at the bottom of the steps.

Jack swallowed and held his breath. Any moment now the darkness would erupt into stone and bone and blood.

'Come on.'

It was Leila, but she wasn't talking to him or Paddy.

Again, she whispered, '*Come on,*' and even with terror pounding in his ears, there was no mistaking the excitement in her voice.

What the hell are you asking it to come on *for?* Jack would have liked to ask, but his tongue was riveted to the back of his mouth.

'Jack, think of something.' It was Paddy, calm and steady. 'You've got the brains.'

'I have?'

'Yeah, you have. And unless you want them smeared all round the walls of this cellar, you'd better think of something *fast*.'

The rush of blood in his head and the sound of the rushing waters outside the mill made it hard to think.

Come on. Come on. Think.

River water rushing. River water.

That was it!

RIVER WATER.

The words tumbled out of his mouth. 'Paddy, get to the wall. To the broken wall.'

Paddy must have realized what he had in mind because he shouted, 'Leila! The light. On the wall. *Now!*'

The beam clicked on and illuminated the column of debris heaped against the far wall. Jack and Paddy ran to it and together they heaved at the large stones at its foot.

'We get out. We cross the river,' panted Jack. 'The witch can't cross water.'

'Right,' grunted Paddy, embracing a huge chunk of stone and pulling.

The torch beamed out of the darkness like a lost star.

'Over here, Leila,' Paddy gasped as he wrenched back on a boulder. 'Help us.'

They had seconds to get out.

Jack felt his spine arch to snapping point and his fingernails tear as he hauled on a slab. He cried out as it began to tilt back. From high up there came a fall of rubble.

'Leila!' shouted Paddy. His lips were drawn tight across his teeth and in the torchlight, the muscles of his neck stood out like whipcord. 'What's wrong with you?'

Leila didn't move, but the yellow beam did. It turned away from Jack and Paddy, so that they were plunged back into darkness. It turned towards the archway that led into the cellar.

Blood and night thumping in his eyes, Jack stared at where the beam lit the arch in a yellow circle. Something reached from the darkness and into the torchlight: a draping wing of leaves ending in long, white claws. With a scrape of stone on stone, the claws closed on the corner of the entrance. Then, below them, a gaping skull of cracked rock peered into the cellar. The skull angled towards the beam of light, sockets trained on where Leila was standing. The claws tightened on the wall, crunching brick to dust.

'Jesus Christ,' gulped Jack. Then, 'Leila!' he yelled and with a muscle-ripping heave, the huge slab of stone came free.

The cellar was filled with the crash of tumbling debris. Jack spun backwards, like a spring recoiling, clear of the burst of stones but cracking his head on the floor hard enough to see stars.

Blinking, rubbing his eyes, he scrambled to his feet. To his left there was a jagged hole in the wall, and through it came cold air, the raucous rush of the river and the violet of night. Facing him was the swearing, staggering silhouette of Paddy Rakhman. And to his right . . . to his right he could see Leila, poker in one hand and torch in the other.

'Come on,' she growled at the gaunt phantom that unfurled itself over her. 'I've been waiting for you.'

Waiting for you? Had she gone mad? Jack wondered if he was seeing things. But the claws of stone that shot towards Leila's head looked real enough.

'You're not van Huygens,' roared Paddy, rugby-tackling Leila to the ground. The poker clattered free.

The lank arm of the witch unspooled, talons slicing the space where Leila had been standing and only coming to a halt when they had embedded themselves in the floor.

'Get out of here,' Paddy shouted at Jack, hauling Leila's arm over his shoulders and half-running, half-dragging her towards the gaping hole in the wall. They stumbled drunkenly over the chunks of rock that covered the floor.

Tearing its claws free, the witch came after them.

Another swipe with a tentacle of an arm and this time nothing could stop the stone blades from ripping Leila.

A razor hiss cut the air.

Stone sliced flesh. Jack's flesh. Jack dropped the poker he had snatched up to block the witch's claws and he clutched the gash across the back of his hand where one claw had slipped down the iron to rake him.

'Get out,' shouted Paddy again. He had caught sight of Jack's dive for the poker and his upwards lash at the witch's talons.

'Get off,' yelled Leila, who was struggling against Paddy. But Paddy had his arm around her waist now and nothing was going to stop him from reaching the river. His headlong charge took them both through the gap in the wall and into the waters that surged below.

Jack sprinted the short distance to the broken wall. He knew the witch was right behind him. Before he was out of the cellar, he was diving headlong, arms flailing. The river was a short drop below. All balance lost, Jack somersaulted down. He glimpsed the ragged apparition clutching the edges of the broken masonry like shipwreck rigging. Cheated. Then he smashed into roaring, cold water.

Bubbles streamed past his ears. His pulse was pounding. He kicked upwards, arms windmilling. His head broke the surface and he sucked in air. The torrent rolled him, dragged at his legs. He had time to see the sky, the moon caught between a rip in the clouds, the skeleton boughs of the willows leaning over him and then he was under again.

Rushing water filled his head. Jack struggled to right himself, guessing at which way was up. His clothes and the grip of the swollen river pulled him down but he fought back. The world above water came in bursts of spray, gulped air and the night-shapes of the riverbank. The world below was cold and black and spinning.

He couldn't see Paddy or Leila. He couldn't focus on anything. But he knew that if he didn't get out quickly he would be swept into the gurgling throat of the Cauldron. Caught in that whirlpool, he would be sucked under for good, his body released only when the floodwaters had subsided, or, even worse, he would be pulled down and down, swallowed within the watery caverns of the Deepfold; lost beneath the earth forever.

Gasping, Jack broke up from the clutch of the current and kicked for the far bank. It wasn't far to go but the pull of the water was a gravity all of its own, a gravity that swept him sidelong or dragged him down. He hauled his arms free and reached forwards, frog-kicking. Then something hard struck his foot, or his foot struck against something hard.

The riverbed.

Jack drove his feet downwards, used the bottom to spring against the flow. Even as he floundered into the shallows, the force of the water nearly upended him. But the bank was within reach now and his hands fastened onto rocks and roots.

Coughing until his chest hurt, and with the water streaming from him, Jack threw himself up and onto the far bank. The river roared beside him. Kneeling, with his palms flat to the grassy floor, he could see the churning well of the Cauldron.

'Leila,' he choked. 'Paddy.' Then, coughing out the last of the water and finding his lungs, *'Leila! Paddy!'* But he nearly sprang back into the river when he felt a hand on his back.

'Hell, Jack,' said Paddy. 'We thought we'd lost you.'

Leila was standing beside Paddy, their shapes sodden and dripping in the shredded moonlight. She was silent. Jack sensed how her silence burned. But that didn't stop him from rolling onto his back, rolling onto his back and laughing with the exhilaration of still being alive.

'I'm happy you're enjoying yourself.' But Paddy was almost laughing too. 'What were you doing? The water's deep, but not *that* deep. We waded across. But you dived in; went straight under.'

'I didn't have time to *stroll* away.' Jack panted and wiped water from his face. The air was still humid and although the clouds were gathered in cliffs, moonlight occasionally broke through, watery as the river.

'Well, thanks.' Paddy nodded darkly, as if he had no

alternative but to acknowledge what Jack had done. But Jack knew he meant it.

'I owed you,' said Jack, matter-of-fact. Cool as a buccaneer settling a life debt. Hopefully that was how it sounded. But inside his head a voice yelled at him hysterically, *You nearly got your hand taken off. You nearly got yourself killed. You've become as crazy as* them.

His right hand was hurting a lot now. Blood zig-zagged across his skin and down his arm, inky black in the pale light.

'You OK?' he asked Leila.

Leila was staring across the river, her short, jet hair plastered to her head, her eyes huge: huge and glistening. She was staring at the gap in the retaining wall of the mill through which they'd escaped. Jack looked where she was looking even though he knew there was nothing to see. The witch had gone.

He couldn't believe how she had been ready to take the witch on. It was madness, but it was an amazing, brave madness. Her slight body against that towering spectre of rock and wood? She hadn't stood a chance and she didn't care.

'We should have finished this when we could,' she growled.

Jack spluttered, even though he'd already coughed out the water from his lungs. 'Are you kidding?' He nursed his hand against his chest, staunching the blood with his

T-shirt, astonished at what Leila had said: astonished that she plainly *believed* what she had said. 'That thing would have killed all three of us,' he pointed out.

Leila snorted, contemptuously.

Paddy placed a hand on her shoulder. 'Leila, it isn't your fault the witch is here. Don't think you have to *finish* anything.' He caught Jack's eye.

She's lost it, he was saying. *Don't ask me why, but she's lost it.*

Jack was desperate to come up with something to reassure Leila. 'We can get it exorcised,' he suggested. 'That's what you do with ghosts, isn't it? Maybe the Reverend Weagg could do it.'

Both Paddy and Leila looked at him, silent, unblinking.

OK. The competition is stiff, but that is one of the most stupid things I've ever said, admitted Jack to himself.

'The Reverend Weagg,' repeated Paddy, deadpan, 'versus the Grindle Witch?'

Jack tried not to picture it.

'I'm off,' said Leila, who turned to go, as if ignoring Jack was the best that could be done in the circumstances.

'I don't get it,' muttered Jack to Paddy. 'If she was upset because she's on the witch's to-do list, I'd get that. But she's upset because she didn't get to *fight* it.' He shook his head.

Paddy looked over to where Leila had set off. 'I don't get *her*. Not any more.'

It was uphill to Grindle. Jack took the lead, tramping unevenly as a drunk, up squelching mud tracks that glistened like giant slug trails along the knotted hedgerows but were dark as treacle beneath the trees. The others followed in silence.

Jack was used to Paddy's silence: steady, strong, like a big cat waiting. And Leila could be silent too, but not like this; this was hot, angry, gaping as the void after a bell stops ringing. It made him talk too much and the more he talked, the more he failed to watch his footing, the more he stumbled unsteadily up the steep meadows.

'We got away, that's what matters.' A foot plunged into a still-warm pool of manure.

'At least we know what the witch is after.' A jarring stub of toe into a knuckle of root. And not a very helpful comment since one thing the witch was after was Leila.

'It's so dark when the moon doesn't shine.' When all else fails, state the obvious. A hawthorn branch hooked the seat of his jeans, yanking him backwards. Paddy unhooked him with a kick of the branch.

Sweat trickled down Jack's back and prickled his face: a consequence of shambling uphill in the stormy heat and the agony of talking rubbish at silence.

'I think *all* of us are in danger now.'

Jack stopped, momentarily stunned. Whether that was because Leila had actually spoken or because of what she had said, he wasn't sure.

'*All* of us?' He didn't mean to make it sound as if he'd rather it had just been Leila.

She shrugged. 'You're in this with me. You're too close. It knows.'

'It might know how close you two are,' observed Paddy. 'I'm safe.'

'No, Paddy.' Leila almost smiled, like someone who knows a sad secret. 'You're not safe. None of us are safe now.'

'Come on,' said Paddy, gruffly. 'We're almost home.'

'I can't walk back to Wicton tonight,' said Leila, uncertainly.

'You can call your mum from mine,' suggested Jack. 'She could come over to pick you up.'

'And we could call Liza's mum too. To warn her.'

That might not be so straightforward, thought Jack, imagining the telephone call. 'Hello, Mrs Onecote. There's a witch coming for your little girl. I just thought you ought to know.' But he just said, 'Sure. We can do that.'

Thunder rumbled, distant, stalking the hills. The moon had vanished.

'Thanks,' sighed Leila. She rubbed her eyes. 'It's been a long day.'

She was trying. Jack knew that Leila was trying to ease up. But whatever was going on inside her had her spirit in a vice and she was struggling.

'I don't understand what's happening with me, Jack,' she whispered.

Jack didn't understand either so he held her hand, his blood on her this time.

'Let's just get back,' he said.

They all walked up the hill.

By the time they crested the pasture, Jack could see the straggling lights of Grindle village. Just looking at the shapes of the clustered cottages, the church spire above the trees, the web of lanes that ended with barns, farmhouses and the solitary outer dwellings made him catch his breath and quicken his pace. It had been a long afternoon. It had been a long night. He was wet through, his hand was killing him, he didn't know what to say to Leila and so much had happened. So much.

'I better get home,' said Paddy when they came to where the lane forked; The Old School House was down the village and The January Gallows was up at the top. Fat drops of rain began to fall.

'See you tomorrow,' said Jack.

'You too?' Paddy asked Leila.

Leila laughed unconvincingly. 'Yeah. After a lie-in.'

Jack watched Paddy set off, rain dashing the orange halos of the street lamps. Butter-yellow light leaked from cottage windows.

Leila's hand found his and her head rested against his shoulder. 'I'm sorry,' she said.

'For what? A great-great-great-great-great-grandfather who killed a witch?'

Paddy's lone footsteps vanished behind the rising hiss of rain.

'Not that.' Leila lifted her head from Jack's shoulder to look at him. 'I'm sorry for *me*, for what *I* am.'

They were alone. The falling rain made this part of the lane seem a place apart from everywhere else. To Jack, the murmur of their voices cocooned them even closer. He pushed his wet fringe back to stop the rain running down his forehead and into his eyes, then wiped his hand softly across Leila's pale face.

'I like what you are,' he said.

For once in your life, Jack said to himself, *don't blow this by saying something stupid.*

Jack's face moved closer to Leila's.

'Jack!'

The sound of his mother's voice shattered the moment like a hammer on glass.

'Jack!'

'Mum?'

Mrs Jolly was half-marching, half-galloping up the lane towards them. 'What on earth are you doing?' she demanded when she reached them, and then, since that didn't need any explanation, she shouted, 'Where on earth have you been?'

This was going to be bad. Really bad. In fact, this was going to be so bad it was pointless mounting any defence at all. So Jack's mouth stayed shut while his brain tried hard to find something to say. But that seemed to make Mrs Jolly even angrier.

'It's night. *Night!*'

'I know, Mum. I can see that.'

'And it's raining.'

The rain was irrelevant, but Jack decided not to point that out.

'And who is *this?*' A finger was raised in Leila's direction. 'I don't mean to be rude, but I like to know who my son is hanging about with when it's dark. When it's *night*.'

'Mum, this is Leila. I've *told you* about Leila.' Jack raised a hand to Leila's shoulder.

Mrs Jolly's eyes widened as she saw the bloody gash across the back of his hand. Anger switched to distress. 'Jack, what have you done to your hand?'

'Mum, I'm OK. Everything's fine.'

'No, you're not OK!' exploded Mrs Jolly. 'And everything's not fine.' The words came tumbling from her. 'You have no idea, *no* idea, how worried your father and I have been. It's late, you vanish, not a word of where you're going, what you're doing, *who* you're doing it with,' an accusing glance at Leila, 'and after everything's that happened in this place you just say everything's fine. Well it isn't. It's dark and we've been waiting for you: waiting and worried to death. As I imagine this young lady's parents must be. Then the police come for your father . . .'

'The police?' Jack snapped out of deaf mode. Suddenly this was taking a different turn.

'Yes, Jack, the police.' Mrs Jolly caught her breath. She seemed to steel herself for what she had to say next. In the distance, beyond her shoulder, there was a flash of light in the sky and then a roll of thunder. 'It's happened again, Jack, and this time it's a little girl. A *little girl*.'

'Who?' It was the first time Leila had spoken since Jack's mum had appeared. Mrs Jolly looked at her as if she hadn't really noticed her before.

'I don't know,' she said, trying to master her voice, her emotion. 'But it's a little girl from High Wicton. That's what the police told your father when they came for him. A little girl who had been playing out after dark. She'd told her mum she was going to the mill . . . wherever that is.' Mrs Jolly paused, recalling what she had heard. 'Something about going to where the big children were.'

Liza. She had wanted to go with them. She must have followed them down to the mill. And when the witch had been cheated of Leila . . .

Jack's blood iced.

'They found her there, Jack.' Mrs Jolly's voice cracked. 'They found her body.' She fought back the sobs. 'They found what was *left*.'

Eliza Onecote, descendant of Francis Onecote. Alone at the mill. Jack shut his eyes and tried not to imagine the witch's revenge.

'Where do you think you are going?' It was his mother's voice.

Leila was walking away from them. And Jack knew exactly where she was going.

'Leila!' he shouted.

She stopped. After a moment's hesitation she turned round.

'I'm going to finish this.' Her voice was dead. Her eyes were black and blank.

Jack ran over to her, grabbed her wrists. They were slippery with rain.

'Are you mad? Leila, you can't go back there. You can't. Leave it to the police. Everyone will do something now. There's nothing you can do. You'll get yourself killed.'

His words died against the deadwall of her silence. The sky flickered with electric light.

'Please, Leila,' he whispered. 'Please. Don't go.'

Leila wrenched her wrists from his gentle grasp. 'I can't live like this,' she hissed. Then she ran: into the rain, into the night, into the Deepfold.

Jack ran too, but he didn't run after Leila. Not straight away. Ignoring his mother who was shouting after him, ignoring the pelting rain, ignoring the lightning that held the world in electric suspension as it forked the sky, Jack ran to The January Gallows.

The stout front door was closed. Rain lashed against it. Jack hammered his fists on the wet wood and pulled the bell chain that trailed down the stone wall. He squinted up and rain cascaded down, past the mullioned windows and into his eyes.

There was no time to lose. Leila was out there and they had to get her back.

Jack turned the handle and pushed the door. It opened. He stumbled into the flagstoned hallway, gloomily lit by nicotine-yellow wall lamps. From a doorway to his left came an abrupt peal of arpeggios, played on a piano. Jack ran through the doorway and there was Ezekiel Creek, hatted and all in black, fingers spidering up and down the keyboard of an old upright piano. Thick candles guttered in the brass brackets that protruded from the piano case. Beads of molten wax hung from the brackets like bunches of grapes. Lightning flickered beyond the latticed windows of the drinking lounge; inside all was candle-tinged darkness.

'Jack!' cried Ezekiel Creek in welcome, with a glance over his shoulder. Then he hunched forwards and drove his fingers into the piano keys with renewed vigour. 'Isn't this wonderful?' he shouted over the torrent of notes.

'Where's Paddy?' asked Jack.

'Liszt's Fourth Transcendental Study.' Ezekiel Creek laughed wildly, deaf to Jack, his goblin face demented with delight at the musical ferment his fingers raked from the keyboard. 'A virtuoso piece if ever there was one.'

Thunder cracked outside.

Jack turned up the volume. 'Where's Paddy?' he yelled.

Ezekiel stopped playing, spun round to face Jack, quizzical as a night watchman. 'Paddy? Why do you come looking for your partner in crime on such a night and at such an hour?'

Jack ignored the sardonic curiosity. In fact, he ignored Ezekiel Creek altogether and scanned the room quickly. Wherever Paddy was, it wasn't here. He turned to go.

'What's happening, Jack?' quizzed Creek.

'I need Paddy,' replied Jack, and then, 'Leila's gone into the Deepfold.' He hesitated on the threshold of the drinking parlour, then added for good measure, 'To look for the witch.'

The piano stool crashed to the floor as Creek sprang to his feet. 'Now? Now, Jack? Is it now? Is the time now?' The crooked figure crossed the room, quick as a whip.

'Is *what* now?' Jack heard himself say. Creek's excitement was a distraction. He needed Paddy. He needed to find Leila.

'Wait for me.' Ezekiel Creek grasped Jack's upper arm in a grip that was far tighter than Jack would have expected. 'There are items we need. There is equipment I must fetch.'

Jack shook his arm free. 'There's no time,' he snapped.

And there was no time.

Jack ran from the room. He ran down the hallway. He looked in every room he came to and found only darkness and the skeletal clutter of pub furniture. At the foot of the stairs he ran into Fergus Ben-Nazim Rakhman.

'What in the seven secret names of the Virgin Mary are you doing here, you knob-witted piece of cat puke?' he bellowed, spit flecking his red beard, eyes rolling, fist raised.

'I'm looking for Paddy,' Jack tried to explain.

The landlord booted him in the shin.

'Get out!' he roared, as Jack hopped on one leg, clutching the other. '*Get out!*' He snatched a walking stick from an umbrella stand that stood at the bottom of the bannister rail. 'Get out, or do I have to club your fool head through that door in the forlorn hope that the rest of your scrawny carcass follows it?'

'I just need Paddy,' insisted Jack, backing away from the beetroot-faced fury with the raised walking stick.

'My son's in the cellar,' growled Rakhman. '*Working*. Shifting barrels. And that's where he'll stay until his work's done.'

Jack leant to one side, to glance beyond the landlord, as if he might actually make a dash for the cellars. But he wasn't even sure where they were.

'*Out!*' The walking stick *whoomed* through the air, missing Jack only because he was quicker with his head than Rakhman was with the stick.

'OK. I'm going,' Jack shouted back, palms raised.

He had to go. He had lost too much time already.

And now Jack ran into the night. He ran from the crazy gloom of The January Gallows, he ran down the lane past the graveyard and the silent stone ship of All Saint's Church, he ran by the slumbering cottages, his feet splashing through puddles, and he ran out of the village to where the old fingerpost pointed towards the Deepfold.

And there, for a moment, he stopped. He gulped air. Water streamed down his face. The sky ripped itself apart and in the flash, only Jack and the fingerpost broke the bare back of the hill. Then he was running again, running through the fields, feet pounding over grass and mud, skidding, slipping, careering, running down, always down, down into the trees, into the woods, into the darkness.

Jack was frightened. Not by the night but by the thing that stalked it, a thing that would rip him to pieces if it found him. But thinking of Leila helped to contain his own fear, so Leila was all he thought about as he plunged deeper into the woods. And thinking of Leila made him go even faster because he knew that she wanted to find the thing, and that in her madness, she wanted *it* to find *her*, and he knew that when it did find her, as it surely would, it would tear her apart. Jack couldn't bear the thought of that.

He hit the valley bottom running and crashed flat onto the ground as if he had been coughed out of the woods. Rain hissed over earth and water. He peeled himself up from the mud. 'Leila!' he shouted. His voice was drowned by the river which coursed over its bed and through the valley in full flood.

'Leila!' As loud as he could, but his voice barely made it into the first rank of trees on the far bank.

No smell of wood smoke tonight. It seemed that even Weland had withdrawn from the world in the face of the storm. Leila wouldn't be heading for the forge anyway.

Jack bent over, hands on knees, lungs aching, gashed hand throbbing, rainwater running off his straw hair like it was guttering. This was going to be so much harder than he had thought.

You haven't really thought about this at all, he admitted to himself. *You just ran. But you're here now. Here at the bottom of the Deepfold. And out there, somewhere, is Leila.*

He stood, still panting, eyes screwed against the rain.

And the witch would be out there too.

'OK, Jack,' he said under his breath. 'You can do this. Now get going.'

Find the bridge. Cross it. Look for Leila.

He wasn't sure how he would find her. He wasn't even sure *if* he would find her. But he was sure as hell going to try.

An explosion of thunder, and for an instant the Deepfold filled with light: a stark whiteness that lit the world from the stone hump of the bridge on Jack's right to the towering eyrie of the cave.

'I know. I *know*!' Jack yelled back. Then he dragged his legs towards the bridge that crossed the water.

The bridge that crossed the *running* water. Once over that bridge, he knew that he would be well within the Grindle Witch's reach, but heavy as his legs were, tight as his chest was, he crossed it. He had to cross it. He had to find Leila.

Jack swore as his ankle twisted over a rock.

'Leila!'

It was as much use as shouting into a blanket.

Now began the climb, a climb with legs of lead: leaden with exhaustion, leaden in the knowledge of where they would have to take him. Up, up, always up. Up to that place of darkness, that gaping mouth of rock. The witch's lair. Jack knew that it would be there that he would find Leila.

It was as wet within the trees as it had been in the fields. The hill track was a stream, slippery as oil. Jack had to grasp fringes of weed and narrow tree trunks to work his way up. He slid backwards, fell to his knees and his outstretched palm slapped down onto something that wriggled against his skin like a cold, twitching heart.

Jack whipped back his hand.

A frog. A flipping frog!

'You prat,' Jack snapped at himself, and he continued to stagger upwards.

He didn't have the energy to shout Leila's name. All he had left was the determination to go where he knew she would go. Thunder, lightning, darkness, rain stripped him of his body so that it felt as if he were watching himself slog his way up the wooded hill. But a momentary thrashing of boughs somewhere to the left of him brought his thoughts hurtling back to his body in one terrified bound.

Please be wrong.

He could be wrong because the storm was perfectly capable of shaking the trees. But there was no wind and there had been no wind. And Jack knew that in here there was something else that was perfectly capable of shaking the trees. Shaking them. Splintering them. Smashing them to the ground.

Go faster.

Weak with exhaustion, weak with fear, Jack drove himself on and up. He stumbled onto the right fork that led along the wooded cliffs and up to the cave. Even if he had had the energy, he wouldn't have dared shout Leila's name now. He moved as quietly as he could, holding his heart between his teeth to stop it thudding so loudly.

Foliage moving in the trees below. Something was keeping pace with him.

Tracking him.

Circling him.

'Shut up,' hissed Jack at the thoughts in his head. He clutched a hazel switch as his right foot slipped clumsily off the edge of the path.

He paused. Caught his breath. Listened.

Fast or slow? Do I go fast or slow? Slow's quieter, but what difference does that make?

He went more quickly now, feet tripping over each other as he hurried along the track. He swore as twigs stung his face, then bit his lip to silence himself. And all the time, he knew, he *knew* that the thing was coming closer.

Get off the path.

That was the only alternative: go straight up, aim for the fields on the slopes below the cave, the open pastures that led to High Wicton.

Jack fought his way up through the dense wood, grasping wet branches to pull himself forwards. Lightning flashed, revealing a steep maze of trees that bore down on him like infantry. Then he was blind again. Then another flash of lightning and thunder boomed. In the pitch that followed, Jack felt a wind rushing down through the trees, he heard wood smashing, he sensed the darkness hurtling straight at him.

No.

Oh, no.

Jack ran into the skull. The stone face was inches from his own, black eye sockets like dead pools, jaws gaping hungrily.

Darkness.

Jack broke right, his chest slamming into the nearest tree so hard that his feet shot from under him. He landed flat on his back in time to feel a shower of wood from where the witch's claws tore a wedge from the trunk. Then he was up and running, not caring what he ran into or where he was going, wanting only to stay alive for as long as he could.

When the sky next cracked and flashed, the great hood of Tor Cave reared above him. Jack was at the edge of the trees where the ground swept up to the huge mouth and steeper still to the hill above. He staggered back from the explosion of light, thinking he had glimpsed a solitary figure on the slopes ahead.

The witch came out of the trees.

Here, on the hillside, the giant apparition of wood and leaf and stone swept clear of the woods. Sheened in rain-light, it spun to face him, a trail of woodland wreckage swirling behind it like a cloak.

I'm dead.

'Leave him.' Leila's voice, clear as a knife in the pouring darkness.

The witch had arched over Jack, arm raised like the skeleton bough of a tree, ready to strike down.

'Leave him,' she commanded. 'It's me you want. Me.'

Jack realized that it had been Leila he had glimpsed on the slope in front of the cave mouth. Now she was walking forwards. Approaching them.

With a *whoosh* of leaf and stone, the witch spun to face her. It reared up like a cobra, hooded in bark. Leila stopped feet away. Small.

'Get away,' shouted Jack.

The sky flickered brilliantly and Jack saw a ripped-shroud arm strike down, saw the claws drive across Leila's pale face, saw her slight body smashed clear of the ground, saw it hurtle into the trees, heard the crack of breaking bones.

Thunder.

'No!' gasped Jack, voice choked by the death blow he'd just witnessed. 'No!' he yelled.

The towering spirit lurched over him. But before it

struck, its gaunt skull tipped aslant, as if listening for some distant sound.

'Leave him.'

Leila? No way.

Jack stared into the night beyond the witch. *No way.*

But Leila was standing where she'd landed. Her head was twisted at an impossible angle and her right arm had snapped back on itself by ninety degrees, but with a crack she straightened her arm and with a crunch she wrenched her head back round the way it should have been facing. Blood seeped from where the claws had raked her face.

'Leave him.' A deep, grating growl.

'Leila?' whispered Jack. The voice didn't sound like Leila's voice at all.

The witch swept away from Jack altogether now, turning in a wide circle to face the slender figure that approached it.

Jack stared speechless as Leila and the witch advanced on one another like animals preparing to fight.

Stop! he wanted to shout. He knew there was no way Leila could win this fight. But he knew also there was no way Leila should still be alive. So Jack was speechless because he didn't understand *what* was happening.

There was a moment of stillness. The ragged, jagged silhouette of the witch and, at its foot, the slight form of Leila Jones. The rain fell gently. Then came the boom of the storm and the witch lashed out, breaking Leila's legs, snapping her body, flinging it towards the mouth of the cave.

Jack scrambled forwards, close enough to see the witch lean over the spreadeagled body on the ground. But he scrambled back again as the huge figure of rock and tree crashed backwards, smashed aside by a blow from Leila's arm. It skidded to a halt metres from where he was kneeling.

How? HOW?

Jack watched Leila roll to her feet and come running down the slope. The witch righted itself in one fluid swirl and rushed towards Leila. The two met in a crunching smash of bone and wood and rock but this time Leila remained standing, her hands locked on the arms of the witch.

Bigger. Leila looked bigger. And she seemed to be growing even as Jack watched.

The witch bent backwards, straining against the girl.

What the hell was that?

From out of Leila's side an arm broke free, but not one of the arms she was using to grapple with the witch. This was *another* arm: black, gleaming, ending in claws of its own. It struck the witch in its middle, driving the giant body upwards, then flinging it aside like a doll.

'Jack.' Leila had turned to face him.

'Leila?'

The blood-streaked face was Leila's but it was someone

else's too, as if there were a face within a face, blurred, out of focus: a different shape with different eyes hiding behind the form that was Leila.

'Please, Jack,' she gasped. 'Run.'

'Run?'

'Run. Please. While you still have time.'

The witch came swooping down but Leila didn't even turn to face it. Her eyes remained fixed on Jack's. A black arm lashed out from her body, chopping the witch flat to the earth. She kicked it across the open ground. It crashed into the grassy slopes below the hood of the cave.

'Get away,' she hissed at Jack and, somewhere behind Leila's dark eyes, Jack thought he glimpsed a piercing blue.

There's something else there, Jack realized. *Something inside Leila. Something that's struggling to get out.*

'Jack, get away. Get away from *me*.'

Then Leila turned, turned and marched to where the witch was summoning its broken body back together, the pieces scuttling towards one another like a carpet of crabs.

Up rose the witch and beneath a sky of blasted cloud ripped by lightning, the two figures fought: striking, wrestling, breaking limbs. All the time, Leila grew larger, and all the time, she drove the witch backwards, up the slope to the place where the high escarpment arched over the valley like the nose of an anvil. Her body bristled with limbs: black-plated arms and legs that were thin, hard and jointed as an insect's, but far larger. Far longer. Far stronger.

Jack didn't move. He watched in disbelief, transfixed by what he saw.

Leila towered over the witch now. The spirit broke left, then right, as if trying to escape but finding no way. Leila's limbs moved fast, too fast for the witch. They imprisoned it within their grip while tearing it to shreds.

They were at the highest point now. Leila, or the thing that had been Leila, grasped the witch clear of the ground, holding it aloft, carrying it to the place where the sky plummeted into the abyss of the Deepfold. And there Leila paused. She cried out in a tongue Jack didn't understand and a voice that seemed to have been torn from the storm itself.

The night was streaked by light and rain and darkness.

With a cry that scraped the drums of Jack's ears and ground the nerves of his teeth, Leila hurled the witch into the vault of the sky, one black arm outstretched as if calling down the storm. And in that moment, as the figure of wood and leaf and rock began to hurtle down, a fork of lightning, blue as steel, speared free of the raging clouds and into the spirit-body of the Grindle Witch, blasting it with a boom that cracked the Deepfold from top to bottom.

Then darkness and the falling rain.

The witch was gone, Jack knew that for sure. The witch was gone, but in its place . . .

A figure was walking down the slope, Leila-sized again.

I should go, thought Jack.

But how could he go? He'd risked everything to find Leila.

Yes, but this isn't Leila, Jack told himself. *This is somebody else. You* know *who this is.*

But still, he waited. He waited because he wanted this to be Leila, and he waited because there was nowhere left to go.

'Jack,' cried Leila when she was still some distance from him. Her voice was twisted, raw, broken, not really her voice at all.

Her stride was uneven: not limping but more like two different strides at once.

Flickering between two bodies, thought Jack.

She stopped a few metres from him.

'Jack,' and now she grinned. Or *someone* grinned: that was how it looked to Jack. Leila's face wasn't grinning at all. In Leila's face, Jack saw anguish. But that face faded behind the high cheekbones, the tight, red lips and the long, blond hair of the tall boy who stood opposite. Leila's limbs twitched, flickered and were gone. Now, six, black-armoured insect legs unstretched, joints cracking, claws working like fingers. A thin, reptilian tail twitched along the ground.

'Leila?' gasped Jack.

You idiot. You know *this isn't Leila.*

The boy tipped back his head and laughed and laughed. When he had finished laughing, his face turned sharp as acid. 'You summoned me. My work is done. And now I claim my reward.'

Ashgaroth.

Jack's mind spun back: back through the days, back through the nights. They *had* successfully summoned the demon after all. And all this time, it had been waiting: waiting within Leila. Waiting to destroy the witch as they had demanded.

'How?' choked Jack. How had the demon managed to possess Leila when they had protected themselves exactly as the book had said?

The boy pouted and in a whisper, insisted, 'My reward, Jack.'

The book had said nothing about a reward.

But you didn't exactly read the whole book, did you? Jack admitted to himself. *You didn't read the SMALL PRINT.*

Of course there would have to be a reward. You didn't need to read the book to know that more than anything else, demons were hungry for human souls. And they didn't do favours for free.

Be careful what you wish for, the Reverend Weagg had said.

'Leila,' whispered Jack, hoping that somewhere inside

the demon, Leila's own will survived. He couldn't turn and run. He was drained. He was terrified. But more than that, more than what would happen to him, Jack needed to know what had happened to Leila. Her body. Her soul.

Ashgaroth laughed bitterly and black claws reached towards Jack's chest: reached for his heart. But before the claws touched him, the demon's eyes flamed with fury and he roared out a name.

'CREEK!'

Out of the trees stepped Ezekiel Creek, a rifle cradled in his arms and a cluster of holy pendants dangling from his neck: crucifixes, looped crosses, stars of David and others that Jack had never seen before. Immediately behind him came Paddy, a long bundle held close to his chest and a metal contraption the size of a briefcase chained across his back. Both of them were streaked with mud. Water dripped from the brim of Creek's hat, which he touched in greeting to Jack.

'Step aside, Jack,' said Ezekiel Creek, his Yankee drawl cool as a gunslinger's.

'*Creek!*' roared Ashgaroth. There was hate in that bellow; Jack could feel its heat. But there was something else, and it took Jack a moment to realize what it was.

Fear.

The demon took a step back, and then another, retreating.

Jack caught Paddy's eye.

'Came as quick as he told me,' panted Paddy with a nod towards Creek. 'Where's Leila?'

Jack pointed at the demon. 'There.'

Leila, or Ashgaroth, whichever it was, backed away from Creek, claws flexing, tail twitching. Only Jack stood between them.

'Christ!' Paddy sank to his knees. His long black hair was plastered across his face and hung to his shoulders in thick, wet swathes. Teeth gritted, he slung the metal from his shoulders. It hit the soft earth with a clatter and now Jack could see what it was, a shallow metal box with a loose lid of overlapping metal plates.

'What the hell have you done, Jack?' accused Paddy.

'What the hell is *he* doing?' Jack fired back, with a jerk of his thumb at Creek.

'I'm a hunter, Jack, and right now, I'm hunting.' Ezekiel Creek's eyes were fixed on the creature behind Jack. 'I hunt demons. Don't I, Ashgaroth?'

The answering roar splintered the air.

'He's cleaning up *your* mess,' Paddy growled at Jack.

'Oh, I wouldn't say that, Mr Rakhman,' said Ezekiel Creek. 'I'm merely doing what I have to do. Sooner or later, this was always going to happen. Isn't that right, Ashgaroth?'

The demon bull-snorted in reply.

'Now, you know what happens next,' stated Creek. He was addressing Ashgaroth. The rifle was tucked under one arm and, in his free hand, Jack could see what looked like a bundle of sticks: metal sticks.

'You see, Jacky boy, our friend is currently trapped within the body he has so brutally borrowed.' Creek chuckled drily, oblivious to the pouring rain. 'Until he has concluded his bargain with *you*, he can go nowhere. Am I not right, Ashgaroth?'

The demon's blue eyes were slits of hate, his voice acid. 'As you say, Creek, *nothing* is concluded yet.'

'Seventy-two demons King Solomon imprisoned in a jar.' Creek threw a stick high and it landed like a knife in the ground beyond the demon. 'And inevitably, seventy-two demons were released by some fool's curiosity.' Another metal stick was thrown, landing beyond the demon again and some way off from the other. The old man winked at Jack. 'History fails to tell who that fool was.'

Jack flinched as the next stick spun past his ear to land in the ground near the trees.

'But all of that was a very long time ago.' Ezekiel Creek flung the final stick into the tree line and Jack realized that the four sticks now marked the four corners of a square: a large square within which he, Paddy, Creek and the demon were all standing.

'It has taken a very long time to get all the demons back into that jar,' sighed Ezekiel Creek, and Jack thought of the large urn in the old man's room at The January Gallows, and he realized what he and Leila had nearly released from it. 'And for too many years I have been hunting this *final* demon.' Creek smiled at the blond boy with the armoured body of an insect. 'You were good, Ashgaroth, but you weren't good enough.' Then he pressed a button on a small fob that remained in his hand.

At once, streaks of light flickered out from the metal sticks, joining square with one another and crackling upwards like electric walls. The walls glowed like silver-blue screens and their surfaces swam with signs and symbols, lines and letters. These patterns swam across the ground too and flat overhead so that the whole formed a huge, luminous box that contained them all.

Dwarfed as he was by this vast illumination, Jack knew it was familiar and, when he looked down, he realized why this was. Shimmering beneath his feet was the design that he had drawn with chalk in the attic room of The Gallows: the Pentagram of Solomon. Now it floated above, around and beneath them, repeated many times and forming a perfect seal, shutting them off from the world outside as if they were underwater, and trapping Ashgaroth within a boundary he could not cross.

Jack still stood between the demon and Creek. Just behind Creek, Paddy rested his weight on the long, sack-wrapped bundle he'd carried up to the cave. His face was cast upwards to look at the patterns. They dappled his dark skin with their watery glow.

'You didn't summon me, Jack, though I daresay that is

precisely how it must have looked to you.' Ezekiel Creek's free hand now dug deep in the hip pocket of his long black coat. A muffled clinking came from within.

Rain poured down. The luminous seal didn't shut that out. But the thunder and lightning had rolled distant.

Creek coughed a hoarse laugh and his blue eyes twinkled in the darkness. 'But the timing of my arrival was determined by your act of madness: yours and Miss Jones's. Summoning a demon?' He shook his head and tutted. 'You should *never* play with demons, Jack.'

'We weren't playing,' Jack stated hotly.

'You weren't sufficiently careful, though, were you?'

Creek's words scorched Jack because they were true. Jack had followed the ritual, had drawn the pentagram exactly as the book had shown, but somehow Ashgaroth had got through. So Jack had got it wrong. This was his fault.

Be careful what you wish for, the Reverend Weagg had said.

'Ah, got it!' A smile cracked the corner crease of Creek's mouth and he pulled a sharp-nosed bullet from his pocket. 'You thought the rifle was loaded?' Creek said to the demon and he chuckled. 'Should have run when you could, Ashgaroth.' Then Jack knew, he *knew,* that whatever remained of Leila Jones, it wouldn't be with them for very much longer.

The blond boy stood still: watching, waiting.

Watching me, Jack realized.

When Jack's eyes met the boy's, the boy whispered, 'If he kills me, he kills *her*.'

Creek sniffed and wiped a drop of rainwater from the tip of his goblin nose with the back of the hand that held the bullet. 'I should thank you, Jack. All those years of hiding, and finally it's you who draws Ashgaroth from the shadows. And all over the ghost of a witch. Funny how these things work out.'

'Yeah,' replied Jack, bitterly. 'Hilarious.'

Jack saw that Paddy was watching them, face hard as stone and dark eyes intense, registering all that was passing.

Creek shrugged. 'It's the way of the world, Jack, and trust me, the world doesn't give a two-dime spit for your tender feelings.' He shook his head at the way of the world and the holy symbols that hung from his scrawny, high-collared neck clattered as he did so. 'Ashgaroth, Prince of Demons, summoned to Grindle. And where the demon goes, so must I.'

'What are you going to do now?' asked Jack, voice hot. Breathless. Leila seemed further away than ever.

'This,' explained Creek, 'is a good, old-fashioned hunting rifle.' He cracked back the bolt, slipped the bullet inside the breech, snapped the bolt forwards. Then he nodded with the brim of his hat towards the demon opposite. 'Inside the body of Leila Jones resides the spirit of Ashgaroth. We have to swap that fleshy prison for a more permanent one. Mr Rakhman has brought the trap.' Jack glanced to the metal box that sat by Paddy's feet. 'Once I drop the body, the spirit will be free but caught within these walls. We open the trap and the spirit will be drawn in. Then we all go home and I deposit Ashgaroth back inside the jar with his brethren.'

'So you kill Leila to catch the demon?' asked Jack, slowly.

'There's always a price to pay, Jack. If I want Ashgaroth, Leila is the price. And I want Ashgaroth.'

Jack kept his body between Creek and Ashgaroth, as if his flesh and blood could stop a bullet. 'You can't just kill Leila,' he shouted.

'Yes I can, Jack. I can do whatever it takes.' Ezekiel Creek raised the hunting rifle, and now it was impossible to tell the difference between his blue eyes and Ashgaroth's. 'Step aside, son. The game's over.'

OK, Jack Jolly, Jack said to himself, *you want Leila back? All you have to do is think of a way to outwit Creek* and *the demon.*

The thoughts raced through Jack's mind, their welter measured in heartbeats.

What do I know about Ezekiel Creek? Can I bargain with him? Can I move more quickly than he can pull the trigger on that rifle?

Am I mad?!

And Ashgaroth. Can I bargain with him? *Is he in a position to bargain with me? I summoned him; can I still command him?*

The book had said that the demon's service was in three parts.

For the first part, he will hunt what you would seek. He had done; he had found the witch.

For the second, he will destroy what you would end. He had done; he had destroyed the witch.

And *As to the third part,* the book had said, *It is wiser not to ask, for desire begets despair.*

Desire begets despair? What's that supposed to mean?

Jack's heart thudded behind his ribs.

Paddy was watching him. Ashgaroth was watching him. The wet barrel of the rifle was trained on him. And all the time, like the tolling of a warning bell, the Reverend Weagg's words rang through his head. *Be careful what you wish for.*

'Step aside, son,' repeated Creek, gravely. Head to the rifle stock, his broad-brimmed hat shadowed his face but Jack could feel the trigger finger tightening.

Be careful what you wish for.

Desire begets despair.

Jack's eyes widened as he realized. They meant the same thing. They spoke of the same thing.

A wish.

You had to be careful what you asked for, very careful, but this was the third part of the demon's service: Ashgaroth could grant him a wish.

'Stop!' Jack yelled at Creek.

But Ezekiel Creek's eyes narrowed, his finger pulled and, with a blast that split the Deepfold, the rifle fired.

The bullet hit Jack in his left shoulder. The pain was no worse than a kick, yet the shock knocked him to his knees. But the bullet didn't stop there. Jack heard the screech of the demon as the bullet struck him in the chest.

'Stay back,' commanded Ezekiel as Paddy stepped forwards. Paddy stopped where he was, face like granite. The barrel of the rifle over his shoulder, Creek strode past Jack.

Jack heard a sound like a dog running through long grass. He turned to look. The demon lay flat on its back, all six limbs and its tail thrashing against the earth. A trickle of blood seeped from the boy's mouth, but a torrent pumped from the hole in his insect-chest.

His own mouth dry, breathing in snatches, Jack put a hand to his shoulder. He felt the warm fluid seeping out, but he could move his arm and shoulder and so he knew that this was only a flesh wound. What had happened to him was nothing.

'Leila,' he gasped, as the blond hair and almond face of Ashgaroth receded into Leila's dark features.

Naked, she lay motionless on the ground. The insect limbs had vanished to be replaced by Leila's pale, smooth limbs. The bloody mess in her chest remained and a trickle of red, as red as her lips, spilt from the corner of her mouth. Her eyes were wide open. Specks of dirt smudged her white cheek.

Ezekiel Creek stood over her lifeless body, his long black coat soaked, rain dripping from the brim of his hat and the rifle across his shoulders.

It had been a successful hunt.

'Fetch the trap, Mr Rakhman,' he ordered.

Paddy looked at the box of overlapping metal plates and then to Jack.

Jack shook his head. 'No,' he gasped. 'Don't, Paddy. Don't. I know what to do.'

'No, Jack, you do not know what to do,' stated Ezekiel Creek, stepping back from the body. 'And if we're not quick about this, none of us will be doing anything. Ever.' He reached down and hauled Jack away from Leila's body.

'This is the dangerous bit, son.' Creek's cracked voice was low. 'See that trail of mist?'

Jack could see a haze forming over the dead body: smoke-blue, coiling, thickening, rising upwards.

'The demon's spirit is free now.' Creek shook Jack by his unwounded shoulder. 'Free from the body but trapped inside these walls: trapped with you, and me and Mr Rakhman over there. And unless we catch it now, inside that trap, there'll be a whole lot more corpses than just Miss Jones's.'

The grip was released on Jack's T-shirt. Jack remained kneeling, jaw set in determination.

I know what to do.

He looked across to Paddy. Paddy looked back at him. They were friends; they didn't have to say anything aloud. Jack's eyes spoke for him.

I know what to do.

'The trap please, Mr Rakhman,' requested Ezekiel Creek, calmly, looking up at where the vapours were forming into a towering figure.

Paddy was looking at where Leila lay, his eyes hot. Then he stared hard at Jack. *You sure you've got this all worked out?* he asked, without saying a word.

Jack nodded and stood.

The vapours unfurled and now Ashgaroth loomed over them, flames bursting out along his many limbs, eyes wild.

'Mr Rakhman,' demanded Creek. '*The trap.*'

Paddy left the trap where it was, but he swung the long bundle he'd been carrying into the back of Ezekiel Creek's head with a *crack*, dropping the demon hunter as if he were a log.

He stared down stonily at Creek's unconscious body. 'She was my friend too.'

'Rakhman!'

The roar was like the bellow of a furnace. Ashgaroth laughed, eyes maniacal.

'RAKHMAN!'

Jack hadn't expected the demon to turn on his friend.

Paddy tore the sacking away to reveal the great sword, Gram.

'I guessed we might need this.' He flashed a tight smile at Jack. Then he turned to face the demon, brandishing the sword in both hands, point upwards and towards the demon's chest. 'Back off.'

He took a step forwards.

'Rakhman,' growled the demon, and with flames streaking behind his arm, he plunged his spirit-fist into Paddy's chest.

Paddy dropped the sword and cried out. Laughing, Ashgaroth twisted his buried fist, then ripped it free. Jack half-expected to see the gory chunk of Paddy's heart, but all he caught sight of was a glimmer of liquid silver more brilliant than anything he had ever seen before. The demon devoured it in an ecstasy of slavering. Clutching his chest, Paddy staggered backwards, eyes rolling. Then he fell. His corpse was smoking before it hit the floor.

'Fresh souls!' cried Ashgaroth, blond hair wild, limbs electrified. Then he looked down and his face dissolved into a wolfish grin.

'Jack!' he exclaimed with hungry delight.

Now. Move now.

Jack snatched up the sword from where Paddy had dropped it. The huge blade was as light in his hand as the first time he had held it. It moved with Jack's arms, humming through the air, wanting to be used, which was just as well because the wound in his shoulder sucked hard on his strength. But once Jack had Gram pointing at Ashgaroth, the demon merely laughed at him.

'What now, Jack?' The demon's laughter pounded him. 'Your soul is mine.'

Jack struggled to stop the sword from shaking in his fear-crippled arms. He had never imagined terror like this: a liquid, streaming through his body and mind, unhooking his joints, flaying him to the core, so overwhelming he couldn't breathe, couldn't even think.

The words. What were the words?

Jack needed the final part of the Rite of Summoning, the final command that would put the demon within his power. But he was so frightened, he could remember nothing.

BLANK.

Rain fell, the glimmering symbols swam about them and Ashgaroth's furnace eyes suddenly narrowed.

'You're mine now, Jack.'

What were the words? He'd tried to memorize them. They were just out of reach. But they were in his mind somewhere.

Jack closed his eyes. He wasn't on that blasted crag. He imagined himself back in the attic room at The January Gallows. The sun was warm, Leila was alive and he was reading out the final part of the rite. The words were in his mouth.

He had the words.

Jack wrestled back fear. He stood his ground. He faced the demon prince. He gripped the sword and shouted, 'Obey your master, or I will destroy you in the fire unquenchable.'

Immediately, the crimson ruby set in Gram's pommel blazed red, and all along the mighty blade, flames burst into life.

Ashgaroth hissed and drew back, then roared.

Jack stepped forwards and swung the sword. Gram moved with him, moved for him, moved in his hands with a mind of its own, like a thing alive. Great streaks of flame blazed in its wake.

'Obey your master, or I will destroy you in the fire unquenchable,' yelled Jack with every fibre of his spirit.

The blazing blade roared through the air as Jack carved Ashgaroth's symbol into the darkness. When he had finished, the symbol hung in lines of fire between him and the demon, burning silently. Its bonfire heat singed Jack's hair and roasted his skin.

The demon hissed and twisted as if it were he and not the symbol that was burning.

'What do you want?' growled Ashgaroth, bitterly.

Jack let the tip of the sword fall to the ground, folded his forearms over the upright pommel and leant on it, exhausted. 'I want my wish.'

The first thing to come into focus was the sound of musical instruments and a delicate tinkle of water. Jack blinked in a white light that was painfully bright, and tried to turn the blurred shadows into shapes.

The music became a string quartet played gently and harmoniously, and then Jack saw the players themselves. They were sitting on an outside terrace, dressed formally, the black ensemble broken only by the ginger-brown of their instruments. Jack was standing on the terrace too, and it was bordered by rose trees and small orange trees and beyond it there was a grand building, ornate: a palace built of honey-coloured stone and adorned with balconies and tall windows, pillars and stone carvings.

Blinking, he turned to look the other way, his back to the palace. Now, spread out before him, were formal lawns bisected by neat gravel paths and surrounded by flower gardens. Beyond the lawns there were meadows and woods and rivers. Jack blinked again. It seemed that from where he stood, there was no distance he could not look, nothing he could not see. Beyond the rivers there were towns and cities, then oceans, then sky, moons, planets, stars, galaxies swallowing the horizon. And then he realized that he wasn't just looking; he was actually hurtling headlong into all this vastness.

He gasped and stumbled forwards, grabbing hold of a stone balustrade to stop himself from falling over. The universe shrank back to the terrace, the string quartet and a fountain that danced high and played a glass music all of its own as the water splashed down.

Somebody coughed. Jack looked to his left and saw a small metal garden table and two chairs, painted white. In one of the chairs sat a figure who Jack guessed was Ashgaroth. Ashgaroth raised a hand and motioned to the empty chair.

'Thanks,' said Jack, relieved to take a seat and feeling a little sick after his hurricane trip into the universe.

Ashgaroth looked different, which was good. He looked human, and was dressed in jeans, trainers and a white shirt. His long blond hair was tied back from his boy's face in a ponytail and he was wearing a pair of sunglasses.

I could do with a pair of those, Jack managed to stop himself from saying. He knew that from this point on, he would have to be *very* careful about what he wished for. He didn't want to waste his one wish on a pair of sunglasses.

Ashgaroth chuckled knowingly.

'Thinking of being careful, I suppose you wonder how

I got through?' The demon placed his fingers together and peered at Jack over their tips, thoughtfully.

Jack realized that the demon was reading him, gauging his thoughts, planning how best to outwit him. And he was dead right about Jack wondering how he'd got through. That was something that had baffled Jack since Ashgaroth had first revealed himself. They had followed the ritual precisely. Leila had drawn out the pentagram perfectly. But still Ashgaroth had slipped through and hidden inside Leila until the vital moment.

'How *did* you?' he asked the boy who sat opposite.

The boy leant forwards and tapped the side of his neat nose, confidentially. 'Floorboards,' he said. Then he sat back in his chair and smiled in a superior way. 'Gets them every time. They seal the doors and the windows and say their spells and draw their pictures, but no one ever thinks of the floorboards: all those *gaps*.'

Jack hung his head and shut his eyes.

It was so obvious. And so stupid of them not to have thought about it.

'Don't be too hard on yourself, Jack,' crooned Ashgaroth. 'It's a common mistake. It isn't *entirely* your fault that Leila and Rakhman are dead.'

Leila and Paddy. Jack felt sadder and sicker than ever. And angry with himself: with everything.

Don't get angry. And don't get upset. You've got to keep your wits about you: keep your mind clear.

He lifted his head and stared about with apparent interest. 'We're not in the Deepfold,' he stated.

I sound particularly dumb. Good.

Conversation couldn't be kept simpler than that. But inside he was thinking hard and fast.

The demon leant back and crossed his hands behind his head. 'Correct, Jack. Your powers of observation are truly astounding.' Then he opened his arms wide. 'This is a little place I like to call home.'

'It's very nice,' said Jack, carefully.

Ashgaroth leant forwards again and said, 'Trust me, Jack, if your soul were mine by now, this place would look very different to you.' Then he smiled. 'But, for the time being, your soul is your own and you have a wish.' He waved towards the gardens and the rest of the universe. 'What's it going to be?' Then he took off his sunglasses and stared hard at Jack and Jack felt those eyes bore right down, deep inside his soul. 'You can have anything. *Anything*.'

Ashgaroth's face might have been a boy's but those eyes, those hard, cold, pitiless eyes were old and Jack knew that he was dealing with a power that was very ancient. And Jack also knew this: that Ashgaroth had sat where they were sitting many times before. But this would be the one and only time for *him*.

Be careful what you wish for.

Jack held on to the memory of the Reverend Weagg and her warning as firmly as he would have held Gram, were the sword still with him. But Gram and the Reverend Weagg and Paddy and Leila were very far away. Jack swallowed and fought back the crushing, hopeless sense of loneliness. Paddy and Leila were in the farthest place.

They're in your hands now, he said to himself. *This is all up to you.*

'A drink?'

'What?' Jack had been listening to his own thoughts, not the demon.

'Would you like a drink?' Ashgaroth tilted his boy's head to one side, enquiringly.

Jack was thirsty. His throat was parched as a piece of card. He was about to ask for some water, or maybe some Coke, but he stopped himself before it was too late. He wasn't going to waste his wish on a drink. So he just shook his head.

Ask for nothing until you know exactly what you want, Jack warned himself.

Ashgaroth sniffed, disappointed. 'You're a clever one, aren't you?' he muttered.

In fact, decided Jack, *say nothing at all.* Nothing . . . *until you're ready.* So he stared back at Ashgaroth in silence.

The demon growled with fury and smashed his fist into the metal table-top. 'Every once in a while I get one like you,' he exploded. 'A real smart arse!' Then he shook his head and sighed, his mood shifting as quickly as storm-weather. 'Can't blame you, I suppose. When some-one grants you a wish there's so much you can lose.'

Bring Paddy and Leila back to life.

Jack didn't put it into words. He was careful to keep it a loose thought for the time being. But would a wish like that work? Being brought back alive wasn't necessarily the same as being what they had been before they were dead. Might they come back as zombies? And suppose they were brought to life only to be immediately killed again by the demon? Suppose they were brought back to life by the demon putting them all into a moment *before* they had got rid of the witch? They'd be alive but they'd also be back at square one.

Jack sighed.

'I know,' empathized Ashgaroth. 'It's more difficult than it sounds, isn't it?'

The string quartet played, the water pattered down and the sun was warm.

'Here we sit,' mused the demon, 'on the edge of eternity, and I wager that you would use it all up in trying to get your one wish perfect, if I let you.'

Jack found it best if he ignored Ashgaroth, so that's what he did.

'However,' continued the boy in the dark glasses, 'I have something that will focus your mind.' He put his hand into his jeans pocket and after a moment's searching he pulled out a small object that Jack recognized.

'An hourglass.' Ashgaroth held it up as if inspecting some rare artefact. 'Except that this isn't an hourglass.

This is more like a minute glass. Barely an egg-timer, I suppose.'

Jack swallowed drily and his thoughts began to race.

'I'll give you one minute to make a wish, Jack.'

'I didn't read anything about one minute,' Jack couldn't stop himself from saying.

'You barely read anything at all,' retorted Ashgaroth. 'Anyway, time is at the discretion of the demon. A minute is fair.' Then he leant forwards and whispered, 'But it does go fast. And the faster it goes, the harder it gets to think. Would you believe it? I've known people to sit where you're sitting now and, by the time the sand's run out, they've thought of nothing. Nothing at all.' The demon grinned a boyish grin. 'And then I get their soul for free.' He shrugged. 'Get your wish right and you keep your soul. No pressure.'

Jack closed his eyes.

'You don't have to be watching for the time to run out,' stated the demon. There was a tap as the device was placed on the table. 'Your minute starts now.'

Jack's thoughts tumbled through his mind. Alternative wishes came to the surface like bubbles, only to pop when he tried to put them into words that would work.

Making a wish was a lot harder than it sounded.

'Fifty seconds left,' sang Ashgaroth. 'Just trying to be helpful,' he added in an affronted mutter at Jack's tight-lipped silence. 'You weren't looking at the timer.'

There was only one thing Jack wanted and that was to get Leila and Paddy back, alive, fully human, with their souls intact and the witch still gone. But getting the right words was difficult.

Bring them back alive?

Back where? In what state would they be? *Barely* alive? Alive and without their souls? Could you be alive and not have a soul?

'Forty seconds,' crooned the demon.

I wish you'd shut up, Jack thought, but he didn't breathe a word.

'Sorry,' smiled the demon, who obviously wasn't and who clearly had a good idea of what Jack was thinking.

Wishing that Leila and Paddy *weren't* dead had even more problems. They could be not dead but return disfigured. You could be in a coma for the rest of your life and not be dead. You could return not dead on the other side of the world, or in a desert. Jack wasn't going to trust to Ashgaroth being any more cooperative than the wish compelled him to be.

'I'm not here to make it easy for you. And I hate being made to do this stuff.' The demon sighed. 'Twenty seconds, by the way.'

It was all about using the right words, or using words in the right way. What he wanted counted for nothing if he didn't get the words right.

Desire begets despair.

Be careful what you wish for.

'How the mind doth wander,' observed Ashgaroth. 'Ten seconds.'

There was no more time to juggle ideas. There was no time at all. Jack had to pluck the wish from his spinning thoughts. And he had it: the right words. The wish burst from him in a shout.

'Get Paddy and Leila back to where they'd want to be.'

'Sorry. Can't have it; that's two wishes. Very sneaky. And time's . . . run . . .'

Jack opened his eyes. The last grains were rolling through the neck of the egg-timer as decisively as boulders.

'Get *us* back to where *we'd* want to be,' fired Jack, before Ashgaroth could say '. . . OUT!'

The demon held his hand over the egg-timer, fingers splayed. Looking closely, Jack could see the last grain of sand suspended in the air a fraction above the small heap of granules in the bottom of the device.

Ashgaroth raised a long, blond eyebrow above the level of his dark glasses. 'Get us back to where we'd want to be? Is that it?' he checked.

Jack swallowed and nodded. 'Yes.'

The last grain of sand hit the top of the small heap without a sound and the demon who looked like a boy sat back in his chair. 'That was very close. But, being as fair as I can be, I think you made it. Just. It is a very good wish, Jack. Well done.' He smiled generously and clicked his finger and thumb in the air.

Only now he had made the wish did Jack turn it over in his mind to inspect it from different angles. He was aware of footsteps approaching at a smart pace from behind him.

Get us back to where we'd want to be.

Jack had pictured him and Leila and Paddy alive and safe on the slope below Tor Cave when he had made the wish. That was what he wanted for them. That *had* to be a watertight wish.

Ashgaroth waved a hand impatiently. 'Stop fretting, Jack. You've made your wish.' Then he crossed his arms and scowled across the table. 'You know, it really annoys me how you people summon me so that you can make a wish and then, when you've made it, you sit there agonizing: was it the right wish? Should I have asked for something different? Should I have wished for lots of wishes? You can't by the way, because that amounts to ending up with more than one wish, which is against the rules. I even had one girl who sat there, right where you're sitting now, wondering whether she should have wished that she didn't have to make a wish at all.'

'Really?' asked Jack. He sympathized with the girl. Having just been through the wishing process himself he understood where she was coming from.

'Yup,' nodded Ashgaroth. '*Really*. And she was right. The wish she actually made was rubbish. Riddled with holes and get-out clauses, for me. I had her soul before the sand had even run out. But you . . .' he pointed at Jack and wagged his finger. 'You're smarter than that, Jack.'

Being complimented by a demon didn't make Jack feel smart. He ran his fingers through his hair and realized from its dampness how hard he'd been sweating. He looked out at eternity without actually looking at anything at all.

Would the wish work? That was all that mattered.

A man in dark, formal clothes had appeared by the table. A butler or servant of some sort, guessed Jack; this was a palace and Ashgaroth was a prince, even if right now he looked like a boy. In silence, the man set down a fountain pen and a clipboard to which there was attached a sheet of paper.

'Just tidying up the formalities,' explained Ashgaroth, as he unscrewed the top of the pen. The butler remained by the table, nose in the air, hands folded behind his back. Aloof.

Ashgaroth pushed his sunglasses up to the top of his head and leant forwards to inspect what was written on the sheet of paper. He pursed his lips, nodded to himself, then spun the clipboard round so that Jack could see what had been written.

Get us back to where we'd want to be, inked in small

handwriting. Neat. Precise. One sentence on its own like that looked remote and powerless in the midst of a whole sheet of otherwise empty paper.

Ashgaroth offered Jack the fountain pen. 'Sign.'

Water tinkled but the string quartet had stopped playing.

The wish would bring Leila and Paddy back. It *had* to bring Leila and Paddy back.

Jack wetted his lips and took the pen. The nib scratched loudly on the paper as he wrote his name beneath the wish he had made. When he had finished, Ashgaroth took back the pen, flipped round the board and drew his own mark at the foot of the page in black ink.

Jack half-expected the symbol to smoulder into the paper. But it merely sat there, bold and black: unburning.

'Good.' Ashgaroth twisted the top back onto the pen and, keeping his eyes on Jack, handed pen, paper and clipboard to the dark-suited servant who was waiting in silence by the table. 'Everything nice and legal.' The footsteps snapped away, receding across the terrace. 'All that remains is for me to send you back.'

But the demon hadn't done anything yet. 'The wish hasn't . . .' began Jack.

Ashgaroth held up his hand to silence him. 'The wish will be granted *exactly* as it was made. And it will be granted as if you had never been here.' He indicated the palace, the terrace, the gardens and the rest of eternity with a sweep of his arm. 'You will be back on that hill, beneath that cave, your wish complete.'

'And what about you?' asked Jack, cautiously.

Ashgaroth smiled in a way that made Jack feel as if a nest of worms was wriggling under the skin of his neck. 'Don't worry about me, Jack. I am perfectly content with the agreement we have reached.'

Agreement? thought Jack. *I thought it was a wish.*

'Shall we put it to the test?' smiled the demon.

Agreement?

Ashgaroth stood. His blue eyes remained nailed on Jack as he performed a short bow, almost courtly. Then, tilting his head, he winked up at Jack, slyly.

Before Jack could say another word, the palace had vanished and rain was whipping his face. He was standing on the slope beneath the mouth of Tor Cave and the great sword, Gram, was still in his hand, tongues of fire curling along its bright blade. Immediately in front of him, the towering, insect-limbed spirit of Ashgaroth reared up. His blond hair was wild as the flames that haloed his body.

Jack gasped.

The wish. The wish hasn't been granted, was all that he could think as the spirit rushed down on him, flames streaking in its wake.

The burning sword came to life in Jack's hands, its blade whirling in a great arc. Its strength coursed through his own body and Jack stepped forwards to meet the demon.

'Hold him right there,' came Ezekiel Creek's dry old drawl.

Creek was standing with the trap open at his feet. Its square plates had been fanned apart to reveal a black hole that appeared far deeper than should have been possible: a well of a hole.

'Nice work, Jack.' Ezekiel Creek smacked the dent out of the top of his hat, then swept the hat onto his head. 'Just keep him where he is a little longer while I tend to the final adjustments.'

Jack brandished the flaming sword at the writhing spirit as Creek knelt beside the metal contraption on the ground.

'Hold him steady,' hissed the demon hunter, grasping a small lever that protruded from one side of the shallow box containing the chasm of a hole.

It seemed to Jack that the spirit before him was not menacing so much as it was struggling: struggling and twisting and burning, as if it were trying to retreat.

He wants to get away, Jack realized.

From beside him there came such a shriek of laughter that Jack's teeth hurt to their roots.

'You're going nowhere,' cackled Creek as he pulled the lever.

There was a rush of air, so powerful that the breath

was sucked from Jack's lungs. Flying straight at him came the spirit: spinning, struggling, howling. It passed right through his own body and, with an electrifying shriek, was sucked directly into the black hole of the trap.

Violent dizziness buzzed through Jack, from his toes to his scalp.

I'm falling into the trap too.

The sword slipped from his grasp, his knees buckled and the ground rushed up to hit him. Then rain, darkness, silence.

His own breathing was the first thing Jack became aware of: calm, rising and falling gently. He opened his eyes. On the earth beside him lay Gram, sleeping now, the fist of a jewel in its pommel dull, lifeless. Jack touched the cold metal of the blade in silent gratitude. Then he pushed himself to his knees, hardly daring to see what had happened to his friends.

The demon had gone. The shifting walls of light had gone.

Ezekiel Creek was kicking shut the plates of the trap with the muddy toe of his shoe. He raised a thin, silvery eyebrow at Jack. 'Why, your head must be just as sore as mine now.' He picked the trap up by its chain and held it out in front of them both as if inspecting a freshly caught salmon. 'We know exactly where *you're* going,' he laughed with intense glee. Then he slung the trap over his shoulder and went to retrieve the rifle.

Leila.

Paddy.

Jack staggered to his sodden feet and looked about. Sheets of drizzle blurred his vision but towards the trees he saw movement. He rubbed the rain out of his eyes and recognized the solid shape of Fergus Ben-Nazim Rakhman, kneeling, holding Paddy's motionless body. Head bowed. Silent.

'Leila?' Jack's cry echoed to the cave and back.

He saw her body, not far away, still as the ground.

Back to where we'd want to be, back to where we'd want to be, he chanted to himself.

Paddy and Leila *had* to be alive.

He dropped to his knees beside Leila, gently placed his hand against her cheek. Her face was white, unstained by blood, and there was no wound to her body, but her skin felt like ice.

The rain fell in a soft veil.

'Leila?' whispered Jack, head bowed.

Had the demon cheated him? Jack's eyes were hot and burning. Burning for Leila. Burning for Paddy.

'Leila?'

Nothing.

Nothing? Jack didn't breathe. Beneath his fingers

there was a movement: no more than a ghost creeping, returning to a secret place. But there *was* movement. A tightening of skin, a quickening of muscle and warmth, spreading like light.

Leila's body shuddered, she gasped and her eyes opened wide, bright with life.

'Jack!'

Two mornings later, Jack, Leila and Paddy knelt at the low windows below the eaves of the attic room in The January Gallows. Paddy had forced open one of the windows and cool morning air flowed in, filling the dusty chamber with oxygen and the crisp sweetness of mown grass. Grindle was bathed in the clear light of mid-morning, its ramshackle rooftops and twisting chimneys flattened by the high sun. Beyond the village, the meadows and woods were fresh from the rains: leaves were greener, the limestone cliffs of the valley whiter and even the great scar of Tor Cave had softened. The birds still dived from its rocky prow but it seemed to Jack that the dizzying darkness of its mouth had drawn back, as if swallowed by the plunging caverns within.

'He's leaving. Creek's leaving.'

Paddy had come knocking at The Old School House that morning. Leila was already with Jack and the two of them had headed back to The Gallows with Paddy. Now, from up in the attic, they could watch the departure of Grindle's extraordinary visitor.

'Did you help him pack the car?' asked Jack.

Paddy shook his head. 'Didn't even know he was going.'

'How did he get it all in the back then?' asked Leila, incredulous. The estate boot of the shark-nosed Citroën was crammed with trunks, suitcases and the huge urn that had been such heavy work to unload.

'Don't ask me. One moment it was all in his room, and the next,' he shrugged his broad shoulders, his long hair ebony in the sunlight, 'it was all in his car.'

'Weird,' commented Jack, 'knowing what he's got locked inside that urn.'

After the night of the storm, all of them had trooped back to The January Gallows in the pouring rain. A sleepless villager, peering into the night, would have spied a most bedraggled and outlandish procession: Ezekiel Creek striding at the front, his battered hat sodden and dripping, a rifle over one shoulder and the trap apparatus slung over the other; then Jack Jolly with a sword in one hand and his other arm around Leila Jones, Creek's long black coat wrapped about her, the mud-streaked tails trailing the floor like a magician's robe; and at the rear, Paddy Rakhman tramping beside Fergus Ben-Nazim Rakhman. And such a sleepless villager might have spent the hour before dawn pondering two curious details: the hand of Fergus Ben-Nazim Rakhman, gently placed on his son's shoulder, and the knowing smile on the lips of Ezekiel Creek. A smile unseen by those who followed him.

On entering The Gallows, Ezekiel Creek had gone straight up to his room and Jack had gone with him. *Only* Jack went with him. Leila remained by the stove in the kitchen while the landlord made everybody hot chocolate laced generously with brandy and Paddy dug out warm clothes for Leila to wear.

'The end of the business, Jack,' Ezekiel Creek had said as he approached the great urn in the semi-darkness of the room. Jack hadn't been sure whether this was a statement or a question.

Rain zigzagged down the broad bay window. It was still dark outside.

'Come here, Jack.'

Jack had hesitated.

'I need you to hold the trap for me.'

So Jack had stood by the urn, trap in hand, while Ezekiel Creek took a ring of thick keys from his trouser pocket and undid the padlocks. The chains slid free like snakes and clattered to the wooden floor.

'Hold it high, Jack. Hold it ready,' and the twinkling blue eyes had twinkled exceptionally brightly beneath the sharp silver eyebrows. 'We have to work fast. We don't want anything undesirable to get out.' And then, nose to nose:

'Jack be nimble, Jack be quick,
Or they'll have your soul in half a tick!'

Ezekiel Creek laughed at his ditty, then turned to the great stone jar. His fingers had wiggled and the dial had spun. The light on the locking system turned red. Smoke poured from around the steel plate of a lid and from far away there had come a terrible screaming, a cacophony of caterwauling, a clanging of iron and a crashing of feet. Far away but getting louder, getting closer.

'Now, Jack, now. Hold the trap high!' Creek had cried, eyes ablaze with wild delight.

Jack had stood on tiptoe, arms raised, the trap dangling over the steel plate.

In a blur of speed, and with an agility Jack hadn't seen in him before, Ezekiel Creek had swept the lid clear, flamboyant as a bullfighter, and, spinning on his heel, he had elbowed the lever on the trap.

'No! No! No!' came the scream from the plasmic sheen of spirit that was sucked down from the trap and into the mouth of the urn. Spinning full circle, Creek had slammed the lid back on the urn. Then, dropping to one knee, he had dialled the lock shut before lashing the chains back in place.

The maelstrom of howling cut dead. The huge padlocks were fastened once more and, with a smile that stretched from one wrinkled ear to the other, the sly old hunter had turned to Jack and drawled, 'That's one troublemaker who won't be bothering us for a very long time.'

Now, in the attic, Jack blinked the image away. 'It's good to see him and the urn hitting the road,' he said.

'At least he explained everything to your mum and dad,' Leila pointed out.

'I don't know how,' laughed Jack, remembering the bizarre meeting between Ezekiel Creek and his parents after the fuming hot chocolates had been drunk. Creek had escorted him home, delivered him to his distraught mother and father, and then spent the dawn hour talking to them while Jack had fallen asleep on a sofa in the sitting room.

'If anything has made me believe the unbelievable,' commented Jack, 'it's the fact that Ezekiel Creek explained everything to my parents and they were OK with it. It's amazing.' Jack shook his head, still deeply baffled, and recalled also what Creek had whispered in his ear just before he had left the house.

'After all you've done for me, Jack, it's the least I could do for you.'

But no matter how hard he thought about it, Jack couldn't figure out what he had done for Creek.

There was a stirring of feet on the dusty road below and now the broad-brimmed, battered black hat came into view and, poking out beyond the brim, the tip of a nose.

'Still hate him?' Jack asked Leila.

Leila shook her head, large eyes fixed on the departing figure. 'No. And it wasn't me doing the hating. Not really. It's just that I had his arch-enemy inside my head.'

Paddy looked across to her. 'What was it like, sharing your head with a demon?'

'Frightening.'

But Jack noticed how calm and steady Leila was now: her true character, back to what it had been before Ashgaroth had moved in.

'I didn't know what was happening,' she explained. 'But from when we did the summoning up here, it felt like the inside of my head lost its balance. I didn't notice it right away, but after a bit I found that I couldn't be me.'

Jack could see how this was bringing back difficult memories. 'You don't have to talk about it, Leila.'

Leila shook her head, earnestly. 'I'd prefer to talk about it; it gets rid of it, like getting rid of a poison.'

'Go on then,' said Paddy. 'What was it like?'

'Well,' Leila sucked in a breath, 'after the first bit, when my head just felt . . . wobbly . . . I began to feel angry, getting mad at things when I didn't need to.'

'Yeah,' muttered Paddy, 'we noticed.'

'It was like when you lose your temper,' continued Leila, 'but . . . better? A mad rage that made me feel that if I let go, I could do anything.'

Her eyes were bright.

Excited, thought Jack.

'*Anything.* But,' she took a calming breath, 'the rest of me, the *me* bit of me, didn't want that, and it was hard, like fighting in my head with myself *all the time.* It hurt. It felt like I was going to rip apart.'

Leila rested her forehead against the window. She looked down at Creek. 'When I saw him, I *hated* him. I wanted to *kill* him.'

'We sort of got that impression,' said Jack.

'Yeah, but that wasn't *me.* That was Ashgaroth inside me, hating his old enemy. And when I thought about the witch . . .' Leila shook her head at the violence of the emotion.

'Well, that was what Ashgaroth had been summoned to do,' explained Jack.

'Nearly got us killed in the mill,' Paddy pointed out.

'But that's why I went for it.' Leila half-laughed. 'I just went for it. I couldn't stop myself.'

'We saw,' said Paddy.

Leila ran her fingers through her spiky black hair. 'You know, I can't even remember what happened out there.' Jack knew she was talking about the cave, and the battle with the witch. 'There was rain and lightning and inside me . . .' She searched for the words. 'Exploding brilliance. Like *I* was the storm. One moment I was running into the Deepfold, and the next, it was all over. The witch, the demon, all gone. Just us again.'

Her hand found Jack's and she squeezed it. Jack could tell that she wasn't even thinking about how hard she was squeezing.

'It's weird, sharing the inside of your head with a demon,' said Leila. 'It's difficult. But I'm all right now.'

Jack looked at the chalk pentagram, almost scuffed out of existence already. The gaps between the floorboards looked so obvious now.

I won't make that mistake again, he thought, *because I won't be summoning any more demons.*

His eyes alighted on the great sword, Gram, propped in the far corner. The ruby was lifeless and, in the glancing sunlight, he saw that a spider was already stringing a thread between the pommel and the wall.

Memories gather dust, pondered Jack. *You put them in an attic room, close the door and time wraps them in silence.*

Down below, Fergus Ben-Nazim Rakhman was talking with Ezekiel Creek, his red-headed body as stout as Creek's was lanky. Their voices were a murmur, rising and falling. Then, with a crunch of grit, the long-toed shoes took Ezekiel Creek to the door of his long black car.

'Are things OK here, Paddy?' asked Leila, gently.

Paddy nodded. 'They're better. Much better.' He jerked his head to where his father was standing and grunted a hollow laugh. 'He's still crazy, but not as bad. I had to be dead on that hill first, but I think he actually wants me here now. I'm glad he followed us out there. That he saw what happened.'

Paddy looked at Jack. 'Weird, isn't it? The way things work out. All of this mad stuff happens and at the end of it, *because* of it, my dad's more like a normal dad. Only a bit more, but it's better than it was.'

Paddy didn't make a big deal about anything, but Jack knew what a big deal this was: how much better life was for Paddy.

Get us back to where we'd want to be.

Leila's hand in Jack's. Leila back to being Leila.

Get us back to where we'd want to be.

She even had money now. A king's ransom.

'Not sure what we'll do with it,' Leila had said, 'but at least we won't be bone-skint anymore.'

Get us back to where we'd want to be.

Even the bullet wound in Jack's shoulder had vanished: vanished straight away, although he hadn't realized that until after he'd known that Leila and Paddy were both alive.

Below, Ezekiel Creek placed a hand on the door handle, paused, then looked up, much as he had done on first arriving at The January Gallows. This time, Jack, Leila and Paddy remained at the window. The black-hatted wanderer raised a hand in their direction, a hand raised in parting. But before he ducked into the car, his twinkling eyes looked straight at Jack. And then something happened that made Jack's heart jolt.

Ezekiel Creek bowed.

It was a short, courtly bow and, as he bowed, he tilted up his head and winked. Slyly.

Jack gulped.

I've seen that bow before. I've seen that wink, he thought. *But not from Ezekiel Creek.*

'What is it?' Leila had realized that something had startled Jack.

Do I tell them who I think it really is? wondered Jack.

He opened his mouth, but already Creek was inside the car. If it *was* Creek. And maybe it really was. Maybe that hadn't been a bow at all, just Creek bending to enter his car. Maybe the wink had been a blink, a trick of the light. Maybe . . . maybe . . .

Maybe I'm wrong.

'What?' asked Paddy

Jack scratched his head as they watched the car jolt and bounce up the road and out of the village. After a long pause he sighed. 'Nothing,' he said.

They remained looking out of the window until the car had vanished over the top of the moor, together with Jack's suspicions. Then he heard footfalls, and someone entered the room.

Jack turned and saw Fergus Ben-Nazim Rakhman standing in the doorway, one hand resting on his belly and the other grasping his red beard.

'He still gives me the creeps,' he grumbled, with a brisk nod in the direction that Ezekiel Creek had gone.

Paddy got to his feet. 'What needs doing?' he asked.

The flame-headed landlord of The January Gallows looked at all three of them simultaneously with his two eyes, something that only his goggling eyeballs could achieve. 'I have a task for all of you night-whelps.'

Jack waited. Leila waited. Paddy waited.

'There's a long summer ahead,' growled Fergus Ben-Nazim Rakhman, 'and if you're going to enjoy it, you need to wash the hell of these past weeks out of your dubious souls.' He pointed through the window. 'Out there, there's a river that needs to be taught what rivers are for.' He pulled a pocket watch from his waistcoat. 'If you don't go swimming before I count to half past eleven, I'll have a crack for every one of your helium-pumped, dunce-capped, wit-fossicking heads.'

There was a moment's pause. Then, like a champagne cork bursting, Mr Rakhman yelled, 'Go swimming!'

With an explosion of laughter and limbs, Jack, Leila and Paddy ran. They ran helter-skelter down the flights of stairs, they burst out of The January Gallows and into the sun, they raced through the village, dashed past the fingerpost, charged down the fields and into the woods, laughing helplessly as they hurtled through light and shadow.

Crashing out of the trees, they sprinted up the riverbank.

The dry stone bed, the rowans, the oaks, the mill, the thick meadows, all flashed by as Jack, Leila and Paddy raced to where the river ran slow and broad. Behind them they left the witch and the demon. Ahead of them was the river and the summer. And there was no stopping. Fully clothed, laughing because they couldn't wait, they dived headlong into the shimmering waters of the Deepfold.

Epilogue

It is night. All is quiet in the Deepfold. The summer is over. Once more, the river is a murmur, whispering its way beneath rock and earth. Once more, the wooded hillsides stir only to the creak of the high trees and the scrape of the foxes who ghost beneath them. The bell of All Souls chimes the small hours and the chimes roll distant over hill and field, tree and valley, to be answered by a dog barking in High Wicton. But no one hears. Everyone sleeps. Everyone except Weland. The blacksmith is working, his hammer beating, his forge glowing: the hot heart of the Deepfold. He has been here longer than the stones and he will be here long after the sleeping souls in the surrounding villages are dust. The summer passes, seasons become years, years become memories and memories become legends, but Weland remains.

But our business this night is not with Weland. Our business is with those who sleep. Look to Grindle. Look to The Old School House. Look to a boy in a low-beamed room, who sleeps undisturbed despite this summer's wild darkness.

Jack.

Let me tell you something about Jack.

Some people are brave their whole life through. But sometimes a person has to squeeze a whole lifetime of bravery into one moment. When Jack faced the demon with only his wits to save his soul, that was one of those moments.

It was a rare piece of bravery.

And he won his wish.

So, Jack and Leila are back together now. And if you look close, even in the slumbering darkness you can see the scars down his cheek and down the back of his hand. This summer will always leave its mark upon him. The price he had to pay, you might say.

So let him sleep. He has earned it.

And Leila? Leila is sleeping too. But asleep or awake, she loves Jack: loves him, in her deep, dark way. And her family has wealth now: greater wealth than she could ever have imagined, courtesy of her illustrious ancestor, the sea captain Johannes van Huygens and his gold. She can buy whatever clothes she likes (although she doesn't) and her parents can fill their kitchen with as much food as they like (which they do). They could even sell their cottage in High Wicton and move to a much grander place, maybe somewhere with a swimming pool, a cinema room, a hot tub . . . But they don't. They like being where they are. But Leila does wear her family ring on a necklace now. And whenever she feels it against her skin, even when she sleeps, she thinks of this hot summer and the Grindle Witch and the darkness that was inside her, a darkness that will always leave a little splinter all of its own. And she thinks of how Jack saved her and Paddy, and how much she loves him.

But what about Paddy?

Rakhman.

The days he spends with his great friend Jack, or he works. He works in The January Gallows. He works alongside that madman of a father, Fergus Ben-Nazim Rakhman, who doesn't seem quite so mad any more, at least not to Paddy. The Rakhmans work together; they have become a team. Together they haul barrels, they chop wood, they serve beer, they break up fights.

But now, in the lost reaches of the night, Paddy sleeps and he dreams. He dreams of the wide world. He dreams of wandering, of adventure, of roads beyond sight, of tearing oceans, of plunging the burning rage of destiny into the ice waters of fate. When the light of morning blows away the fog of night he won't remember these dreams but they will stir deep inside him and one day they will become his path. For now, he keeps the great sword Gram wrapped in that attic room. Waiting.

I know.

I KNOW.

What of Ezekiel Creek? you ask.

Be patient.

We've been through so much, you and I. We have only these pages left together and I feel that we barely know one another. But we have come to my part of the story at last: the ending, the narrator's reward, you might say. And like all good stories, this ending comes down to words. Words are so important: the *right* words. Words, and the person who speaks them.

So may I give you a piece of advice? If you are going to bargain with demons, be careful to use the right words, in the right way. At the very least, you should get yourself an excellent lawyer. One little slip, an unfortunate phrase, a moment of carelessness . . . disaster! When it comes to demons, a little carelessness goes a very long way.

You have to possess an eye for detail. You have to look at the agreement from *every* angle.

Get us back to where we'd want to be.

Well, as you see from this night's sleepers, we end this story exactly where Jack wanted to be, or perhaps I should say, exactly where *those who were making the wish* wanted to be.

But it was Jack's *wish!* you cry.

Well, you're right. It *was* Jack's wish. But, as I recall, he allowed Ashgaroth to repeat it.

Get us back to where we'd want to be.

So it wasn't only *Jack's* wish, was it?

Why did Jack allow *Ashgaroth* to utter those words? Because Jack was frightened, because he was distracted, because he was careless. Because he was human. But the consequences, the consequences of those words in the mouth of a demon . . .

Don't be angry. Don't feel betrayed. When it comes to bargaining with demons, this is what happens.

Jack and Leila are certainly back where they would have wanted to be: alive and in love with each other. And Paddy Rakhman is back and living a life that is as normal as any life could be with Fergus Ben-Nazim Rakhman for a father.

And Ashgaroth?

Ah, this is the point when we return to Ezekiel Creek.

You see, there has been a swap: Ashgaroth's spirit for Creek's. In accordance with the wish that Jack allowed him to make, Ashgaroth's spirit is exactly where Ashgaroth wanted it to be: inside the body of Ezekiel Creek. And Ezekiel Creek? Why, Ezekiel Creek's spirit is precisely where Ashgaroth wanted *it* to be too: caught in the trap, then secured inside the prison with those other seventy-one demons.

What a neat swap that was.

Now, Ashgaroth can masquerade as Ezekiel Creek and come and go as he pleases. And with the other seventy-one demons out of the way, he has the whole world to himself.

So, I am pleased to announce officially that we have a happy ending. As happy as any ending can reasonably be expected to be. Happy for all, except Ezekiel Creek. Now, don't complain. If it was happy for *everyone*, it wouldn't be realistic. The world doesn't work like that.

Listen, my friend. A cock crows. Even on the great hood of Tor Cave you can hear it. Soon the sun will creep out of the eastern hills and our sleepers will stir. Morning will come in all its raw and hopeful glory. So our time together is over. I thank you for your eyes and your ears. And I am pleased to have set down these events, to have placed them on the record, so to speak. To have given you the true history of the Grindle Witch.

But, you may ask, how do I, your narrator, know all of this to be true? How do I know what happened? How can I speak with such certainty of all these things?

Because I saw them.

Because I was *there*.

And to this, I leave my mark . . .

the orion star

CALLING ALL GROWN-UPS!

Sign up for **the orion star** newsletter to hear about your favourite authors and exclusive competitions, plus details of how children can join our 'Story Stars' review panel.

Sign up at:

www.orionbooks.co.uk/orionstar

Follow us @the_orionstar

Find us facebook.com/TheOrionStar